# RELENTLESS

## SHAWN WILSON

OCEANVIEW PUBLISHING
SARASOTA, FLORIDA

ISBN  978-1-60809-370-0

Cover Design by Christian Fuenfhausen

Published in the United States of America by Oceanview Publishing

Sarasota, Florida

www.oceanviewpub.com

10 9 8 7 6 5 4 3 2 1

PRINTED IN THE UNITED STATES OF AMERICA

*For Lady*

*"To be Irish is to know that in the end the world will break your heart."*

—Daniel Patrick Moynihan

# ACKNOWLEDGMENTS

My thanks and gratitude go to:

Bob and Pat Gussin and the Oceanview Team for making *Relentless* a reality.

Anne Dubuisson for your expertise and encouragement. Third time's a charm!

The organizers of Santa Barbara Writer's Conference, Bouchercon, Left Coast Crime, Sleuthfest, and Killer Nashville where I learned so much and always had a great time.

A group hug to my family and friends for sharing the good times and bad, the laughter and tears. I am so blessed to have you in my life.

A very special thank you to Ruth Ann for letting me have the creative writing gene.

And, of course, to Bob for introducing me to Chicago, a place that felt like home from day one and for turning this Yankees fan into a Cubs fan forever.

# CHAPTER ONE

*Washington, D.C.*
*April 2013*

PINK SNOW.

A gentle breeze sent the fragile, two-days-past-prime cherry blossoms cascading to the ground.

Detective Brian Kavanagh ignored the petals falling around him. As he peered past the railing toward the east side of the Tidal Basin, he was focused on one thing. He adjusted his binoculars. A naked body floating facedown in the murky water came into view. What he saw was long dark hair and a petite build. Odds were the body was female, but he knew better than to assume. Another slight adjustment provided a clearer look. He noticed something unusual. The skin on the right shoulder and extending partway down the arm appeared inflamed. There were lots of possible explanations, but Kavanagh knew the only way to find out was to get a close-up look.

At roll call, seven hours earlier, the lieutenant had announced that the weekend triple shooting in Southeast brought the number of homicides up to forty-one. Would this add another to the tally? Murders were running ahead of last year's total, and at this rate, could start creeping back up to the bad years—those years when D.C. had the distinction of not just being the nation's capital—but its homicide capital as well.

Kavanagh didn't believe in numerology any more than he believed in psychics solving crimes, but for some reason, the number forty-two seemed to be stalking him. He had turned forty-two last month and celebrated by watching a couple of spring training games at Stein-brenner Field in Tampa. For a split-second he thought about his chance coffee-shop encounter with Mariano Rivera. Many times, he'd watched the Yankees' number 42 take the mound at the top of the ninth. Calm and confidant with nerves of steel, the Sandman would face his opponent and then almost always strike him out. Kavanagh hadn't thought of it before, and even though it might be a stretch, realized he had something in common with the future Hall of Famer. After all, their goal was pretty much the same—close the inning or close the case; do your job and put another one in the win column.

"Hey, Brick."

Kavanagh's red hair was now laced with strands of gray, but the nickname from his youth would probably stick with him to his grave. He turned toward the sound of his partner's voice. Brick had been working with Ron Hayes for a little over a year. They were a good fit even though Ron was ten years younger and this was his first stint in Homicide. He was a quick study, eager to learn, but only time would tell if his enthusiasm would last or he would burn out like several of his predecessors.

"They've got the area by the bridge taped off and uniforms posted. A couple of squirrel chasers are over there, too."

Brick smiled. He didn't always agree with Ron, but when it came to the Park Police, they were of the same mind. Still, the presence of mounted officers might help discourage curious onlookers. "What's going on with the harbor patrol?" Brick asked.

"The dive team is suiting up; they should be here in about twenty, twenty-five minutes." Ron glanced at his watch. "Ten bucks says the media gets here first."

Brick shook his head. Only a sucker would make that bet. "I'm surprised they're not here already." He glanced toward a dock where a fleet of light blue, plastic-shelled paddle boats were moored. In a few hours, tourists and locals would pay a nominal fee to don life jackets and pedal around the Tidal Basin. Before long, this annual rite of spring would lose its appeal when summer temperatures soar and the smell of fish hangs heavy in the humid air. Brick pointed toward the boat dock. "Let's go."

For a moment, Ron hesitated. He lagged a few steps behind his partner. "Please tell me you're not considering hopping into one of those boats."

"You got a better idea?" Brick shouted over his shoulder.

"C'mon, man, it's the Tidal Basin. The body's not going to get washed out to sea. I say wait for the Harbor Patrol."

Brick turned in Ron's direction. "That's because you've never worked with them. Some guys are okay, but a few are known for finding new ways to screw things up."

Ron shook his head. "Guess I should have figured that's not happening on your watch." His dark dreads swayed from side to side as he stepped up his pace. He caught up to Brick in front of an eight-foot fence surrounding the area where the boats were stored. A heavy padlock secured the rusted metal gate where a sign listed the operating hours for boat rental. "Looks like we're out of luck."

"I can see how disappointed you are." Brick studied the lock for a minute. "You want to shoot it, or should I?"

"Whoa." Ron took a step back. "Last time I checked, shooting locks isn't on the approved list."

Whether Ron realized it or not, the suggestion was meant as a test. Brick was pleased his protégé passed. "I'm kidding. You've learned how to scale a fence, haven't you?"

Ron nodded as a smug smile crossed his lips. "Are you really going to risk those fancy threads you're wearing?"

Brick was used to being teased about his wardrobe. There was no denying he was a clotheshorse, more likely to shop at Brooks Brothers than the Men's Wearhouse. "It's called taking one for the team."

"Okay, then." Ron deferred to Brick with a sweeping hand gesture. "Age before beauty."

This wouldn't be the first time Brick scaled a fence, but silently he hoped it might be his last. He took a deep breath, grabbed hold of two iron bars, and pulled himself up to get a foothold on a narrow ledge. He hesitated for a moment, then launched himself over the top. The landing wouldn't earn points for style, but he made it without damage to himself or his favorite suit. He was grateful on both counts.

Ron took a running start, leapt onto the ledge and over the top of the fence sticking the landing with the grace of a well-trained athlete. Being in his early thirties gave him an edge as did his college days at University of Maryland where he had been a track star and the hours he still spent working out.

"What?" Ron shrugged his shoulders. "Unfair height advantage?" At six-foot-four, Ron was a good five inches taller than Brick.

"First time today you've reminded me," Brick said.

Ron sneered and lowered his voice to a growl. "Day ain't over yet."

Brick shook his head. A line from a movie—Ron's constant challenge—who said it—what movie? But Brick wasn't taking the bait. Unlike a lot of guys, he didn't have an endless supply of movie quotes at his disposal. Except for *Field of Dreams*, he'd rarely watched a movie more than once.

Together, they walked down the weathered dock past the row of boats to the last one tied securely to the one next to it. Brick went to work on the thick rope with a Swiss Army knife. Once freed, Ron held onto the back of the boat, keeping it steady as Brick stepped aboard. Carefully, he moved over to the left and sat, positioning his feet on the pedals.

Ron followed his lead but with more difficulty. "This is worse than squeezing into an airplane seat."

"Would you rather swim?" Brick asked.

Ron shifted as if to find a more comfortable position. "Goddamn, my knees are hitting my chin."

"Really? Well, how's that height advantage working for you now?"

"Guess I deserved that." Ron started to laugh but stopped abruptly. "Oh, man, I got a charley horse." He winced as he tried to stretch his left leg. "Why is it in movies cops get to commandeer Lexuses and Jaguars?"

Brick thought about how ridiculous they must look. "Do you really think anyone would pay ten or eleven bucks to see a couple of cops in a paddleboat?"

"My wife would if one of them was Denzel." Ron shifted again. "And right now, I wish it was his ass in this boat instead of mine."

Brick and Ron drew closer and stopped pedaling. The wake from the paddleboat caused the body to bob up and down giving them their best chance to get a look at the victim before the Harbor Patrol arrived. Ron craned his neck as if trying to get a better view of the victim's upper body, which was closer to Brick's side of the boat.

"What the hell is that—some kind of bruise or burn?" Ron pointed to the patch of reddish-purple skin Brick had spotted earlier.

"Looks like a birthmark," Brick said.

"Probably one of those, what's it called . . . port wine?"

Brick nodded and pointed toward the victim's collarbone. "See how it starts there and travels over the right shoulder and down the arm?"

"Yeah. I was about to say she was lucky it didn't cover her face, but even if lucky described her before, it sure doesn't anymore."

"She? You're sure about that?"

Ron hesitated before responding. "I'm basing it on what I didn't see, rather than what I did. Know what I mean?"

"Water's cold enough to cause shrinkage."

"Provided there's something to shrink, and it doesn't look like there is."

Ron furrowed his brow as his eyes once again scanned the body from head to toe. For a minute, it appeared he might be second-guessing himself. "I'm as sure as I can be, but if the ME says otherwise, he's the man."

There was a reason Brick was quizzing his partner. Part of being a detective meant being open-minded and paying attention to details, especially ones you may have to someday testify about. Being on the witness stand was nerve-wracking. Hopefully, the prosecutor wouldn't hang you out to dry, but you could count on the defense attorney doing exactly that.

"Wish I could get a better look at her face." Ron's voice had a pensive quality, almost as if he was thinking out loud. "She's thin, almost no body fat. Probably weighs less than a hundred pounds. And she's short—maybe five feet." Ron continued to lean over the side of the paddleboat and scanned the victim's body. "Aside from the birthmark, I don't see anything remarkable. Do you?"

"No."

"So, unless she decided to go skinny dipping and drowned, which I seriously doubt, we've got a secondary crime scene." Ron settled back into his seat. "And, of course, they had to dump her in the water. Sucks, doesn't it?"

"Big-time. Unlikely we'll get any useful trace evidence off of her."

"How long do you think she's been here?"

"Not long—a few hours, tops." Brick glanced down at his watch. "The call came in just after five. It's possible she got dumped sometime after midnight. This area is pretty deserted between then and daybreak."

"There's got to be security cameras around here," Ron said.

"Given the budget cuts, don't count on it. And even if there are tapes, they might be useless since it was so foggy last night."

"Wouldn't you know, for once the weather guy on Channel 7 got it right." Ron sighed loudly. "We're just batting a thousand, aren't we, partner. No clothes or driver's license—she's young, could be a runaway from anywhere. How long do we have before the Medical Examiner's Office buries the body?"

"Thirty days."

"Damn. That's what I thought."

Brick nodded. "And the time starts now."

# CHAPTER TWO

"Jesus, I've seen some sights out here, but you two take the cake." Sergeant Phil Jones, better known as "Jonesy," laughed as Brick stepped from the paddleboat onto the ladder attached to the side of the Harbor Patrol rescue boat. "Had to do a double take, thought it was Carrot Top and Bob Marley."

Brick could have been offended; instead he was impressed by Jonesy's knowledge of pop culture. He carefully climbed the narrow rungs one by one, then stepped onto the deck. Ron followed, no doubt grateful to be able to stand and stretch his cramped muscles. Jonesy pointed toward the opposite end on the boat where four members of the Water Search and Rescue Squad were checking their equipment. "Most cops would have waited on the shore and just let us do our thing."

"Have you ever known me to be like most cops?" Brick asked.

Jonesy shook his head. "Now that you mention it, nah." He turned his stocky frame toward Ron and introduced himself. "Who'd you piss off to get stuck with this guy?" He didn't give Ron time to respond. "Just kidding. Hey, did he ever tell you about the time—"

"Jonesy, you don't need to tell that story."

"Okay, okay." He squinted in the early morning sun. "Well, Ron, you'll have to take my word for it—it's a good one." He turned back toward Brick. "Oh, by the way, did you hear my news?"

Brick shook his head, knowing he was about to get the lowdown.

"I'm hanging it up. Twenty-seven days and three hours to go, but who's counting."

"Congratulations."

"Thanks. I filed my retirement papers last week, and I gotta tell you, it's like the weight of the world's been lifted from my shoulders." He patted the boat's railing. "Yeah, I'm ready to trade this one in for one I can sail on the Chesapeake. Figure I'll keep it docked up in Annapolis. You're welcome any time." Immediately, he appeared to regret what he had just said. "But the Bay can get kind of choppy. You don't get seasick, do you? I remember one time, think it was mid-October—no wait, it was first week in November—"

"Thanks, Jonesy. I appreciate the invite." Brick knew if he didn't interrupt, Jonesy's sea adventure would make *Moby Dick* seem like a short story. "Looks like your guys are ready. How about if Ron and I get out of the way."

"You're fine where you are. I'm getting some coffee—feel free to help yourself, but I gotta warn you, it tastes like it was made with water straight out of the Tidal Basin." Both men declined.

Although Brick had worked several cases involving floaters, he didn't recognize the four guys who were suited up and going over a checklist. Considering the physical demands of being on the dive team, it wasn't surprising that the members tended to be young. No doubt, rescues from capsized canoes or boats and cars that had plunged into the water were rewarding. Recoveries—not so much. Still, diving into the murky water was, to Brick's way of thinking, preferable to searching pipes and sewers, which was something else they were called upon to do. Wading through sludge and mud, and God knows what kind of toxins—no wonder the turnover rate was high. Their twofold mission this morning—retrieve the body then look for evidence using metal detectors and sonar.

As two of the divers jumped into the water, Jonesy unzipped the body bag that had been laid out on the deck. The two divers on the deck lowered a basket large enough to accommodate an adult much larger than the victim. The divers in the water quickly positioned the body into the basket and signaled it was ready to be raised. Jonesy supervised as his officers quickly transferred the body from the basket to the bag.

"Nice work, guys," Brick shouted and gave a thumbs-up. Before zipping the bag, he and Ron checked the body for any clues as to how she died. "What do you think?" Brick asked his partner.

"No obvious wounds as far as I can see. I'd say she was probably dead before she hit the water. We won't know until the ME determines whether or not there's water in her lungs."

Brick was about to compliment Ron but didn't get a chance.

"Don't envy you, guys." Jonesy leaned in, close enough for Brick to smell the coffee on his breath. "The White Shirts down at Headquarters will be shitting plaid rabbits over this one. Young girl, cherry blossom time—better hope she's not some cheerleader from Iowa on a school trip."

The thought had crossed Brick's mind. Jonesy was right. Already this case had the potential to make lots of people nervous, from the mayor on down. And Brick knew from experience, when the powers-that-be got nervous, his job got a whole lot more stressful.

"I've called the ME's office—they're sending a wagon," Jonesy said. "With any luck, they'll be waiting for us at the dock." He looked over at Ron. "Good thing you had time to rest—it's always harder pedaling back."

"Say what?" Ron asked with obvious disbelief. "You mean—"

"Hey, you can't just leave that paddleboat out here." Jonesy started to laugh. "I'm pulling your leg. We'll run you two back, then my guys can get on with it."

As Jonesy was talking, Brick watched one of the guys check his face mask and strap on an array of knives. He would be the primary conducting the search for evidence. The secondary would keep a close eye on him, ready to spring into action if the diver got into trouble. Soon they would bring out the sonar and metal detectors. Brick waved toward the back of the boat. "Thanks, guys."

Brick felt reasonably confident the search would be conducted properly, but that didn't ensure anything useful would be recovered. As far as he was concerned, the odds were about the same as the Cubs getting to the World Series.

Jonesy steered the boat toward the dock, and just as he had anticipated, a medical examiner's van was waiting in the parking lot adjacent to the building housing the Harbor Patrol.

"Home sweet home—at least for the next twenty-three days"— Jonesy checked his watch— "and two hours."

Two guys wearing blue jumpsuits leaned against the van. One was smoking; the other playing air guitar. The smoker ground out his cigarette and the guitarist stopped playing as the boat came to rest at the dock. They retrieved a gurney from the back of the van and proceeded to wheel it toward the boat.

Brick signed the required paperwork to transfer the body to the custody of the medical examiner's agents. It was a routine procedure that had to be followed, but it always made him uneasy. Even though he'd never had kids, in an odd way, he felt parental-like responsibility toward the victim. The guys in the blue jumpsuits wouldn't have been his first choice for babysitters.

Along with Ron, Brick watched as the body bag was loaded into the back of the van. The door slammed shut and the air guitarist double-checked to make sure it was locked. "Guess we're good to go."

"Wait a minute," Brick said. "Our cruiser is parked on the other side of the Tidal Basin. Can we hitch a ride with you?"

"No problemo. We gotta go past there anyway. I'll get in the back; you guys can ride up front."

At least for a few more minutes, Brick still had the illusion of control.

\* \* \*

After dropping Ron off at the Archives Metro Station, Brick turned onto Indiana Avenue and pulled into a parking space reserved for police vehicles. He jaywalked across the street and made his way up the stairs of the Henry J. Daly Building. Usually referred to simply as Police Headquarters, the building was named for a veteran police sergeant who was killed along with two FBI agents when an armed intruder entered the building, proceeded to the Cold Case Squad, and opened fire. Brick had been a rookie assigned to the Third District on that fateful November afternoon. Still, it would always be a day when he'd remember exactly where he was when he heard the news.

"Watch your step there, Brick, my man."

Brick recognized the voice of Otis Johnson, the night janitor. He turned to see the older man grimace as he bent to position the "Caution—Wet Floor" sign.

"Looks like your shift's about over," Brick said.

"Yours, too?" Otis straightened up, but it was evident he was still in pain. "Arthritis is kickin' my ass today. Bet I know where you'll be going."

His comment stopped Brick in his tracks. With all that had happened in the past few hours, he'd forgotten it was Opening Day at Nationals Park. How was that possible? He'd been looking forward to this for weeks. He had suffered through the early years at RFK and now was reaping the reward of watching a competitive team in a beautiful park. But not today. He reached for the ticket in his pocket and handed it to Otis. "Got a new case; I'm going to be here for a while."

Otis looked at the ticket and shook his head. "Club level. Too rich for my wallet." He tried to hand the ticket back, but Brick waved him off.

"It's yours for the taking. Just one condition—if you catch a foul ball, it's mine."

Otis smiled broadly. "You got it, man, you got it."

In an ideal world, Brick would have his own windowed office with a view of waves crashing on a rocky shore. From the time he was a kid, he was drawn to water, especially the ocean, and the more dramatic the coastline, the better. As it were, he was grateful for a battered gunmetal-gray desk in a three-sided cubicle he didn't have to share with another detective when the shift changed. Although Brick didn't see himself as a neat freak, comparing his standards to those of some guys in the squad, the label might apply. He checked his voicemail and listened to a message from an assistant U.S. attorney who wanted to meet with him before an upcoming witness conference. It would have to wait. For now, he was on his own time and other matters were more pressing. Ron had offered to stay until he remembered he had promised his pregnant wife to accompany her to a doctor's appointment. Brick smiled as he recalled Ron's words: "I'd rather face down a junkyard dog who hasn't eaten for three days than be a no-show."

Brick drummed his fingers on the keyboard as he waited for his computer to boot up. Finally, he was able to log on. When budget time rolled around, maybe this would be the year for upgrades and the existing computers could be retired to the Smithsonian. Starting with the current date and working backwards over a six-month period, he searched a database of local missing persons. He got a few hits, but no one who even remotely resembled the young woman in the Tidal Basin. Still, it was possible she could be an out-of-town high schooler whose information had been reported but hadn't been loaded into the database. If that proved to be the case, Brick was fairly certain he would know within a few hours. The report of a missing tourist, especially a

kid, would be flagged. In the meantime, he expanded the date param-
eters and refined his search criteria: Caucasian, female, 15–25 years
old, 90–140 pounds, 4'10" to 5'5". When prompted, he checked black
hair and hit "enter." On the next screen, a pull-down menu listed specific identifying characteristics. He scrolled past tattoos and piercings
to birthmark. Under that heading, he clicked on "shoulder." He hit
"search" and sat back while the computer matched his specifications
against an expanded database containing missing person reports from
the D.C.-Virginia-Maryland region.

Three hits. Brick's reaction was Pavlovian. He felt his heart beat
faster as he leaned forward to read what was displayed on the screen.
His excitement waned as he eliminated each possibility based on the
accompanying photographs.

"Fuck."

"Only if you take me to dinner first."

Even before Brick swiveled in his chair, he knew who had made the
remark. Travis Allen, one-half of a pair known as "The A-Team,"
slouched against the cubicle divider. He and his partner, Paul Adkins,
were the only detectives who had been in Homicide longer than
Brick. For the most part, Brick got along with the others in the squad
but a little bit of Allen went a long way. He was like the obnoxious
brother-in-law family members tolerate at the holiday dinner only because it's Christmas.

Allen pulled the tab on a can of Coke. The soda bubbled up over
the side of the can and dripped onto the floor. Allen didn't seem to
notice. He raised the can to his mouth and took a drink. "Heard
about your floater—know who she is?"

"Not yet, but it's only been a couple of hours." Brick deliberately
sounded more optimistic than he felt. He wasn't about to give Allen
the satisfaction of knowing he was frustrated. "Is that your phone
ringing?"

"Yeah, guess it is." Allen started to walk away then stopped. "Almost forgot, Blancato needs to see you."

Nice that the lieutenant sent his messenger boy, Brick thought. He turned his computer off and headed down the hall.

*   *   *

"Is Lieutenant Blancato expecting you?" The secretary's stiff formality always seemed out of place, better suited for a District Court judge's chambers than a police squad room, but then again, she was probably following Blancato's orders.

"Yes."

Brick walked past her desk and opened the door leading to the lieutenant's office. Everything about the office, from the newly installed carpet and drapes to the leather chairs and Blancato's highly polished walnut desk, shouted "rank has its privilege." And if anyone didn't get the message, they probably would by glancing around at photos of Blancato shaking hands with politicians, law enforcement officials, and actors playing cops on TV. Brick always made a point to look around to see if anyone new had been added to the gallery.

"Is that you with Joe Biden?" Brick asked.

"Yeah, he was the keynote . . . anyway, we got to make this quick. I'm meeting with the chief in five minutes."

Brick figured the "got to make it quick" comment was code for "don't sit down, just stand there and tell me what I need to know." He pulled up a chair and made himself comfortable.

Blancato glanced up at the clock on the wall. "Bring me up to speed on this body in the Tidal Basin."

Brick complied.

"And the media wasn't all over this?"

"We managed to get out of there before they arrived. That's not to say they won't find out about it."

Blancato seemed to mull that over. "Yeah, and when they do—we're screwed. The timing couldn't be worse. Tourists are overrunning the city like a swarm of locusts. And of all places, there's a body floating in the Tidal Basin. Why couldn't they drop her in Chesapeake Bay, then she'd be Baltimore's problem." Blancato reached up as if to scratch his curly hair but stopped short. He glanced down at his shoulder and brushed his uniform sleeve with his hand. "Holy Christ, the networks live for stories like this. We don't need that kind of publicity."

Brick wasn't sure who Blancato meant by "we" but he suspected the reference included the mayor. One of the worst-kept secrets in the department was the borderline incestuous relationship between Blancato and the mayor's office. When it came to decision-making, Brick often wondered who was calling the shots.

"Keep me informed and under no circumstances are you to talk to the press. That's my responsibility." Blancato popped a couple of Tic Tacs in his mouth. "Hey, let's hope she's just a crack whore who went for a swim."

And that from the guy who would handle the press. Brick didn't respond. He just shook his head as he left Blancato's office.

# CHAPTER THREE

*"Then one foggy Christmas Eve . . ."* The words stuck in his head even though several hours had passed. Ear worm . . . yeah, that's what it's called, he'd found the term on Wikipedia. A few times he even sang along as the words played on a seemingly endless loop. He was grateful for the fog. And just like it had been for Rudolph, it was a game changer.

At first, he wasn't sure where he would dump her body. But when he saw the monuments shrouded in fog, he didn't have to look any further. Disguising himself as a street person was always part of the plan. It was a no-brainer. You can stand in a crowd and still be invisible. Kind of like being a mailbox. People walk right by and don't even know you're there.

All he had to do now was get rid of the shopping cart. That would be easy. He drove his van to a suburban Giant and parked near a designated cart-return place. Just for good measure he wiped down the handle before shoving the cart into the queue behind the others.

He was hungry, and as long as he was here, he might as well get something to eat. He had plenty of cash in his pocket. Only an idiot would use a credit or debit card and leave a paper trail. What sounded good? He thought about it for a minute or two.

Pop-Tarts. He hadn't had a Pop-Tart since he was a kid. Blueberry or cherry? He'd get a box of each and eat as many as he wanted. And he wouldn't burn them like his mother used to. She had to be the stupidest woman on earth. She couldn't even toast a Pop-Tart without fucking it up.

# CHAPTER FOUR

At Judiciary Square, Brick boarded the Red Line bound for Shady Grove. After a sixteen-hour day, he should have been exhausted. He wasn't. New-case adrenaline coursed through his veins. There was a time when winding down after work meant a couple of beers and swapping stories at the Fraternal Order of Police Lodge located a few blocks from Headquarters. That ended when he was assigned to Internal Affairs. It was obvious he wasn't welcomed at the FOP when he walked in just after his appointment and other cops walked out leaving untouched drinks on the bar. And there was another time when the end of a shift meant going home to his fiancée. That ended when he went undercover in Narcotics at the height of the crack epidemic. His bride-to-be said she had agreed to be his wife not his widow. Nothing he said convinced her otherwise. Over the years, as his options dwindled, Brick found a place that provided refuge. For him, Boland's Mill was much more than an Irish bar.

Brick exited the Woodley Park Metro Station and headed north on Connecticut Avenue. He walked past his circa 1920 condo building, crossed the street, and continued on for two blocks. Just before walking in the door of Boland's Mill he rolled his shoulders up and back a couple of times, a move he had learned from a Pilates instructor he used to date. The brief exercise along with the anticipation of a slow-poured Guinness did the trick; he felt the tension in his muscles ease.

Brick's barstool of choice allowed him to keep his back to the wall with a clear view of the door. He was glad to see it was vacant. Despite the ceiling fan whirling overhead, it was warm inside, but the gun holstered at his waist prevented him from taking off his suit coat. He compensated by pulling off his tie and loosening the collar of his shirt. He glanced up at the new big-screened TV in time to catch the bottom of the ninth. The Nats left two men on base, losing 3–0. He could only hope this wasn't a harbinger of the season ahead. He watched other scores scroll across the bottom of the screen as he waited for Rory, the day manager and bartender, to put down his cellphone. Finally, Rory turned in Brick's direction and held up his index finger in a wait-a-minute gesture. Still holding the phone to his ear, he set a glass under the tap. Just after pulling the spigot, Rory must have realized his mistake. He dumped the Harp and set a clean glass under the Guinness tap. He continued holding the phone as the dark liquid filled the glass. Before it had settled, he put it in front of Brick.

"Sorry, I'm a bit distracted."

Brick nodded. "You know, if I want bad service, I'll go to Mulligan's." Rory didn't crack a smile. Something wasn't right. Brick looked around the room expecting to see Eamonn Boland holding court with a couple of regulars in the back corner. Not today. Except for a table of four who appeared to be tourists having a late lunch, the place was empty.

"Where's Eamonn?"

"He had another doctor's appointment."

Brick didn't like the sound of that. "Is he okay?"

"Yeah, he's supposed to take it easy for another week but he's going stir crazy. It's just—"

The sound of the tri-tone from Rory's cellphone stopped him mid-sentence. He snatched the phone from where it had been lying on the bar. Brick watched as he apparently read a text message before exhaling loudly. "Feck!"

"Rory, what's going on? Girlfriend trouble?"

Rory shook his head. "It's Jose—he hasn't shown up for work."

Brick knew who Rory was talking about. Jose was the young guy who had been bussing tables at Boland's for a couple of years.

Rory continued to stare at his phone. "And he hasn't answered the voicemail and text messages I've left."

Brick's pint of Guinness had settled. He took a sip then wiped the back of his hand across his mouth.

"It's none of my business, but aren't you overreacting?"

Rory reached under the bar and retrieved a bottle of Gatorade. He unscrewed the cap and took a swig from the bottle before stowing it back under the bar. "Today's the third day. I was off over the weekend so I didn't know he hadn't shown up until this morning. It's not like him—he's never missed a day since he's been working here."

Brick took another swig of Guinness. The stress of the day was beginning to fade. "Cut him some slack. He's young."

"I know, but he's more responsible than some of the guys we've had that were twice his age." Rory shrugged his broad shoulders. "He's more feckin' responsible than I am."

Brick knew that wasn't true, but the self-deprecation spoke volumes about how Rory felt toward Jose. He wasn't the only one. Several of the regulars recognized what a hard worker Jose was and did what they could to help him in different ways. A retired schoolteacher tutored him in English. Brick, on the other hand, tutored him in baseball, something Jose knew little about since he had grown up playing soccer in Guatemala. Another of the regulars with a window treatment business hired Jose to install blinds. He always seemed eager to do whatever he could to earn extra money to send back home to his mother.

"What about his sister? I remember him saying something about her coming here," Brick said.

"She did, a couple of weeks ago, but I don't have a number for her."

Brick picked up his glass, took a drink, then another. "Any issues with his work status?"

Rory shook his head. "Not that I know of, but Eamonn handles all that." He glanced over Brick's head, toward the front window. "And speak of the devil."

As if on cue, the door flung wide and Eamonn limped toward the bar carrying a zippered money bag. Brick hadn't seen the owner of Boland's in over a week and was surprised by Eamonn's condition. Well into his seventies, he always seemed younger than his years, but now it appeared his health problems were taking a toll.

"Have you heard anything, lad?" Eamonn sounded out of breath.

"Not a word."

Eamonn raised the hinged section of the bar and made his way over to the cash register. He opened the drawer and filled the designated slots with ones, fives, tens, and twenties. It wasn't until he finished and turned around that he acknowledged Brick.

"Aw, jaysus, I didn't even see you there. How are you, Brick?" Eamonn struck a roll of quarters on the side of the cash drawer before dumping the coins into the tray. "Did Rory tell you about Jose?"

Brick nodded his head. "I was asking about his work status—you're sure his papers are in order?"

"They are, for feck's sake." Eamonn closed the cash register drawer with more force than was necessary. "The last thing I need is to get involved in some illegal shite and lose the liquor license I've had for thirty years."

"Eamonn, I didn't mean to imply—"

Eamonn waved his hand in a dismissive gesture. "And I didn't mean to rip you a new one. It's just that I'm worried about the kid."

Brick understood. Rory was Eamonn's nephew, but Eamonn tended to treat all of his employees like family. "Do you have an address for him?"

"He lives in an apartment building over on Columbia Road. Rory dropped him off there a couple of times."

"Then let's check it out," Brick said.

Eamonn nodded in agreement as he poured himself a shot of Jameson. "Go ahead, I'll cover the bar."

Rory looked sternly at his uncle. "You know what the doctor said; you're supposed to stay off your foot."

"He also told me to give up the gargle." Eamonn raised his shot glass. "Here's to the young doctor I have every intention of outliving." The Jameson disappeared in one swallow.

Rory opened his mouth as if to say something but laughed instead. He threw his arm around his uncle's bony shoulder. "I've no doubt you will, Eamonn, no doubt at all."

"That makes two of us." Brick chugged the rest of his Guinness. "C'mon, Rory, let's go."

*  *  *

"That's it, the one on the left."

Rory pointed to an eight-story building on the corner of Columbia Road and 18th Street. Unlike several buildings in the neighborhood that had been rehabbed and turned into high-end condos, this one had been neglected. But even though plywood covered some broken windowpanes and a couple of air conditioners teetered precariously on crumbling ledges, it was still possible to see the original architectural details. Back in the day, the building had been elegant. It was probably just a matter of time before an investor saw the potential, snatched it up, and sent thirty-day vacate notices displacing the low-income residents who had few housing options left in Northwest Washington.

The cab driver pulled over to the curb. Brick climbed out as Rory paid the fare. It had been years since he had done a well-being check, but it was a fairly common occurrence when he had been in uniform. Most of his experiences had been uneventful, ending with the concerned relative or friend apologizing for having bothered the police when the missing party showed up safe and sound. But there had been one. To this day, every time he saw a roach, he thought of the hoarder who suffocated after a pile of trash fell on him. The eighty-year-old man was dead, but the walls of the apartment were alive with roaches, hundreds and hundreds of roaches. It never failed; the memory alone made his skin crawl.

"Here goes." The sound of Rory's voice snapped Brick out of his reverie. At the front door, Brick watched as he scrolled through the names on the intercom until he found Jose's. He entered a three-digit code, stepped back, and waited. Six or seven static-filled rings went unanswered. "Now what?" Rory asked.

"See if there's a code for the building manager and enter that. Hopefully, he's on-site."

After three rings, a groggy-sounding voice responded. "Who's there?"

Brick spoke into the intercom. "Metropolitan Police—doing a well-being check on one of your tenants."

With that the intercom went dead. Brick looked over at Rory. "I think I interrupted his siesta." He was about to redial when a man who looked to be in his early forties shuffled toward the door. He was dressed in paint-splattered jeans and flip-flops. A wifebeater t-shirt stretched over his protruding belly, and a large cross hung from a chain he wore around his neck. It appeared he hadn't taken time to comb his hair, maybe in several days.

Brick held up his badge for inspection. The man nodded his head and yawned as he opened the door.

"I'm Detective Kavanagh." Brick extended his hand and the two men shook.

"Carlos Garcia."

"We're looking for Jose Delgado. I understand he lives here."

"*Si*." Carlos looked skeptical. "Everything okay?"

"As far as we know, but he hasn't shown up for work in a couple of days." Brick gestured toward Rory. "This is his boss; he's worried about him."

"*Si*." Carlos yawned, again exposing a front tooth capped with gold.

"Have you seen him recently?" Brick asked.

Carlos scratched the stubble on his cheek. "A week, maybe two. He work a lot so I don't see him much." He fumbled with a large key ring before removing one. "He live in 307 with his sister. She just move in." Carlos shrugged his shoulders. "He said his sister. I don't know if she really is—I don't care. He pays rent on time and don't cause no trouble."

"Any neighbors ever complain about noise coming from his apartment?"

Carlos shook his head. "Like I told you, he don't cause no trouble. Some living here do. Big-time, like the one across the hall in 306, ay yi yi when he's drinking." Another yawn. "Want to take the elevator or stairs?"

It was a no-brainer. In a building like this, Brick figured the elevator hadn't been inspected since Jimmy Carter was president. Carlos led the way up the dark, narrow stairwell. They exited to the sound of Ricky Martin's "Livin' La Vida Loca." If ever the Homicide Squad needed a theme song, that would be Brick's choice. A baby wailed from the next apartment they passed. As the three men made their way down the hall, the aroma of Mexican food competed with the smell of old musty carpet. By the time they reached Jose's apartment, the carpet was the undisputed winner.

Brick and Rory stepped aside as Carlos knocked loudly on the door. "Jose, is Carlos." There was no response and he knocked again before turning toward Brick. "You want I unlock the door?"

"Yes."

He slipped the key into the lock and tried to turn it. He looked surprised. "Is not locked." He reached toward the doorknob.

"No, don't—"

It was too late. Carlos gripped the knob and turned it to the right before pulling his hand back as if he had touched a hot potato. "What?"

"It's okay." It really wasn't. The unlocked door concerned Brick. He knew there could be a simple explanation—Jose or his sister could have left and forgotten to lock the door. Or something more sinister could be in play. Someone who didn't have a key was the last person to leave the apartment. If that was the case, the doorknob might have been a source of useful fingerprints. Even though Brick was off-duty, the detective wheels were beginning to turn in his head, but he knew better than to get ahead of himself.

"What's the layout of the apartment?" Brick asked, but Carlos didn't seem to understand. He tried again. "Is it a one-bedroom?"

"*Si.* The bedroom in back across from bathroom."

"Okay. Both of you need to wait out here."

Neither Carlos nor Rory objected.

Brick reached in his pocket and retrieved a pair of latex gloves. He slipped them on before pushing the door open. A blast of cold air greeted him. All three windows in the room were wide open. He stepped inside and loudly announced his presence. Silence reigned except for the low hum of the refrigerator in the galley kitchen off to the left. Quickly, he glanced around the room. It was pretty much what

Brick expected and not all that different from the kind of apartment he had shared with roommates back in college—mismatched chairs surrounded a card table and a rumpled futon had seen better days. The only extravagance was a small flat-screen TV sitting atop a wooden trunk.

Nothing struck Brick as unusual until he glanced down at the floor. Little reddish-brown paw prints led from what he guessed was the bathroom into the bedroom. Both doors were ajar. He felt his heart rate accelerate; the refrigerator hum drowned out by the sound of his own pulse pounding in his ears. Instinctively, Brick reached inside his jacket to where his gun was secured in its holster. It had been over three years since he had shot a suspect; he hoped today wouldn't be the day to reset the counter.

Brick took a deep breath. That's when he smelled it. It was faint, barely discernible, but it was there, like the lingering metallic after-taste from a clotted bloody nose. With his foot, he eased the bath-room door open.

# CHAPTER FIVE

TWELVE YEARS ON the Homicide Squad had prepared Brick for anything and everything, or so he thought. But up until now, with one exception, the dead bodies he had encountered all belonged to strangers. He felt weak in the knees as he glanced down at Jose's battered body crumpled between the bathtub and toilet. From the blood splatter and what looked to be brain tissue on the wall, it appeared he had taken several blows to the head. Jose was still wearing his shamrock green polo shirt from Boland's Mill. The front was drenched in blood, but Brick could still see the pub's logo and Jose's name embroidered above the breast pocket. An unexpected wave of sadness mixed with anger washed over Brick like a tsunami. There would be time to grieve, but it would have to wait. He paused and listened for any movement but heard nothing. With his gun drawn, Brick headed toward the bedroom following the paw prints that faded before disappearing altogether.

Brick's eyes scanned the room before focusing on the closed closet door. He positioned himself so the door would provide a makeshift shield. He jerked it open with his free hand. He held his breath and again listened for any indication of movement. Nothing. He peered around the edge of the door into the small walk-in closet. He could clearly see all the contents—men's clothes on one side; women's on the other. Two large suitcases took up most of the floor space. Brick felt the hair on the back of his neck stand up. He knew from experience a body or body parts could be hidden inside the bags. Without actually touching either suitcase, he looked for suspicious stains but found only normal wear and tear. He nudged one suitcase then the other. Neither seemed heavy enough to cause concern. That wasn't to say they were empty, but it would be the responsibility of the evidence guys to check out what was inside.

Brick was relieved not to find another body, but the whereabouts of Jose's sister needed to be established. Was she capable of inflicting the injuries that had killed Jose or was she a victim, too? Brick glanced down and realized he was still holding his gun. Suddenly it felt heavy and superfluous in his hand. He stuck it back in its holster.

Rory and Carlos were waiting in the hall, but Brick needed to call this in before delivering the awful news. His hand shook as he punched the numbers into his cellphone.

"Nine-one-one. What's your emergency?"

Brick recognized the operator's two-packs-a-day raspy voice. "Hey, Caroline, it's Brick Kavanagh." He proceeded to give her all the pertinent details.

"Guess you won't be needing an amb'lance."

"Too late . . ." Brick paused, trying to get the words past the lump in his throat. "Afraid it's too late for that."

"Are you okay, hon?"

Caroline's Baltimore roots were showing. Brick found comfort in her voice, and he knew her concern was genuine. It was why she was one of the best 9-1-1 operators the department ever had. An image of Jose cheerfully bussing tables at Boland's flashed in front of his mind's eye. "I knew him, Caroline. He was a good kid . . . a real good kid."

"I'm sorry, hon."

* * *

The Grim Reaper's messenger. That's how Brick felt every time he had to deliver devastating news to a victim's family or friends. It was part of the job, and over the years, he had come to realize the best way to deliver the news was as directly as possible. Then be prepared for a reaction that could run the gamut from stunned silence to ear-splitting shrieking. He took a deep breath, stepped out into the hallway, and closed the door behind him.

"I'm sorry, Rory. Jose's dead."

"Dead? I knew . . . I knew something was wrong, but dead?" Rory paced in front of Jose's door. "How . . . what . . . I mean, how did it happen?"

It was obvious to Brick that Rory was having trouble processing what he had heard. Brick wasn't surprised. It often took hours or days for someone to wrap their head around something so shocking. Brick had no intentions of sharing the specific details, but he owed Rory some information.

"Rory, this wasn't an accident or a suicide. Someone killed him."

"What about his sister?" Rory asked.

"I don't know. All I can tell you is she's not in the apartment."

Carlos clutched the cross he wore around his neck. He started speaking in a mixture of Spanish and English. Brick made out enough words to recognize the prayer. Apparently, Rory did as well. Although only slightly louder than a whisper, he added his voice: "Holy Mary, Mother of God, pray for us sinners, now and at the hour of our death. Amen."

Brick turned toward Carlos. "The police will be here any minute. I need you to go downstairs to let them in."

"*Si* . . . yes . . . *si* . . . I go now . . . downstairs."

Rory took a deep breath and exhaled slowly. "Killed—that makes no sense. He was just a hardworking kid." Rory continued to pace. "Should I call Eamonn?"

"That's up to you, but it might be better to tell him in person. The homicide detectives assigned to the case will want to talk to you, but I'm guessing that won't take very long."

"Yeah, what's another hour or so? It'd be different if it was good news and he could stop worrying." Rory put his phone back in his pocket. He leaned against the opposite wall for a little while then slid halfway down and rested on his haunches.

# CHAPTER SIX

BRICK CHECKED HIS watch. It was just after three p.m., which meant the eight-to-four shift was still on duty. As the minutes ticked by, he tried to recall which teams were assigned to work days this week. Then he remembered his brief encounter with Travis Allen. The A-Team. Paul Adkins was the other half. By himself, he was okay, but when paired with Allen, his personality changed; he became the straight man to his partner's routine while evaluating crime scenes. There was no sense in pretending otherwise—Travis Allen annoyed the hell out of Brick. But he also recognized the A-Team were experienced detectives with an impressive closure rate. That counted for more than their personalities. Still, Brick would have been okay with another team catching the case.

Two uniformed cops, one male and one female from the Third District, were the first to arrive. For now, their job was to protect the scene. Later, they may be directed to canvass the building to see if anyone heard or saw something that might be useful. Brick introduced himself and together they made small talk while they waited for the detectives and the Mobile Crime officers to arrive.

Brick's speculation as to which homicide detectives would respond ended when the elevator doors opened.

"Brick?" Adkins appeared to be taken aback. "We were up in the rotation. What are you doing here?" Allen seemed less interested. He lagged behind sweet talking into his cellphone.

"It's your case, I'm off-duty." Brick went on to explain his involvement. Halfway through his explanation, he heard Allen wrapping up his conversation with the kind of kissing noises more appropriately exchanged between teenage lovers. Brick would have confidently bet the rent Allen's wife wasn't on the receiving end of his lip smacking. Despite being overweight and balding, Travis Allen had a reputation as a ladies' man. Based solely on looks, Brick could understand if women were attracted to Adkins. The guy ran marathons and bore a resemblance to Steve Carell. But Allen . . . it didn't make sense.

"So, what are you doing here?" Allen asked.

Brick took the high road and patiently repeated what he had already told Adkins. When he finished, he introduced Rory. To their credit, both detectives expressed their condolences.

It was obvious to Brick, Adkins was taking the lead. Adkins asked Rory to wait in the hall while he and Allen went into the apartment indicating one of them would be out shortly to ask him some questions. He then turned in Brick's direction.

"Want to show us the way?"

Brick opened the door and stepped inside. He knew it was his imagination playing tricks, but the smell of dried blood seemed far more pronounced than it had just minutes before. The three detectives paused while scanning the living room, committing it to memory.

"Nothing to indicate a struggle." Adkins pointed toward the TV. "And if it were a burglary gone bad, chances are that wouldn't still be sitting there."

Allen added his two cents. "I'm just glad someone opened the windows. Otherwise this place might reek as bad as that one over on

Florida Avenue." His cellphone rang, but he ignored it. "Hey, Paul, remember?"

"The place where the dead woman had sixty-some cats? Yeah, we needed hazmat suits, but the best we could do was put big garbage bags over our clothes."

"That's the one," Allen said.

"I hope to God I never smell anything that bad again."

"Me, too. I was shoving Vicks up my nose like it was going out of style. Burned like a motherfucker, but I didn't care."

The conversation was quintessential Travis Allen. Brick felt his blood pressure rising, but he didn't say anything for now.

Adkins pointed toward the floor. "Speaking of cats, those look like paw prints. Did Jose have a cat?"

"Yes." Brick didn't elaborate, but for a moment, he thought about the frigid night Jose found the kitten abandoned in the alley behind Boland's. He was the only one who believed the tiny cat would survive. Somehow Jose nursed it back to health. Elvis. Brick smiled at the memory. Jose had named the cat Elvis before he realized it was female. It didn't matter, the name stuck.

"Brick?"

He turned toward Adkins. "What was your question?"

"Know where the cat is?"

"No. Maybe with Jose's sister? The tracks fade and disappear in the bedroom, but there was no sign of either one of them when I checked." Brick stifled a yawn. "I'm not telling you how to run your case, but if it were mine, I'd get an APB out on the sister. The building manager can give you a description."

"Yeah, we'll take care of that." Adkins looked down the short hallway. "So is the bathroom on the right or left?"

"The right."

Adkins nodded toward his partner. "C'mon, Travis, let's go take a look."

# CHAPTER SEVEN

BRICK HAD BEEN up for almost twenty hours and fatigue was setting in. He was about to take a break and step outside for some fresh air in hopes that it would revive him enough to get through a couple more hours.

"Hey, Brick," Adkins called out from the bathroom. "Come here for a minute."

He complied even though he wasn't eager to revisit the scene. Sometimes it's worse knowing what to expect.

"It's probably tough for you since you knew Jose—"

"It's okay."

"Was Jose a member of a gang?" Adkins asked.

"Not that I know of. Why?"

"Look down on the floor, just beyond his right foot." Adkins handed him a flashlight.

Brick shone the light toward the floor illuminating what had previously been in shadow. On the side of the tub something had been scribbled in what looked like blood. Brick cocked his head to get a better angle but it was still difficult to read. As best he could tell, it looked like MSX.

"It could be a gang signature, I guess."

Adkins nodded. "Yeah, that's what I thought, but gangs aren't my area of expertise. Where is Jose from?"

"Guatemala."

Adkins wrote something in his notebook. "I think there's a special gang task force that's teamed up with ICE. Have you worked with them on any cases?"

Brick shook his head. All he knew about Immigration and Customs Enforcement was what he had read in the papers. And lately they had been getting some bad press. Rounding up and deporting aliens who hadn't committed any crime other than failing to renew their visas was creating a lot of controversy. A couple of cases involved pending deportation of women who had given birth in the U.S. and their potential separation from their children who were American citizens. The ACLU and other civil rights groups were taking up their cause.

Adkins finished taking notes. He stuck his pen back in his pocket. "Whether this was gang-related remains to be seen, but I've got a few ideas about how it might have gone down. I'm betting you do, too."

Brick wasn't convinced Adkins really did, but he was willing to brainstorm. If his ideas put them on the right path, the A-Team would, no doubt, claim the credit. But as far as Brick was concerned, this wasn't about who got the credit. All he was interested in was getting the perpetrator and the sooner, the better. Brick pointed at the metal towel bar that had been ripped from the wall and was now lying in the bathtub. "My sense is that the killer did not come here with the intent to kill Jose. If he had, he would have brought a weapon rather than bash in Jose's head with that thing."

"You said 'he.' Any chance it could be a woman, maybe his sister?"

"Not likely. From the way the building manager described Jose's sister, she's tiny. Could she have been in an adrenaline-fueled rage and had the strength to pull the bar off the wall and beat her brother to death? It's possible but not very likely."

"That's kind of what I've been thinking. Could be Jose's sister had a boyfriend and, for whatever reason, he went after Jose."

"Maybe . . . but she's only been here for a couple of weeks. And from the sound of things, she was totally dependent on Jose."

"Yeah, she probably—" Adkins didn't finish his thought. There was a knock at the door and Brick stepped aside so Adkins could see who was there.

Brick glanced at his watch. Less than an hour had elapsed since the A-Team showed up, but it definitely seemed longer. The door to the apartment was open now, and Brick heard multiple voices coming from the hallway. A team of Mobile Crime officers had arrived along with the same two guys from the Medical Examiner's Office who had responded to the Tidal Basin. The air guitarist seemed perplexed when he saw Brick.

"You, again?"

"Afraid so . . . it's been a long day."

"Tell me about it, man."

Brick saw Rory standing off by himself. He looked around to see where Allen was, but didn't spot him anywhere. It was possible he had gone downstairs to talk to Carlos or to return a call from one of his girlfriends. Brick went over to Rory.

"Is that detective finished talking to you?"

"Yeah, he has my phone number if he has any other questions. He said I could go, but I was waiting for you."

"Hey, Brick." Adkins stuck his head out the door. "We need you in here."

"Just a minute." Brick turned back in Rory's direction. "I'm going to be here a little longer. There's no reason for you to stay."

"Okay." Rory sighed. "Guess it's my turn to be the bearer of bad news."

Brick didn't envy Rory. Eamonn, no doubt, would be devastated. He was good to all his employees, but it seemed he had taken Jose under his wing. Brick headed back inside the apartment to see what Adkins wanted.

"Looks like we've found the cat."

Brick figured he knew the answer, but asked anyway. "Dead?"

"No, he's alive. Do you have a number for Animal Control?"

He didn't, but even if he did, he wasn't about to have Elvis taken to the city pound. "Where is he . . . she?"

"In the kitchen, under the sink."

Brick went back into the apartment and found a Mobile Crime officer on his hands and knees in front of the cabinet below the sink. Fingerprint dust had been brushed on a couple of glasses on the counter.

"I thought I heard a meow while I was printing those glasses so I opened the door and looked inside . . . sure enough. I tried to get him out but he's not having it."

"Let me try." The officer stood up and stepped aside. Brick bent down on one knee and reached back into the corner of the cabinet. "Come on, Elvis, it's okay." He stroked the cat's orange head, but Elvis backed away, retreating further into the corner. "Can you get me an evidence bag, one that's about the size of a grocery bag?"

"Yeah, sure."

"Elvis, c'mon, come on out." Brick shifted his weight to his left knee. "Where's a mouse when you really need one?"

"Excuse me?"

Brick didn't realize the officer had returned. "Nothing—guess I'm getting a little punchy."

"Is this okay?" The officer handed the bag to Brick.

"Thanks." Brick unfolded the bag and placed the opened end in front of Elvis. He waited for a few minutes, hoping the cat would decide to check out what was inside, but no such luck. Brick wasn't about to give up. He raked his fingernails along the side of the bag. He noticed the cat's ears perk up and then, suddenly, the cat pounced. Elvis landed squarely in the bag. As cat carriers go, it wasn't ideal, but with a couple of air holes it would do the job. Brick picked up the bag. It was light, eight or nine pounds, and, at least for now, Elvis wasn't struggling to escape.

Adkins had been watching from the doorway. He was joined by Allen who started to laugh. "I've heard of the cat in the hat, but pussy in the—"

"Travis, not now." It was one of the few times Brick had heard Adkins discourage his partner from going off on a riff. He turned in Brick's direction. "If you want to take responsibility for it, I'm okay with that."

It was what Brick had hoped to hear. "Once we find Jose's sister, it'll be her responsibility. In the meantime, I'm sure Rory and Eamonn will look after her. If not, I will." Brick felt the cat move around. "Unless there's anything else you need from me, I'll get go . . ." Brick's voice trailed off as he spied a photograph on the refrigerator door.

He stepped closer and bent down to get a better look. He couldn't believe what he was seeing. Maybe it was the bad lighting or maybe sleep deprivation was causing him to hallucinate.

"You okay?" Adkins sounded uneasy.

"You're not going cat-a-tonic, are you?" Despite the pun, even Allen's voice had a hint of concern.

Brick pointed toward the photo. "Look at this picture." He stepped aside so Adkins and Allen could move in closer. "That's Jose on the left."

"The one with his arm around the older woman in the middle?" Adkins asked as he studied the photo. "Yeah, I can see a resemblance. I'm guessing that's his mother, and the girl next to her, she's got to be related, too. Looks like a family day at the beach—where did you say he's from? Mexico?"

"Guatemala," Brick said. "Look closer at the girl."

"Mexico, Guatemala, anyplace south of Texas, it's all the same." Allen leaned in toward the photo. "Not bad-looking. She's got a nice body, but that bathing suit looks like something her mother should be wearing. It's about as sexy as granny panties."

Brick ignored Allen. The suit was a modest one-piece, but ironically, as far as Brick was concerned, every bit as revealing as the skimpiest bikini. "Look closely at her shoulder."

Allen looked again. "Oh, I see what you mean. One of those birthmarks, I forget what they're called." He looked back toward Brick. "Yeah, so?"

"She's the girl . . . the girl in the Tidal Basin."

# CHAPTER EIGHT

"ANOTHER SHOT, BRICK?" Eamonn held the bottle of Jameson, ready to pour if Brick said the word.

"No, thanks." One shot on an empty stomach was probably a mistake; a second one definitely would be. The two men were sitting in the corner of the storeroom that doubled as Eamonn's office. Elvis had taken up residence on his desk. She alternated between lapping up water and eating chopped-up pieces of boiled chicken Rory had gotten from the kitchen before going out to get some cans of cat food and a bag of kitty litter. Taking care of Elvis seemed a welcomed distraction in the same way the grief-stricken find comfort in preparing food for sharing.

"Jose and his sister." Eamonn shook his head. "A mother should never have to bury a child, and this poor woman will have to do it twice." Eamonn swiped at his cheek with the back of his big, beefy hand but not before Brick noticed a tear trickle from his eye. "What is this crazy feckin' world coming to? The violence has become an epidemic."

Brick agreed. Finding logical explanations for irrational acts could be as elusive as a winning lottery ticket, but that didn't mean the killer or killers wouldn't get caught. For Brick and Ron, and now the A-Team, their job was to find "who." The reason "why" might always be the subject of speculation. Brick had a couple of questions for Eamonn, but Rory's return preempted his opportunity.

"Jaysus, I didn't know it would be so complicated. There were all different flavors and some sounded gross like pate liver and turkey giblets. Maybe if you're a cat, that sounds good, but I just grabbed a couple of cans of chicken in gravy and a bag of dry food." Rory set his purchases down on the desk. "And I got this litter because it's supposed to control the odor. They better feckin' not be lying. We don't want this place smelling like cat shit." Rory glanced around the room. "What should I use, Eamonn? One of the rubber dish pans?" He didn't wait for a response. Rory left, presumably in search of a makeshift litter box.

"It's not like him to be so hyper." Eamonn shook his head. "Guess it's his way of coping."

"I think you're right," Brick said. Now was his chance to ask a couple of questions before Rory returned. "Eamonn, do you think Jose was involved in any type of gang activity?"

"I never saw anything to make me think he might be." Eamonn hesitated before he continued. "Given how much the kid worked, he hardly had time to sleep much less hang out with friends. I worried about him not having any real fun, but he was determined to save enough money to bring his sister here."

"What about drugs?"

Eamonn shook his head. "No, like I said, he worked all the time. You knew him pretty well; did you ever suspect anything?"

"No, but we have to consider all possibilities. It's too early to rule anything out."

"So, what happens now?" Eamonn asked.

"Autopsies. Maybe as early as tomorrow depending on the backlog at the Medical Examiner's Office. Once the bodies are released, the family is free to claim them. But in this case, it's complicated by the next-of-kin being in Guatemala unless Jose had other family here."

"No one he ever mentioned." Eamonn shook his head. "He always spent Thanksgiving and Christmas with Rory and me and whoever else we'd round up."

"There's a liaison at the State Department who will be contacted and will work with someone from the Guatemalan Embassy or Consulate. Hopefully, they'll help the family arrange for the bodies to be flown home. Unfortunately, I'm pretty sure it will be very expensive." Brick pushed back his chair and stood up. Only then did he realize how exhausted he was.

"Will you let me know what you find out? I mean, if there's something I can do. I thought a lot of the kid."

"I know, Eamonn. We all did."

# CHAPTER NINE

IT WAS STILL dark when Brick walked into the Starbucks at Judiciary Square. Usually he drank tea, but not this morning. He ordered a venti coffee.

"Should I leave room for cream?" the barista asked.

"No, fill it to the brim."

"Uh-oh, one of those days?"

Brick turned at the familiar sound of his partner's voice. "More like one of those nights."

"Glad somebody's getting some."

Brick shook his head. "It's not what you're thinking." The barista slipped the steaming cup into a sleeve and handed it to Brick. "Thanks." He put his change in the tip jar and turned back in Ron's direction. "Get your coffee and I'll tell you what's up."

Ron joined Brick at a counter looking out on Indiana Avenue. For now, there was little activity on the street, but that would soon change when the day shift officers started arriving for roll call.

Brick stirred a packet of sugar into his coffee and took a sip. He glanced over at his partner. "Our Tidal Basin girl—her name is Maria Delgado. She's here from Guatemala on a work visa. I should say, she *was* here."

"Way to go!" Ron raised his hand in a high-five gesture but let it drop when Brick didn't slap his hand. "How'd you identify her so fast?"

"Not the way I would have chosen." While Brick waited for his coffee to cool, he told Ron about finding Jose's body and then seeing the photograph of him and Maria.

Ron raised his latte but set it down without drinking. "Whoa, man, I don't know what to say. I mean, what are the odds?" He shook his head. "Wait, is Jose the kid who works at the Irish bar—the one you took to a Nats game last year?"

"Yeah." Brick smiled at the recollection. "I had forgotten about that. Rory and I took him. We were trying to help him understand baseball and it was just after the All-Star Game. So Jose was expecting another home run derby and instead Scherzer took a no-hitter into the eighth. I tried to explain to him that it was actually exciting, not boring." Again, Brick smiled. "I'm not sure he was convinced, but we had a good time."

"I'm sorry for your loss, man. I pray to God I never arrive at a scene and recognize the victim, but I guess if I stay on the job long enough, there's a good chance it will happen."

*Or happen again*, was the thought crossing Brick's mind, but he wasn't about to share the previous experience with his partner. It was something he thought of often but rarely spoke about. His coffee had cooled slightly. He took a sip before continuing. "So, like it or not, we're going to be working closely with the A-Team."

"How closely is closely?" Ron looked as though he had swallowed a mouthful of curdled milk.

"I'm not sure—that will be up to Blancato. And speaking of the lieutenant, keep in mind that anything you say to Allen will find its way to him. Not sure about Adkins, but watch your step around him, too."

"Got it." He stared into his cup for a moment. "I bet Travis Allen was a brown-noser in kindergarten, and all these years later, he still is." Ron finished his latte and tossed the empty cup into the trash. "Proves a theory of mine."

"That being?" Brick asked.

"The only way some guys can be bigger assholes is to gain weight."

Brick paused then handed Ron the keys to the cruiser he'd signed out. "How about I finish my coffee and ponder that while you drive."

* * *

The sun was up, and at least for now, it was the kind of morning that tempts lots of government employees to call in sick. As Ron drove past the Capitol and the Supreme Court, Brick envied the tourists who would spend the day enjoying all the beauty the city had to offer, oblivious to what lay just beyond the tour-mobile route. If it was possible for a city to be described as schizophrenic, D.C. would meet the criteria. Looking out the window, it was almost inconceivable that this, too, was Pennsylvania Avenue. The Southeast suffix added to addresses in this quadrant definitely distinguished them from those in the affluent Northwest section of the city. Instead of a Starbucks on every corner, boarded-up storefronts flourished.

"They should have built the stadium right there." Ron pointed to the area between the Armory and RFK Stadium.

Brick laughed at his partner. "You say that every time we pass by here."

"It still pisses me off. They're not the Maryland Redskins, they're the Washington Redskins."

"Given the controversy over their name, maybe not for long."

"Then move them back to the city and call them the D.C. Redskins—problem solved."

"I think you're missing the point."

"I know, I'm kidding. Personally, I don't care what they call the team as long as they have a winning season." Ron drummed his fingers on the steering wheel as he waited for the light to turn green. "And, I think some people take the whole political correctness thing too far. I'm surprised they still call Notre Dame the Fighting Irish. Are you offended by that?"

"That's better than the 'Drunken Irish,' which might be more accurate."

Ron was still laughing as he pulled the cruiser into a parking space next to a medical examiner's van. He took the keys out of the ignition and dropped them into his pocket. "This has gotta be my least favorite place on earth."

Brick unbuckled his seat belt. "I thought that was Fed Ex Field."

"You're right. Okay, my second least favorite."

Together they walked up the steps of the nondescript structure known simply as Building Twenty-Seven. Ron hesitated before opening the frosted glass double doors. He took a deep breath and motioned to Brick as he held the door. "After you."

"No way. If I turn my back, you're liable to bolt."

Reluctantly, Ron led the way.

"Morning, boys." Denise Jackson smiled broadly as Brick and Ron approached the receptionist's desk. She was a large woman in her mid-fifties with a sunny disposition and a preference for bright colored clothes. Today's outfit was a tropical floral printed dress that would be more appropriate at a luau. By the end of the day, it would probably smell like formaldehyde and other strong chemicals.

Brick signed in first. "You're looking lovely as always."

"Thanks. I bought this in the Bahamas last month." Denise sighed. "Eleven months until the next vacation."

"It'll be here before you know it," Brick said.

"You really think so?"

"No."

Denise laughed as she put an "X" through another day on her calendar. "Still, it gives me something to look forward to. Working here, I need it."

"Amen to that." Ron took the pen from Brick. He looked at his watch and recorded the time before signing his name and noting his badge number.

"Let's see, you'll be in room—" Denise checked her computer screen "—three with Dr. Park."

Brick was glad to hear that. Until Dr. Sammy Park was hired as Chief Medical Examiner, the office had been a disgrace. Botched autopsies resulted in acquittals that frustrated police and prosecutors. It wasn't until an investigative reporter's story that the deplorable conditions were revealed. Over breakfast, Washingtonians read about maggots and the stench of decomposing bodies. Recognizing this was a place where either they or a loved one could ultimately end up created a firestorm, the likes of which the city hadn't seen in a long time. In less than forty-eight hours, the staff was gone and Dr. Park took over. Under his leadership, the turnaround was accomplished in less time than anyone thought possible.

Ron followed Brick into the assigned autopsy room—a stark, cold, impersonal florescent-lit temple of stainless steel where social status was no longer a commodity. Georgetown resident or street person, the procedure was the same. The technician placing a hard rubber body post beneath Maria's back acknowledged the detectives with a nod but continued with his task. Once the body post was in place, he adjusted the white sheet covering her from just below her chin to above her ankles.

Brick had stood in this very spot more times than he cared to count. Normally he could detach emotionally as the body, usually that of a homicide victim, was subjected to necessary but extremely intrusive procedures. Not so under these circumstances. Even though he had never met Maria, knowing Jose placed him at one degree of separation from her. And now, staring at her sheet-covered corpse, Brick felt he was violating her privacy like some kind of voyeur. But he had no choice—this was his job. This was his case and he was required to be present.

"Good morning, gentlemen."

All three men turned as Dr. Park entered the room. He was carrying a clipboard, and, before proceeding, checked the tag attached to Maria's big toe on her right foot. Apparently satisfied that the identifying information was correct, Dr. Park put on a pair of gloves and a headset microphone. He looked directly at Brick and Ron.

"Any questions before we get started?"

"No, sir," Brick answered for both of them.

"Very well, let's proceed." With that as his cue, the technician turned on the audio and video recording devices.

Brick watched as Dr. Park studied Maria's body for signs of injuries or trauma, stopping to take photos from different angles. He worked quickly until he zeroed in on a bruise on Maria's left hip. He adjusted an overhead light and took several photos from different angles before setting the camera aside.

As Dr. Park reached for his face shield, Brick braced himself for what was coming next. He swallowed hard, trying to get rid of the excess saliva pooling in his mouth. He wasn't very successful so he swallowed again as the buzz from the Stryker saw sent chills down his spine. He knew it would be used to cut through Maria's ribs and collarbone so that her breastplate could be removed. Dr. Park was verbally documenting everything he was doing, but Brick couldn't bring himself to concentrate on what was being said. Later, he could rely on the findings in the written report. For now, he spent much of the next hour staring down at his shoes. At one point, he glanced over and saw Ron was doing the same. Technically, they were meeting their attendance requirement; nothing said they had to watch every gory detail. One by one, the internal organs were removed and weighed. This was an indicator the autopsy was almost complete and for that he was grateful, but Maria's brain still needed to be removed. Once again, the sound of the Stryker saw filled the room as the blade cut across the top of her head. There was no way Brick could bring himself to watch. Instead, he focused his eyes on the clock mounted on the wall across the room, mesmerized by the second hand's orbit.

\* \* \*

"You okay, partner?" Ron asked as the two detectives walked down the hall toward the exit.

Brick nodded and exhaled for what felt like the first time in over an hour.

"Sure? You look a little pale. And that's saying a lot because you're one of the whitest white guys I've ever seen."

"Not everyone is lucky enough to have a natural tan."

"He shoots, he scores." Ron's hearty laugh echoed in the drab hallway as he tossed an imaginary basketball into an imaginary hoop. "Seriously, Brick, I get the feeling this one was tough for you."

"I'll let you in on a secret. When I was in college, I almost flunked biology because I couldn't dissect a fetal pig. So, when it comes to autopsies, they're all tough."

"I hear ya, but since you have a connection to the vic—to Maria—I don't mean to be out of line here, but are you too close to this case?"

Brick stopped short of the exit. "To be objective? Is that what you're asking?"

"Yeah, I guess I am. It's just everyone in the squad knows you take your cases to heart, and since you're sort of connected—hey, forget it." Ron looked embarrassed. "I shouldn't have brought it up."

"No, it's okay. The thought crossed my mind, and it's probably why I didn't get much sleep last night." Brick stifled a yawn before looking Ron straight in the eye. "If I said this is just another case, I'd be lying. I'm counting on you to make sure I keep everything in perspective."

Ron nodded. "No problem." He reached in his pocket and pulled out the keys to the cruiser. He handed them to Brick. "Let's grab some breakfast before we head back."

# CHAPTER TEN

"Lieutenant Blancato will see you now." His secretary delivered the words in the same robotic voice Brick had heard many times. He was beginning to think she had a limited repertoire of phrases and facial expressions. Whether she had a pulse was questionable.

Brick led the way; Ron followed. They had decided beforehand Brick would do the talking unless Blancato specifically addressed Ron.

"Okay, guys, take a seat." Blancato looked at his watch. "I've got a conference call at ten, and I need to bring everyone up-to-date at that time."

"Who's everyone?" Brick asked.

"The chief." Blancato answered quickly. "And the uh . . . the deputy chief."

Blancato wasn't fooling Brick. He was sure there were others—the mayor, for one.

"No need to tell me about the brother's murder. Travis has already briefed me, but how was it you were there?"

Brick was glad he had an opportunity to explain in case Travis Allen had misrepresented the circumstances, deliberately or otherwise.

"What are the odds?" Blancato looked first at Brick and then at Ron. "But like I've often said, sometimes it's better to be lucky than smart."

"Excuse me?"

"Well, given a body with no ID and no hits on missing persons, she might have never been identified if it weren't for her brother turning up dead." Blancato twisted the cap on a bottle of Coke and took a swig. He got up and walked around to the front of his desk. "Who did her autopsy?"

Brick was still taken aback by what Blancato considered to be a lucky break, but he let it go. "Dr. Park."

"Good. He knows what he's doing, not like a couple of those medical examiners we used to have. Can't remember the guy's name, but he was so incompetent, he couldn't find his ass with both hands." Blancato took another sip of soda. "Anyway, I digress. What did Park find? Any surprises?"

"The autopsy confirmed she was dead before she hit the water, which is what we suspected."

"So we're dealing with a secondary crime scene." Blancato glanced in Ron's direction. "Double the fun."

Brick suspected Blancato was spending too much time with Allen. "The way I see it, there's at least three—the Tidal Basin, the apartment Maria shared with Jose, and the place where she was killed. Nothing at Jose's apartment indicates she was killed there."

"Well, if there's a third crime scene—you need to find it."

Brick was used to hearing Blancato state the obvious. He overlooked the comment just as he had done many times before. "According to Dr. Park, the hyoid bone was fractured. Cause of death was asphyxiation. Other than a bruise on her left hip, no significant trauma to the body. Dr. Park concluded—"

"Was she raped?" Blancato got up from his desk and started to pace.

Brick hated being interrupted. "That's what I was getting to." Despite his best effort, Blancato was starting to get to him. He took a second and tried to control the sarcastic tone he heard creeping into his voice. "There was no conclusive evidence that she was sexually assaulted. Pelvic examination indicated she was a virgin."

"How old was she?"

"According to her passport, she was twenty years old."

"And a virgin? Is that possible?"

Brick assumed that was Blancato's feeble attempt at a joke. Neither he nor Ron laughed. "Toxicology results are pending."

Blancato checked his watch again. "What's your gut telling you—how did this go down?"

It wasn't a question Brick was expecting. "It's just over twenty-four hours since Maria's body was pulled out of the Tidal Basin. Less time than that since Jose's body was found. At this point, I don't have a theory."

"Okay, okay . . . it's probably too early to figure out if there's a gang or drug connection, but with them being from Mexico—"

"Guatemala!" Brick had had enough. He stood up so he would be at eye level with Blancato. "Do you think Travis Allen has ever looked at a map? There are several countries between Mexico and South America—one of them is Guatemala."

Blancato smiled. "When Travis was in school, he was probably more interested in girls than he was in geography. Hey, I know you two don't always get along, but you're going to have to. You've got to play nice on this one. We need closure."

As if we don't strive for closure on every case, Brick thought. "Then how about some extra resources?"

"You know my hands are tied because of the budget." Blancato checked his watch. "I've got my call in five minutes—we're finished here."

Ron headed toward the door, but Brick hesitated. "Doesn't cost anything to have recruits from the Academy scour the grounds around the Tidal Basin. They might find something that belonged to Maria."

"You're talking needle in a haystack. I don't think that's how we should be using our resources."

"Why don't you run it by the mayor—see what he thinks."

Brick had made his point. There was no need to wait for a response. He and Ron headed back to the squad room.

"What just happened in there?" Ron asked.

Brick ushered Ron into his cubicle and kept his voice low. "It's what I call QB—quintessential Blancato. Cases like this with the potential to be high profile screw with his head because he probably figures they could make or break his career."

"Good to know because I was beginning to think either he forgot to take his meds or he took too many. And, by the way, I need to correct something I said back at the ME's office."

"What's that?"

"I was wrong about you being the whitest white man—your face has more shades of red than a jumbo box of crayons."

Brick laughed now even though he had felt his face flush and his blood pressure rise while he was in Blancato's office. And at this moment, his cubicle felt claustrophobic. "C'mon, let's go for a ride."

* * *

This time Brick drove and Ron rode shotgun. Their destination was Jose's apartment building. They got as far as Connecticut Avenue and K Street before traffic ground to a halt in all directions.

"Know what this means?" Brick drummed his fingers on the steering wheel.

"Yeah . . . motorcade."

Both detectives used the delay time to check their phones. Brick listened to a message from the prosecutor's paralegal about an

upcoming trial. He'd return the call later. He slipped the phone back
into his pocket just as the sound of sirens would have drowned out
any conversation he might have been having anyway. A convoy led by
three MPD cars sped north on Connecticut Avenue. A black limo
with small flags attached to either side of the front of the car was next
in line.

"Decoy vehicle," Brick and Ron said in unison.

An identical limo was right behind. Five SUVs, a hazmat vehicle,
and two press vans flew through the intersection followed by an ambulance serving a dual function as a caboose. Taillights sped away, but
it would still be a few minutes before the roads reopened to regular
traffic.

"Man, they could save the taxpayers a lot of money if they just drove
him around in a Fed Ex truck," Ron said.

Brick gave his partner a skeptical look.

"Think about it. How many Fed Ex trucks do you see on any given
day?"

"I don't know."

"Okay, you have to agree, they're a common sight." Brick nodded,
mostly to appease his partner. "If the President was in one of them,
who would know?"

"Good point. If Blancato becomes head of the Secret Service, why
don't you suggest it?"

"Whoa . . . is that really a possibility?"

"I've heard rumors mentioning that or the Capitol Police."

"He'd leave MPD?"

"For a job with the Feds—in a heartbeat." Brick noticed a uniformed officer removing the sawhorse-type barricade that had blocked
the street. "Looks like we're about to start moving."

What should have taken fifteen minutes took twice that, but finally, Brick pulled into an alley behind Jose's apartment building. His

options were limited forcing him to park behind a dumpster. Before getting out of the car, he checked where he was about to step. He wasn't taking any chances. It had already been a dog shit kind of day.

Brick stood where Rory had several hours ago and entered the manager's code into the intercom. "Does it feel like déjà vu all over again?" Ron asked.

"Yeah, in some ways it does." Brick didn't get a chance to elaborate.

"Who there?" Carlos answered on the third ring.

"Detective Kavanagh."

"*Si.* I be right there."

While they waited, Brick looked around to see if there were any security cameras recording people entering and exiting the building. He wasn't surprised to see that none existed. The intercom system was about as state-of-the-art as a manual typewriter.

Carlos appeared a few minutes later wearing the clothes he had worn the day before, and his hair had the same wild look. He opened the door and motioned for the guys to enter.

"Since what happened, I tell everyone not to buzz people in. They need to be sure who they let in."

"I understand." Brick stepped into the lobby and Ron followed. "This is my partner, Detective Hayes. We've got a couple of questions for you." Just then the elevator door opened. A young woman pushing a stroller exited. A crying toddler clung to her leg refusing to go any further. "Is there somewhere we can talk?"

Carlos nodded. "*Si.*" He led Brick and Ron down the hall. On the last door on the right, the nameplate below the peephole read "Manager." There was no mistaking the pride in his voice. "My office and casa."

Cops get to see how people live much more so than the average person. Usually, as in this case, it's an unannounced visit, and what lies beyond a front door is anyone's guess. Given that Carlos looked like a walking unmade bed, that's what Brick expected to see. He was wrong. Instead, the studio apartment reminded Brick of an interview he once conducted at the Marine Barracks. Carlos would have easily passed a white-glove inspection. Even the floor looked as if it had recently been mopped and waxed.

"Have a seat." Carlos pointed to the folding chairs surrounding a small round table. "You want coffee—is fresh."

"No thanks, I'm fine," Brick said.

"So am I," Ron added.

Carlos poured himself a cup from a Mr. Coffee machine on the counter next to the stove before joining Brick and Ron at the table. He picked up the TV remote and hit power. A Spanish-speaking talk show faded as the screen went dark.

"Carlos, we know what happened to Jose's sister." Brick watched his expression, trying to gauge any reaction. He didn't pick up on anything.

"Is okay?" Carlos raised his cup and took a sip of coffee.

"No. She's dead, too."

Carlos started to cough as if the coffee had gone down the wrong way. To Brick's way of thinking, it was either a very convincing performance or Carlos may be on the verge of choking. "Are you all right?"

Carlos nodded his head but continued to cough. Finally, he seemed to catch his breath. "What happened to her?"

"Do you watch the local news?" Brick asked.

"No, mostly I watch Telemundo."

"The body of a young woman was found floating in the Tidal Basin—it was Maria Delgado."

Carlos set his mug down with a shaky hand. Some coffee sloshed over the rim and landed on his pants. He didn't seem to notice. "Oh my . . . dead, too. Who . . . who would do this?"

"That's what we intend to find out. We're assigned to her case."

"And to Jose?"

"No, his case is assigned to Detectives Allen and Adkins who were here yesterday. But whatever you tell them, you should tell me, too."

"*Sí.*"

"Did Jose or Maria have trouble with anyone in the building?"

"No. If they did, I don't know. Jose . . ." Carlos sighed. "Jose work a lot. Always, I see him going to work. The girl, his sister, I only see her two, maybe three times."

"When you did see her, was she by herself?"

"No, she always with Jose. She seemed shy, she don't say nothing."

"Okay, we'll need to talk to people here in the building. Do you have a list of tenants?"

Carlos pushed back from the table and walked across the room to a file cabinet. He opened the top drawer, pulled out a file, and returned to the table. He handed Brick a spreadsheet. The tenant information for several units was blank.

"Are a lot of apartments empty?"

"*Sí.* When someone move out, that's it."

"Why?"

"The owner want to sell. That's why he no want me to fix things, only if something really bad. I worry I no have this job much longer."

Brick felt his cellphone vibrate. The caller ID displayed a number he didn't recognize. He ignored it for now. "Can I get a copy of this list?"

"Take it. I print another."

"Thanks." Brick started to get up and Ron followed his cue. He handed Carlos his business card. "If you think of anything that we should know, anything at all—that's my number. We're going to go knock on a couple of doors."

After leaving Carlos's apartment, Brick checked his voicemail. He listened to one of the messages twice. "Listen to this." He handed the phone to Ron.

"Sounds promising." Ron gave the phone back to Brick.

"Yeah, let's go check that out first."

# CHAPTER ELEVEN

IT WAS CLOSE to noon when Brick and Ron arrived at the Central District Station of the Park Police. They identified themselves to the officer of the day who then directed them to the Crime Prevention Unit on the second floor. Unlike MPD headquarters, the stairwell was clean and smelled like air freshener rather than body odor. Upon opening the door, they stepped into a large bright room with windows looking out on the Potomac River.

"Maybe I should reconsider squirrel chasing," Ron muttered under his breath.

"You and me both," Brick said. He stepped up to the counter where a receptionist was seated.

"May I help you?"

"I'm Detective Kavanagh. We're here to see Sergeant Fischer."

"I'll let him know you're here." She picked up her phone. "Okay, I'll send them back." She hung up and smiled at Brick. "His office is the second door on the left, just past the exit sign."

"Thanks."

"Sure." She smiled again.

As they headed down the hall, Ron elbowed his partner. "She's into you." Brick gave him an exasperated look. It wasn't the first time Ron had made such an observation.

"Didn't you see her looking at your left hand?"

"No."

Ron's dreads swayed as he shook his head. "It was obvious, man."

Brick rolled his eyes. "If you say so, but I need you to be my partner not my pimp."

The door to Sergeant Fischer's office was open. He was seated behind a neatly organized desk that looked as though it had recently been polished. He stood when Brick and Ron appeared in the doorway. "Please, come in. Have a seat."

Brick made the introductions before sitting down.

"As you probably know, we have several cameras set up around the Mall and Tidal Basin. I went through the footage for the past couple of nights. I gotta warn you, the quality isn't great, but there's one tape that might be significant. Let me get it here on the screen." Fischer started typing. "Here we go." He turned the computer screen so Brick and Ron could view the images. The date and time stamp indicated it was approximately three hours before the call came in about a body floating in the Tidal Basin.

Brick pulled his chair closer to the screen and Ron stood behind him. Fischer was right about the poor quality of the film, but it was still possible to make out a shadowy figure pushing a grocery cart.

"Looks like a street person with all his worldly goods," Brick said.

"Yeah, there's a core group that hang around that area. When it's cold, they spend the night on the heating grates along Constitution Avenue, but now that it's warmer, they've moved to the Monument Grounds and down near the 14th Street Bridge."

Brick kept watching even though all he saw was a narrow segment of the Tidal Basin on a moonless, foggy night. He was beginning to think he and Ron would have been better off spending their time canvassing tenants at Jose's apartment building.

"There." Fischer sounded excited as he pointed toward the screen.

From the edge of the frame, Brick saw the street person enter the picture heading in the opposite direction. He was still pushing the grocery cart. "Can you freeze this frame?" Brick asked Fischer.

"Sure."

Brick studied the image. "Now, go back to where we first see him." Fischer complied and Brick scrutinized this image as well.

"Want to see them side by side?" Fischer asked.

"Yes." Brick had already mentally done that but needed confirmation his eyes weren't playing tricks on him.

"You see it, too, don't you?"

Brick nodded. "Appears the street person lightened his load."

"Exactly!" Fischer had become quite animated.

Ron bent down to get a better view. "Damn . . . that could explain how our girl ended up in the water."

"It could," Brick said. He turned in Fischer's direction. "She was petite, right around a hundred pounds."

"Then she could have easily fit into that cart," Fischer said. A perplexed look crossed his face. "I'm surprised, though. We've never had any serious problem with the street people who congregate in that area. An occasional disorderly, public intoxication, but I don't even recall any aggressive panhandling reports."

"Maybe it wasn't a street person," Brick said. "If you want to hide in plain sight, that's a smart disguise. For the most part, they're invisible except to each other."

"I got a feeling I know where this is going." Ron looked over at Brick. "Think we'll be making the rounds tonight talking to a bunch of homeless guys."

"My partner is psychic."

"That's better than psycho . . . I had a female partner who was." Brick and Ron laughed but Fischer didn't. "Unfortunately, I didn't figure that out until I married her. Still burns my ass I'm paying alimony. Just last month—"

"Ah, is it possible to get those images blown up?" Brick asked.

"What? Oh yeah, we don't have the capacity here, but I can send a request to our photo lab. But I'll be honest with you, I'm not optimistic anything helpful will show up. One homeless guy pushing a cart looks pretty much like every homeless guy."

"True, but it's worth a try."

"Yeah, can't hurt and you might want to check with the Center for Creative Non-Violence. Their volunteers deliver meals to the homeless on a regular schedule. I've seen the guys milling around waiting for the van to arrive."

"Thanks, that's a good idea."

*   *   *

Before heading back to the car, Brick and Ron stopped at a hotdog vendor set up near the public tennis courts. Carefully, they made their way across the bike path. During the week it was still fairly tame, but on weekends it seemed a lot of cyclists were in training for the Tour de France. Brick pointed toward an empty bench shaded by one of the late-blooming cherry trees.

Ron popped the tab on a can of Pepsi. He took a swig then proceeded to unwrap his hotdog. Brick did the same. For a few minutes, they sat silently eating lunch and watching planes taking off and landing at Reagan National Airport located directly across the Potomac.

"If ever there was a day to play hooky, it's today." Ron raised the soda can and gestured toward the river.

"Spring fever?" Brick asked. It occurred to him Ron hadn't taken any leave since being assigned to Homicide. "Take some time if you need it."

"Saving it for when the babies arrive." For a minute or two, Ron seemed lost in thought. "I've had a few months now to get used to the idea, but I still can't wrap my head around being a father. Lately, I've been waking up at night in a cold sweat."

"I understand." Brick thought about what he had just said. "No, actually I don't because when it comes to kids, I'm clueless. None of my own, and since I don't have any brothers or sisters, no nieces or nephews either. But I think I know you well enough to know you'll rise to the occasion."

"I guess if I just show up, I'm bound to do a better job than my old man." Ron shrugged. "But who am I to judge, maybe he did the best he could." He picked up his napkin and dabbed at the corner of his eye. "Man, sometimes I think I'm having hormone issues like Jasmine."

"Another subject where I'm clueless." Brick looked over at Ron and shrugged. "But it's got to be an emotional time for you, too. Cut yourself some slack."

Ron seemed to consider that for a moment. "It's just I've been thinking about my father a lot. He died when I was seven, so I can't say I knew him well, but I wonder how much of his DNA is in me. Didn't get his musical talent, that I know for sure. But it's his demons . . . that's what worries me."

It was common knowledge Ron was the son of a musician who, at one time, had played with some jazz greats before dying from a heroin overdose in his mid-thirties. Up until now, Ron had never mentioned the man. Brick wasn't sure how to respond. He had enough unresolved issues when it came to his own father.

"You're your own man, Ron. My advice, stop worrying and enjoy this time." Brick checked his watch. It was after one p.m. "We should get back to Headquarters. I have to return a couple of calls and I need you to run an NCIC check on Carlos."

"I got a pretty good idea what I'll find—he's dirty."

"What makes you so sure?" Brick asked.

"I'm suspicious of a guy who looks like a slob but keeps his place like a neat freak. I figure he's used to having his wardrobe provided and living in a confined space subject to regular inspections."

Brick nodded. He was pleased with Ron's observations. Some things can be learned but others can only be discerned through gut feelings. It wasn't the first time Ron had shown he had the kind of instincts that would serve him well, especially if he chose to stay in Homicide. Brick was about to compliment his partner when he noticed Ron seemed to be checking his appearance before a mirror that didn't exist.

"Do these horizontal stripes make my ass look fat?"

Brick shook his head and laughed. "Might want to lay off the nachos."

# CHAPTER TWELVE

BRICK AND RON stepped off the elevator just as the A-Team stepped on. Travis Allen held the door open with his left foot.

"Looks like we're going to be double-dating for a while." The elevator door started to buzz. "Can't dance now, we're headed to the grand—" The elevator doors banged shut, and as far as Brick was concerned, not a second too soon.

Brick was leaving a voicemail message when Ron appeared with a printout in hand. He waited for Brick to hang up before handing him the paper. Brick scanned it quickly.

"Let's go." Brick grabbed his jacket from the back of his chair.

"I figured that's what you would say." Ron held up a set of car keys. "Already signed out a set of wheels."

\* \* \*

For the second time in less than six hours, Brick and Ron sat opposite Carlos Garcia at his kitchen table. This time Carlos didn't offer them coffee. He avoided eye contact. His attention was focused on the skin around his right thumbnail, picking at a hangnail with his index finger.

"Is not what it seems." Carlos looked up briefly before looking away.

"Carlos." Brick spoke softly. "I've heard that too many times. If it's not what it seems, you need to tell me what it is."

Carlos scratched the back of his neck. "It was Fourth of July and it was hot, man. Me and a couple of buddies, we were drinking some beers. And all of a sudden, I had to pee real bad, and there was no place to go 'cept this alley. I no see this woman up in the window looking down, but she see me. Next thing I know the police come, and she say I disposed myself."

Brick glanced over at his partner. Ron's hand was clasped over his mouth and Brick suspected he was trying hard not to laugh. Brick could see the humor but would be the first to admit that Carlos's command of English far exceeded his own Spanish.

"You mean, *exposed* yourself."

"*Si.*" For the first time, Carlos made eye contact with Brick. "But I no do that. I just had to pee."

"I understand. But according to your record, you pled guilty to indecent exposure. Why would you do that if you weren't guilty?"

"My lawyer, the one the court gave me, he say that would be best. He tell me the judge will go easy, but I got sent to jail. And now—" Carlos cleared his throat before continuing. "I have to, how you say, sign up?"

"Register?"

"*Si.* Register as a sex offender." A tear rolled down his cheek, but Carlos didn't seem to notice. "I am not a sex offender." He shrugged his shoulders. "I just had to pee that day."

"I believe what you're saying, Carlos. And I need you to continue to be honest with me. Okay?"

"*Si.*"

"Did you have anything to do with the death of Jose and Maria?"

"No!" Carlos's face registered shock.

"But you had keys to the apartment. You could have gone there at any time. Maria was young and pretty—"

"I am telling the truth . . . about everything you ask."

* * *

"Did your bullshit detector go off?" Brick waited until he and Ron were in the stairwell before he posed the question to his partner.

"No, I think he's telling the truth."

"Why?"

"The way he talked about peeing in the alley—it was almost like a kid. That made me think he was being honest. And when he denied having anything to do with Jose and Maria's murders, he answered straight up and looked you right in the eye. If he's lying, he's a hell of a good actor." Ron paused as if considering what he had just said. "Still, I'm not saying he should be ruled out as a suspect."

"Good. How about you take the second floor, I'll take the third. Text when you're done and we'll meet in the lobby."

* * *

Unlike a couple of days ago, the musty hallway was eerily quiet—no music, no crying baby. The first two doors Brick knocked on went unanswered. He had learned from Carlos that four of the units on this floor were unoccupied. The apartment directly across from Jose's was his last chance to talk to anyone, assuming someone was home and willing to speak to him. Brick knocked loudly and waited. He was about to knock again when he heard footsteps approaching the door.

"Who is it?" The voice was female.

"Detective Kavanagh, Metropolitan Police." Brick's badge was hanging from a black lanyard he wore around his neck. He stepped back and held the badge up in front of the peephole. Slowly, the door opened as far as the security chain would allow. A young woman was on the other side. He could only see her in profile, but she appeared frightened. Brick held up his identification again to reassure her that he was who he claimed to be. "I'm one of the detectives assigned to the case involving your neighbors across the hall. I'd like to ask you a few questions."

Before the young woman could respond, someone within the apartment called out to her. "Who's at the door, Lourdes?"

"Police."

"Police?" A woman who appeared to be about ten years older than the first woman joined her at the door.

Brick introduced himself and explained his reason for being there. "May I come in?"

"One second."

Brick heard the security chain being slid back before the door was opened. He extended his right hand. "And you're—"

"Alma Gonzales. Lourdes and I are sisters."

Brick smiled. "I see the resemblance." The two women did look alike except Lourdes was pregnant and appeared as though she could deliver at any minute. That wasn't the only distinguishing characteristic Brick noticed. "What happened to your eye?" He was expecting to hear the standard I-walked-into-a-door response from Lourdes, but her sister didn't give her a chance to answer.

"The son of a bitch she's married to—that's his handiwork. Nice, isn't it?" Alma glanced around the room. "See these boxes and those suitcases? We're packing up and gonna be out of here before he gets home from work. Ask your questions, but we've got to keep working."

"I understand. Do you live here with Lourdes and her husband?"

"No, and it's a good thing for him because if I did, well, I'd better not go there." She was using a screwdriver to loosen the legs on a crib but not making much headway. "Damn, I can't get this to budge."

"Let me try." Brick motioned for Alma to hand him the screwdriver. "Hold on to it, there at the top." Over the next few minutes Brick managed to disassemble the crib and ask Lourdes about Jose and Maria. She didn't see Jose often but said he was always friendly and helpful. He'd help her with her groceries or if she were carrying her laundry basket. That sounded exactly like the kind of thing Brick would expect from Jose. "Did you get to know Maria after she moved in?"

"Yes, a little. She didn't have any friends here so she would come over sometimes while Jose was working. She'd help me cook and do some cleaning. I've been really tired, but Roberto still expects me to do everything like before."

"Asshole," Alma said. "Excuse my language, but that's the nicest name I can call him. What kind of a man hits his wife, especially his pregnant wife?"

"An asshole." Brick handed the screwdriver back to Alma along with the screws he had freed. "You might want to put these in a bag and tape them to the crib."

"Thanks. Otherwise, they'll get lost for sure."

Brick turned toward Lourdes. "Is there anything else you can tell me about Maria?"

"No, not really."

"Did you ever see anyone coming or going from Jose's apartment?" Lourdes shook her head, but Brick continued questioning her, hoping something would jog her memory. "What about noises—loud voices, people arguing?"

"No, nothing."

"What about a boyfriend. Did Maria ever talk about having a boyfriend?"

"No." Lourdes glanced at her watch before brushing her hair out of her eyes. "I need to go pack the baby clothes."

"Just one more question. Did Maria seem worried about her safety or Jose's?"

"No, she never mentioned anything like that."

When Lourdes left the room, Brick lowered his voice so she wouldn't hear the question he was about to ask Alma. "Tell me about Roberto. Is he involved in a gang?"

Alma shook her head. "No, that's about the only good thing I can say about him. He works and he provides for her, but it's the drinking. He's a nasty drunk."

"Does he get in fights with other people?"

"Not that I know of. He's not stupid; he doesn't want to get his ass kicked, and mostly, he drinks at home. It's gotten worse since Lourdes is pregnant, but hitting her—that crossed the line."

Brick had heard stories like this way too many times. But at least it sounded like Lourdes and her baby had the family support she needed to escape a situation that could escalate. Still, for his own peace of mind, he needed confirmation. "Is she going to be safe with you?"

"Yes, we'll be fine." Alma smiled confidently. "Roberto's afraid of my husband and with good reason. It's one thing to hit a woman, but he knows better than to take on a guy who is bigger, stronger, and hates his guts. Roberto's a coward . . . and an asshole."

"Do you think it's possible Roberto could have been involved in any way with Jose and Maria's murders?"

Alma shook her head. "I'd like to say yes so you could lock him up, but honestly, I don't think so."

Brick wished everyone he talked to was as forthcoming as Alma. "Where does Roberto work?"

"He manages the bodega at the corner of Columbia Road and 18th Street. He's there now or at least he should be."

"What do you mean by that?"

"He's the daytime boss, so I wouldn't put it past him to sneak away for an hour or two." Alma shrugged her shoulders. "I've stopped by there a few times and got the old 'he'll-be-right-back' routine. I don't think he's at noon Mass, if you know what I mean?"

"Is he cheating on your sister?"

"I don't have proof, but I've got intuition. Sometimes women just know things."

Brick couldn't argue with that. He felt his cellphone vibrate but ignored it for the moment. He took out one of his business cards and handed it to Alma. "I'm going to go to the bodega and talk to Roberto."

The color drained from Alma's face. "Oh my God, please don't tell him—I mean I want to get her out of here before—"

"It's okay. I won't let on that I've been here or that I've talked to you or Lourdes."

Alma didn't look convinced.

"I give you my word."

Alma managed a half smile. "Thank you." She slipped Brick's business card into her pocket.

"If you or Lourdes think of anything else, anything at all, give me a call."

Brick wrote down a number and address for Alma in his notebook. Something told him he'd be talking to her again. The apartment door closed behind him as he checked his phone for text messages. Ron was waiting in the lobby.

# CHAPTER THIRTEEN

"WHAT DID YOU find out?" Brick asked Ron.

"Nada. That's Spanish for nothing, right? 'Cause that's exactly what I've got. And 'nothing from nothing leaves nothing.'"

"Is that a quote from a movie I'm supposed to know?"

Ron shook his head. "No, man, song lyrics. Go ahead, take a guess."

"Tony Bennett."

Ron burst out laughing. "Tony Bennett . . . please tell me you aren't serious." Ron glanced over at his partner. "Want to try again?"

"No."

"Okay, it was Billy Preston."

"Never heard of him."

"Sure, you have. Among other things, he played keyboards on Abbey Road for The Beatles."

"Them I've heard of."

"I'd be real worried if you hadn't." Ron rolled his eyes. "So, did you have better luck than me?"

Brick relayed what he learned from talking with Alma and Lourdes. Nothing seemed all that significant, but he was concerned about the apparent domestic abuse. Brick believed Alma knew her brother-in-law well, but she wasn't around him 24/7. For that matter, neither was Lourdes.

"This Roberto guy sounds like a total douchebag," Ron said.

"You're right, but just remember we can't let on that we know any of this."

Brick and Ron left the cruiser parked in the alley and walked the two blocks to the intersection of Columbia Road and 18th Street. The El Mercado Bodega was located between a Zagat-rated Ethiopian restaurant and a vintage clothing store. Across the street, a two-story mural of Toulouse Latrec adorned the side of what otherwise would have been a nondescript building housing a French café.

The aroma of freshly baked pan dulce greeted the detectives as they stepped inside the bodega. Customers with plastic trays in one hand and metal tongs in the other selected items from the bakery cases. Brick was tempted to grab a tray and join them. Instead, he zigzagged his way around the cases and past the fresh produce. Ron followed close behind. They stopped in front of the cash register. A health department certificate was posted on the wall. Next to it, a sign indicated the manager-on-duty was Roberto Morales.

Brick waited while the guy behind the counter finished printing computer-pick lottery tickets for an elderly man whose attempt at small talk was being ignored.

"Are you Roberto Morales?" Brick asked.

"Who wants to know?"

Brick wasn't about to swap attitude with Roberto. Instead, he identified himself formally but in a louder voice than Roberto may have appreciated. "And this is Detective Hayes. We'd like to ask you a few questions."

"About what?"

Before Brick could respond, a man approached the counter from the opposite side and pointed to a pack of cigarettes on a shelf behind the cash register. Roberto retrieved the pack, handed it to the guy, and rang up the sale.

"The murder that happened across the hall from your apartment," Brick said.

The answer seemed to catch Roberto off-guard. His eyes narrowed. "How do you know where I live?"

"We checked the rental applications for all the tenants. This was listed as your place of employment." It wasn't the truth, but it was an explanation that worked for Brick in the past. He hoped it would again.

"So what do you want to know?" Not exactly polite, but Roberto had dialed down the surly tone.

Brick glanced around. "Is there someplace where we can talk?"

"Guess you haven't noticed, I'm working here."

"I have noticed. And this will take less time if we're not interrupted."

Roberto exhaled dramatically. He turned and looked toward a young man stocking a shelf with canned food. "Miguel." He motioned for him to come over to the counter. A young guy in a white Real Madrid jersey quickly complied. "Take over for me . . . and don't screw up."

Roberto popped the top on a can of Inca Kola before leading Brick and Ron to a stock room at the back of the bodega. He sat down on top of a stack of fifty-pound bags of rice.

Brick took the lead. Even though Jose's murder wasn't their case, he decided to start there and transition to Maria's at the appropriate time. "Did you know your neighbor, Jose Delgado?"

"Yeah, I knew him. So?"

"How well did you know him?"

"I knew who he was, that's all."

"Did you ever hang out, watch a game together?"

"No."

"Did you ever notice anything going on across the hall? People coming and going at all hours, anything like that?"

"No."

"Loud voices, people arguing?"

"No." Roberto started to get up. "I need to get back to work, man."

"Take it easy, just a couple more questions. Do you know if Jose belonged to a gang?" Brick noticed a smirk on Roberto's face. "Is there something funny about that?"

"Yeah. If he belonged to a gang, it'd be a gang of fags."

Brick was taken aback. He never got the impression Jose was gay. "Why do you say that?"

"I know a fag when I see one—he was a fag." Roberto took a long swig of soda and then another. "Only girl I ever seen him with was his sister."

Brick wasn't convinced Roberto was an expert on sexual orientation, but the mention of Jose's sister was the segue he was waiting for. "Are you aware that Maria Delgado was also found dead?"

"Yeah."

"Did you know her?"

"Not really."

"What does that mean—you either knew her or you didn't."

"She spent some time with my wife."

"Like shopping, partying..."

"No. My wife's knocked up. Maria helped her with stuff, laundry and cleaning."

Like an experienced tag-team member, Brick gave his partner a familiar head nod. Ron immediately picked up on the cue and took over the questioning. "Did Maria ever help you with stuff?"

Roberto shifted his position. "What do you mean?"

"C'mon, Roberto." Ron stepped a little closer. "You're a smart guy, you know what I mean." Roberto didn't respond, but a muscle in his jaw started to twitch. Ron leaned in. "I can tell you're a macho guy. You said your wife's pregnant, probably been a while since you've gotten any." Ron shook his head. "That's tough on a guy . . . right? And there's Maria, young and pretty, and all you got to do is walk across the hall."

Roberto jumped to his feet. "Man, you're full of shit. I don't know what happened to Jose and Maria, but I know I didn't have anything to do with it." He crumpled the empty soda can and tossed it into a trash can. "And I know something else—I'm done talking to you." Roberto brushed past the two detectives and out of the stock room.

Ron glanced over at Brick. "Think I hit a nerve."

"Like a dentist with a jackhammer." Brick smiled. On the suspect list he was keeping in his head, Roberto Morales just joined Carlos Garcia.

*       *       *

It was around nine p.m. when Brick arrived at the Tidal Basin near the paddleboat launch. Five minutes later, Ron showed up. Officially, the detectives were off-duty, but Brick never let that stop him from pursuing a lead. And in order to talk to the street people who spent their nights near the Tidal Basin, he had to accommodate their schedule. Swapping out the Brooks Brothers suit with some old jeans and with a backpack slung over his shoulder, Brick could easily pass as a tourist. Although, it was unlikely a tourist would be wearing a Kevlar vest under a hooded sweatshirt as Brick was. For the most part, he found street people to be harmless, but it was impossible to know when someone would turn violent.

At first, Brick and Ron went in opposite directions looking for anyone who might have been in the area on the night Maria's body was dumped in the water. It didn't take long for Brick to realize their timing was off. From the number of Styrofoam cups spilling out of a trash can, it appeared the soup truck had been there earlier. It wasn't unusual for recipients to dine-and-dash in order to secure a place on a steam grate or, as a last resort, a bed at one of the city-run shelters. Brick continued along 15th Street toward the Jefferson Memorial, stopping only once to talk with a heavily tattooed guy who said he took the train from Philadelphia earlier in the day. Brick kept walking, wondering if he was nearing the infamous spot where, back in the '70s, Fanne Foxe, an Argentine stripper, leapt from a car and jumped in the water. In the back seat of the car was Congressman Wilbur Mills, Chairman of the House Ways and Means Committee. What would Washington be if not for scandals, Brick thought.

After about forty-five minutes, Brick felt his phone vibrate. He read the text message and headed toward the 14th Street Bridge. Ron was waiting under a cherry tree that had lost most of its blossoms. "What's up?"

"I talked to two guys who claimed they weren't here that night because it was foggy and damp. Said they spent the night down at the shelter on Indiana Avenue. Anyway, they told me there's a guy who goes by the name of 'Ranger' who's staked a claim in the culvert under the bridge. If anyone saw something, it'd be him. I was about to go look for him, but they told me he doesn't like black guys ever since he got rolled by a couple of teenagers."

"Does he have anything against redheaded Irishmen?"

Ron laughed. "Don't know, but I'm guessing you're about to find out. Should I watch your back but keep out of view?"

"No. Let's go check it out."

Brick and Ron walked in the direction of the bridge. As they got closer, they saw pieces of clothing hanging from a tree limb. Just beyond was a sleeping bag atop what appeared to be a paint-splattered drop cloth. Brick shone his flashlight over the sleeping bag. It moved slightly.

"Ranger." Brick listened but heard nothing. "Ranger, are you in there?" Still no response. Brick handed the flashlight to Ron. He needed to get closer, but he also wanted his hands free. Ron trained the flashlight on the sleeping bag.

"Ranger, we're from the police. Put your hands where I can see them. Do it now." Whoever was in the sleeping bag complied. "That's good. Keep your hands up and slide on out of there."

The man who emerged was rail thin. He looked to be in his late sixties, but the wizened face could have belonged to a younger man. He rubbed his rheumy eyes with hands that appeared to be deformed, probably by arthritis. "Get that goddamned light out of my face." He blinked a couple of times. "How'd you know my name?"

"You're famous around here."

"Guess I am at that." Ranger started laughing, which triggered a phlegmy coughing fit. "Am I under arrest?"

"No."

"Damn."

"You're disappointed?"

"Yeah. I could use a couple of nights indoors. Food's better at the jail. Plus, I can sleep there with both eyes closed 'cause the cops aren't going to steal my stuff like the riffraff at the shelter."

"When's the last time you ate?"

"Yesterday." He scratched the back of his head. "Maybe the day before."

Brick unzipped his backpack and pulled out a bag from McDonald's. Several times testimony from a street person had been useful in prosecuting a case. Unlike paid informants, they didn't expect to be compensated, but a sandwich or cup of coffee often proved to be a good investment. "You can put your hands down. Here's a couple of cheeseburgers and some fries. How about you eat those while we ask you a few questions? I'm Detective Kavanagh and this is my partner, Detective Hayes."

"You sure he's a cop?"

Brick nodded.

"See this scar over my eye. Got that from a black guy. Two of them beat me up last summer."

Ron spoke up for the first time. "I'm sorry, man. Why do they call you Ranger?"

The guy struggled to get to his feet. He shifted his cheeseburger to his left hand. With his right, he saluted. "82nd Airborne, Fort Benning, Georgia. Went to 'Nam in '69 and '71."

Brick wondered if it was true or a lie told so many times Ranger probably believed it himself. Either way, it was the kind of response that tugged at Brick's heartstrings. The second tour would have put this guy in the country around the same time as his own father. Brick felt like he was staring at another casualty of war.

Ranger sat back down and went to work on the fries.

"How long have you been living on the street?" Brick asked.

Ranger shrugged his bony shoulders. "Stopped counting a few years ago."

"Were you here every night last week?"

"Yeah, 'cept for the night I went to the opera at the Kennedy Center." Ranger laughed heartily, once again sending himself into a coughing fit.

"Are you okay?" Brick feared Ranger might be choking, and despite the compassion he felt for the guy, performing CPR was not something he wanted to do.

Ranger nodded. "Think I'm allergic to these fucking cherry blossoms."

"That could be," Brick agreed. "Anyway, are you aware of anything unusual that happened here a couple of days ago?"

"Duh—I saw the whole thing."

Brick exchanged a quick glance with Ron. "Go ahead; tell me where you were and what you saw."

"Okay." Ranger exhaled loudly. "Let me get my bearings." He looked around before pointing to a spot facing the river. "There, that's where I was standing. Sounded like it came right over my head, close enough I could reach up and touch it. I figured something was wrong, then BAM—it hit the water and—"

"Whoa, stop right there. What are you talking about?" Brick asked

"The crash—Air Florida."

"Ranger, that happened over thirty years ago."

"No way." A look of shock crossed Ranger's weathered face. "Seems like yesterday to me."

"I'm sure it does," Brick said. "I'm sure it does."

# CHAPTER FOURTEEN

"This is it, my home away from home," Brick said.

Ron swiveled on his barstool and looked around. "I've probably passed here a thousand times but never stopped in. Feels like a neighborhood bar, something you're more apt to find in Baltimore than D.C." Ron turned back around. "You know, sometimes I think Washington is a city without a soul."

"Can't argue with that," Brick said. "Especially when I think about where we were tonight. With all the stuff I've seen over the years, it's the homeless that get to me the most."

"Really? More than the murdered?"

"When I figure out who killed someone, I've made a meaningful contribution. I've done everything I can."

"You gave Ranger food; that counts for something."

"But tomorrow, he'll be hungry again."

Ron seemed to think about that for a minute. "I hear ya, partner. There but for the grace of God . . ."

Brick looked past Ron toward the end of the bar. He hadn't noticed it when he first sat down, but a small shrine honoring Jose and his sister had been set up. He got up to take a closer look. Ron joined him.

"Most of these pictures were taken right here at Boland's." Brick pointed out several regulars and recalled some of the occasions—

Halloween, the customer appreciation Christmas party, watching sporting events like the Super Bowl and World Cup.

Ron stepped closer and studied the photos. "He looked like he was having a good time. No doubt living his American dream."

"Come to think of it, I never heard him complain about anything."

Brick glanced at the words on a jar next to a flickering votive candle. "Help send Jose and Maria home." It was going to take a lot more than was in the jar, but every dollar would help. Brick pulled a ten from his wallet and dropped it in the jar. Ron did the same before they both headed back to their barstools.

"Hey, Brick. The usual?" Rory placed cardboard coasters in front of Brick and Ron.

Brick nodded. "Rory, this is my partner, Ron Hayes."

The two men shook hands. "What can I get you?"

"What's the usual?"

"Guinness."

"Not much of a stout drinker, but I'll give it a try."

Rory set two pint glasses under the tap. "You'll not be disappointed."

"Did you put together the photos of Jose?" Brick asked.

Rory nodded as he picked up the two glasses of Guinness. He set one in front of Brick and the other in front of Ron. "You'll want to let that settle for a minute or so." He turned back toward Brick. "I figured it was the right thing to do. Everybody's asking about his family and how they can contribute, that's why the jar is there. We've already collected a couple of hundred."

"That's good." Brick raised his glass and took a sip. "Has anyone been here to talk to you and Eamonn about Jose?"

"Yeah, yesterday. The same detective who talked to me at Jose's apartment and his partner." Rory pulled a business card out of his wallet. "Paul Adkins. He did most of the talking. Allen seemed more interested in checking out a couple of girls at the bar."

Brick looked at his partner. "Why am I not surprised."

"There's not much I could tell him other than Jose was reliable and respectful, a hardworking kid. How he spent his time away from here, I can't say other than he did some jobs with Declan and he took ESL classes. He had to eat and sleep sometime so there weren't a whole lot of unaccountable hours."

"Is Declan back from Ireland?"

"Not yet. I tried to get ahold of him, but no luck; seems he decided to go over to the Aran Islands. Cellphones are pretty much useless there. I know he'll be shocked when he hears the news."

Brick turned toward Ron. "Declan is an independent contractor who comes in here a lot. He renovates kitchens and bathrooms and was teaching Jose carpentry, hanging drywall, stuff like that. Isn't that right, Rory?"

"Yeah. Jose would leave here and then go to a work site for several hours. I gave the detectives Declan's number, but it's probably not doing them any good. It was kind of weird—they asked me a couple of times if I thought Jose might have been into drugs or a gang. I never saw any indication of either one. Then I guess it was Allen—is he the pudgy one?"

Brick and Ron both nodded.

"Anyway, he asked if Jose was into the occult. The *occult*—what the feck?"

Brick realized this was one of the longest conversations he and Rory had ever had before Rory dropped an Irish-accented f-bomb. For a moment, he was distracted but then focused on what Rory had said. Why would the A-Team think Jose was dabbling in the occult?

"You got me—I don't know what that's about." Brick took a sip of Guinness, then another. "How's Elvis?"

"Good. She's in the office with Eamonn. Why don't you go back there—Himself's taking this pretty hard."

Brick and Ron picked up their glasses and headed down the narrow hallway past the kitchen and restrooms.

"*Himself?*" Ron asked.

"It's kind of an Irish term of endearment. Eamonn is Rory's uncle."

The door to the office was closed. Brick knocked lightly. "Eamonn, its Brick."

"Come in but don't let the cat out."

Brick eased the door open so he and Ron could enter. Elvis rubbed up against Brick's leg, purring loudly. Brick bent down and stroked the cat. Elvis arched her back as if requesting more pats. Brick complied and was rewarded with a head butt.

"Eamonn, this is my partner, Ron Hayes."

Eamonn attempted to stand but it was obvious he was struggling.

"Please, don't get up." Ron extended his hand across the desk.

"Seems my foot fell asleep." Eamonn shook hands with Ron. "Nice to meet you, lad. I've heard lots of good things about you."

"Careful, Eamonn," Brick said. "Don't want him to get a swelled head."

"Don't think that will happen," Ron said. "With this job, when you think you're on to something, it can turn out to be absolutely nothing."

"Like tonight?" Brick asked.

"Exactly." Ron looked at his watch. "I'd better get going. It was nice meeting you, Eamonn. Partner, I'll see you in the morning."

Eamonn had been counting a stack of money. He put a rubber band around it and slipped it inside his desk. "Did Rory tell you we've already collected a couple hundred dollars? A lot of generous people, shows they cared." Eamonn took a sip of what looked to be an Irish coffee. "Any idea when the bodies will be released?"

"Should be soon. This case is complicated because there's no designated next-of-kin. I know the liaison from the consulate has been contacted so hopefully the details can be worked out quickly." Brick sat down and Elvis immediately leapt onto his lap. "It may be that the bodies will be released to the Guatemalan Embassy and they will take responsibility for making the arrangements."

"Can you find out?" Eamonn asked.

"I can try," Brick said.

"Good. Those kids shouldn't make that journey alone."

Brick noticed tears threatening to spill from the old man's eyes. "Eamonn, you're not thinking about . . ."

"Never mind what I'm thinking."

"Too late," Brick said. "I already know."

# CHAPTER FIFTEEN

IMMEDIATELY FOLLOWING ROLL call, Brick and Ron headed to Lieutenant Blancato's office. The A-Team were already there seated at the conference table across from Blancato. A box of Krispy Kreme donuts was within easy reach of Travis Allen.

Blancato acknowledged Brick and Ron with a nod. "Have a seat. I need to brief the chief so let's get started." Blancato looked around the table. "Travis?"

Allen had just stuffed half a donut into his mouth, but that didn't stop him from responding. "Got the autopsy report from the ME." He licked some jelly from his fingers before handing a copy to Blancato. "No surprise, Jose died from blunt force trauma to the head. Appears he had been dead at least thirty-six hours, which means he was killed before his sister. Right, Brick?"

"Yes. According to Maria's autopsy, she had been dead for approximately twelve hours. That leaves twenty-four hours that she was alive after Jose was killed."

"Did you do that math without a calculator?" Allen reached for another donut. "I'm impressed."

"So it would seem Jose was the primary target," Blancato said.

"That's the way Paul and I see it. Can't speak for anyone else."

Blancato looked at Brick and Ron. "How about you guys, do you agree with that?"

Brick spoke up. "I think it's equally possible Maria was the target."

"How so?" Blancato asked.

"Jose may have walked in on a sexual assault in progress."

"Aren't you forgetting her autopsy showed she wasn't raped?"

Brick picked up on Blancato's dismissive tone. "No, it only proves there wasn't penetration."

"Oh, I love it when you talk dirty." Allen leaned over to his partner. "Don't you, Paul?"

Brick ignored Allen and continued. "As I was about to say, if Jose walked in to find his sister in any kind of danger, I'm sure he'd do everything he could to defend her."

Blancato seemed to think about that possibility for a moment. "Suppose we can't rule out a burglary gone bad. Some guy breaks in not expecting anyone to be there, but he encounters Maria. That presents an opportunity he hadn't planned on, but then Jose comes home and messes up the whole thing." Blancato seemed very pleased with himself as he looked around the table.

"It's possible, but there was nothing to indicate forcible entry so the perp would have needed a key or been let in by Maria or Jose. Also, what little of value there was in the apartment, like the TV, was still there. If burglary was the motive, there's more affluent buildings to hit nearby."

"So you're saying it couldn't have happened the way I described?" Blancato asked.

Allen put down the donut he was eating and jumped in before Brick had a chance to respond. "Or he's being contrary just to be contrary?"

Brick dug deep to be diplomatic. "I'm not saying it couldn't happen that way, I'm just saying ,given the evidence, it's less likely. And, Travis, let's get something straight right now." Brick looked around the table.

"Probably more than anyone in this room, I want the bastard who's responsible. I'm not about to undermine the investigation by disagreeing with something just to disagree."

"Okay," Blancato said. "We need to move on. What do we know about Maria, other than the autopsy findings?"

Ron responded. "Not a whole lot. According to the apartment building manager, she had only been in D.C. for a couple of weeks. He claimed she was quiet, kind of shy. When he saw her, she was always with Jose. We spoke to the owner and manager of Boland's Mill where Jose worked, and they indicated they had only met Maria once—on the day she arrived from Guatemala."

"Any indication she was involved in any high-risk activity?" Blancato asked.

"No. From what we've been able to find, her only friend seemed to be her pregnant neighbor across the hall. Maria helped her with cooking and cleaning." Ron turned toward his partner. "Brick interviewed the neighbor."

"I figured if she was going to confide in anyone it would be her neighbor," Brick said. "But when I spoke to Lourdes Morales, she couldn't recall anything Maria said indicating she was unhappy or worried or afraid. There's two other men she came in contact with that bear watching—Carlos Garcia, the building manager, is a registered sex offender. And her neighbor's husband, Roberto Morales. According to Lourdes's sister, Roberto is volatile and she suspects he's been cheating on Lourdes. I don't think she's totally objective, but the black eye Lourdes was sporting confirmed her husband has anger management issues, to say the least."

"Have you talked to this guy?" Blancato asked.

"We have. He was arrogant, somewhat defensive, and when Ron bore down on any connection he might have to the murders, he abruptly ended the interview."

Blancato didn't say anything, but he appeared to be processing what he had heard. He made a couple of notes on a yellow legal pad. "Anything else?"

Brick recapped viewing the Park Police tape and their unsuccessful mission to identify the person pushing the grocery cart.

Blancato glanced at his watch. "Travis, Paul, what have you got?"

It was the first time Paul Adkins had spoken. "We've been looking into Jose's background and trying to establish a timeline from when he was last seen alive. At the scene, we spoke with Rory Boland and then again at Boland's Mill. Eamonn Boland indicated he last saw Jose eating fish and chips the last night he was at work. It helped establish the ME's finding as to time of death."

Blancato nodded. "Yeah, stomach contents are pretty reliable."

Allen piped up. "Gnawed-up fish and chips—probably looked as nasty as some of the stuff my wife cooks," Travis said.

Blancato laughed. "Don't believe him, guys. I've had dinner at their place plenty of times; Karen's a good cook. Go ahead, Paul, what were you saying about Jose?"

"Just that no one we've talked to had anything derogatory to say about him. But we have to consider how well they really knew him. There was the gang graffiti scrawled on the side of the tub and Travis found something interesting."

"Yeah, I'm not sure what to make of it, but I think Jose might have been into some kind of voodoo shit."

That would account for the occult question posed to Eamonn, Brick thought. "What makes you think that?" he asked.

"There was this nightstand next to his bed, so I opened the drawer expecting to find condoms or drugs, maybe a gun, but instead, there's a couple of miniature voodoo dolls. They were pretty crude, just made out of wire in the shape of a doll with some cloth and yarn wrapped around the frame. No pins or anything sticking out of them, but, c'mon, what's up with that?"

"They're called Guatemalan worry dolls."

Allen leaned back in his chair. "Say what?"

"It goes back to a Mayan tradition. At night, a child tells the doll what he's worried about and slips it under his pillow. Then he can sleep without worrying."

"If you say so, but it still sounds like some weird voodoo shit to me."

Brick saw no point trying to convince Allen otherwise. Instead, he wondered what Jose was worried about. Realizing he may never know would undoubtedly be his own source of worry.

\* \* \*

"How did you know that?" Ron asked as he and Brick headed back to their cubicles in the Squad Room.

"Know what?"

"About the worry dolls."

"Something I learned from an ex-girlfriend. She taught anthropology, and believe me, if the worry dolls had voodoo power, I'd have been dead years ago."

"Didn't end well?" Ron asked.

"Actually, it did. She moved to California and I never heard from her again."

"And I'm guessing you won't be friending her on Facebook."

"Not her or anybody else. I'll gladly admit it; I'm a dinosaur when it comes to social media."

"Oh man, think of what you're missing. Nothing makes my day like a friend request from some mope I locked up." Ron laughed. "But seriously, what about Jose? Was he into social media?"

"I asked Rory about that. He said Jose was saving money to buy a computer, but it wasn't a priority since his family back in Guatemala didn't have internet access. Apparently, he had a cellphone, but it was outdated—none of the latest bells and whistles. So far, it hasn't turned up."

Ron shook his head. "It's a shame. Sounds like the kid was doing everything right."

"It does, but did he get involved in something he shouldn't have? Even though that would surprise me, people don't always reveal who they really are."

"That's for sure. And then there are the Travis Allens of the world who constantly reveal who they are," Ron said. "I'm going to get some coffee. You want anything?"

"No, thanks."

Brick checked his watch. The meeting had taken just over fifteen minutes, but it seemed much longer. He went back to his desk where he kept a box of Barry's Tea. He dropped a teabag in his mug and headed to the break room for hot water.

"Whoa, where's the fire?" Brick stepped aside as Blancato's secretary nearly collided with him as she ran from the room. She didn't respond. Brick filled his mug and returned to his desk. He let the tea steep for a couple of minutes. He wouldn't have admitted it earlier in the meeting with Blancato and the A-Team, but he was frustrated. He attributed much of his success as a homicide detective to his in-depth study of the victim. Often what looked to be random or a crime of opportunity was anything but. A victim's lifestyle, employment, friends, enemies were all elements that could hold the key to finding the perpetrator. By reputation, Brick was relentless in digging into the victim's background, but to do so, he had to rely on people who knew the victim. Maria's case was complicated by Jose's death and the fact that so few people had had contact with her. Traveling to Guatemala to interview her family and friends would be out of the question. The department would never spring for it. Brick fished out the teabag and threw it in the trash. He guessed he and Ron would have to settle for a trip to the Guatemalan Embassy. Hopefully, the liaison would be cooperative and arrange for the local police to do some digging.

* * *

"That's it," Brick said. "2200 Kalorama Road." He pointed to a white stucco building with bay windows flanking the front door. It could have easily passed for a high-end single-family home had it not been for the Guatemalan flag flying out front.

"For an embassy, looks kind of plain." Ron drove around the block looking for a parking space. Just as he spotted one, Brick's cellphone rang.

Before answering, Brick checked the caller ID. He recognized the number.

"Kavanagh." Brick listened to Lieutenant Blancato's secretary deliver a rapid-fire command. She hung up before he could respond. "I don't know what's going on, but we need to get back to Headquarters."

"Lights and siren?" Ron asked.

"No, that's not necessary."

Ron maneuvered through midday traffic that was only slightly lighter than morning rush hour. When they finally reached Sixth Street, he turned right onto Indiana Avenue and immediately jammed on the brakes. A jaywalker barely missed the edge of the bumper as she darted across the street.

"Hey, wasn't that what's-her-name from Channel Four news?" Ron asked.

"Yeah, it was. She's lucky she's not reporting herself getting run over."

Ron continued down the block then backed into a parking space reserved for police vehicles. He and Brick hesitated before getting out of the Crown Vic. Across the street, the jaywalking reporter had joined a group of her counterparts milling outside of Headquarters. Microphones had been set up in front of the steps and a satellite truck was illegally parked on 5th Street. Ron unhooked his seat belt and reached for the door handle. "You don't suppose—"

"Only one way to find out."

# CHAPTER SIXTEEN

BRICK AND RON zigzagged their way through the minefield of reporters. Up until now the murders of Jose and Maria Delgado hadn't gotten any attention, but hearing the questions being shouted in his direction, Brick felt certain that had changed.

"Detective Kavanagh." A female reporter from WTOP Radio approached Brick and shoved a microphone in his face. "What can you tell us about the girl in the Tidal Basin? Do you know who she is?"

"No comment." Brick picked up his pace. The reporter did, too, but her high heels were no match for his Cole Haans.

"Is she a tourist? Should people stay away from the—" The reporter's voice faded as Brick entered the building with Ron following close behind.

"Man, that's the closest I've ever felt to being a rock star. I think I could get used to it."

"Don't." Brick figured his partner was kidding, but just in case, he wanted to make himself clear. A misstep with the press could end a career. "Don't ever let the attention seduce you—they're cannibals."

Even though they knew the security officer on duty and he knew them, Brick and Ron were required to show their credentials. They did so, then headed down the hall past the out-of-order elevator to the stairwell. As they exited on the third floor, Brick almost smacked Blancato's secretary with the door. She didn't seem to notice.

"Here." She thrust the stack of papers she was clutching in Brick's direction. "Lieutenant Blancato wants to see you two and he needs this stuff right away. I've got more copies to make and the freaking copier keeps jamming."

"Tried kicking it?" Ron asked.

"No." She tucked a loose strand of hair behind her ear. "But if you give me your gun, I'll shoot the motherfucker."

Brick swallowed the gum he was chewing and came close to gagging. In all the time the secretary served as the lieutenant's gatekeeper, he had never heard her utter a swear word. Nor had he ever seen her so frazzled. Before he had a chance to ask what was going on, she headed up the stairs, two at a time.

The short walk to Blancato's office was long enough for Brick to scan the document he was holding. With each word he read, his blood pressure rose a couple of points. Had the office been any farther, he might have had a stroke right then and there. Brick dropped the stack of press releases on Blancato's desk.

"A task force?" Brick didn't try to conceal his disdain. "Isn't this a bit premature? It's only been—"

Blancato didn't let him finish. "The chief believes this is exactly the kind of case that can demonstrate the advantages of multi-agency cooperation."

Brick didn't believe that for a second. This wasn't about the case; it was about publicity for Blancato.

"The Park Police are already involved," Blancato said. "Given the victims are aliens, including Immigration and Customs Enforcement is a no-brainer."

"They were here legally. I don't see what ICE can contribute," Brick said.

Blancato popped a breath mint into his mouth. "That remains to be seen." He brushed the shoulders of his uniform jacket with his hand before slipping it on. "Whether you agree with it or not isn't the point. It's been decided and that's what I'm about to announce. We've been lucky—the press has ignored this story because they've been preoccupied with the murder-suicide in Georgetown, but now they're all over it."

Brick refrained from saying anything, but he suspected Blancato had played a major role in creating the media feeding frenzy outside.

"Okay, what I need from you two and from Allen and Adkins is to stand behind me and show that we're all on the same page in conducting the investigation." Blancato stepped away from his desk. "Grab those press releases. You can hand them out when the news conference is over." He walked over to his coat tree and retrieved his hat. Before leaving, he stopped in front of a mirror mounted next to the door. He ran his tongue back and forth over his front teeth, adjusted his hat, and turned in Brick and Ron's direction. "Let's go."

Brick glanced over at Ron. "All right, Mr. DeMille, I'm ready for my close-up."

"Will wonders never cease?" Ron stopped in his tracks and broke into a broad smile. "My man is channeling Gloria Swanson."

*   *   *

Standing behind Blancato, Brick felt like a prop, every bit as one-dimensional as a life-size cardboard cutout of the President. Like the ones down on Constitution Avenue where the tourists line up to take a selfie. Yes, his presence fell under the other-duties-as-assigned clause in his job description, but he resented the way Blancato was using this case as a launching pad for his next career.

"Can you spell that?" a female reporter shouted at the lieutenant.

Blancato complied, slowly spelling his last name. "First name is A-n-t-h-o-n-y."

Just as Brick had seen Blancato do on previous occasions, he spoke with authority as he made a brief statement summarizing what was known about the Delgado murders. He went on to praise the Park Police then announced the task force being coordinated with ICE. Brick hoped he would leave it at that, but wasn't surprised when Blancato opened it up to questions.

The first few questions were benign, but Brick was nervous. Whenever Blancato went off the script, it was like watching a trapeze artist performing without a net. With two or three questions being shouted simultaneously, Blancato could choose which to answer and which to ignore. Brick hoped he would pick wisely, but he wasn't counting on it. If it had just been microphones, Blancato might have walked away. But he was drawn to the TV cameras like the proverbial moth to the flame.

"No, we do not have a person of interest at this time." Blancato pointed toward a reporter from WRC-TV.

"Should visitors to the Tidal Basin be concerned for their safety?"

"No. Visitors and residents should always use common sense, but the Tidal Basin area is well patrolled, and we have reason to believe this was not a random act."

"Are you saying the victims were targeted?"

"Yes." Blancato pointed to another reporter.

"How can you be so sure?"

If Brick could have telepathically beamed a response to Blancato, it would have been "no comment." Instead, he held his breath as Blancato seemed to contemplate his answer.

"Jose Delgado was killed in his apartment approximately twenty-four hours before his sister's body was discovered floating in the Tidal Basin. Evidence found in the bathroom—" Brick couldn't believe what he was hearing. The gang graffiti found scrawled on the side of the tub was known only to the killer and the police. Brick thought the A-Team intended to keep it that way, but Blancato had just announced it to the world.

Finally, it was over. Blancato stepped back from the microphones. He turned and walked away with the A-Team trailing on his heels. Brick handed half of the stack of press releases to Ron. Several of the reporters didn't bother to wait around. Even those that did dispersed as soon as they got the press release. Now, it was their job to spread the word that, according to Blancato, Jose and Maria were targeted by a possible gang member.

"Miller time?" Ron asked.

Brick glanced at his watch. "I wish but we're still on duty for an hour."

"Starbucks?"

Brick and Ron crossed the street and headed east half a block. They each ordered something to drink then sat at a table where they could talk without being overheard by other caffeine hounds. Not that it seemed to matter; Ron was uncharacteristically quiet. He stared into his coffee cup for a couple of minutes before finally speaking.

"On a scale of one to ten . . . one being no damage and ten . . ." Ron hesitated as if searching for the right qualifier. "Ten being . . . fucked sideways. How much damage did Blancato do?"

"Too soon to tell." Brick took a swallow of tea. As much as he liked it strong and unsweetened, it left an unfamiliar bitter taste in his mouth. "I can almost guarantee the lead on this story will be 'gang graffiti found at murder scene.'" Brick shook his head. "Thanks to Blancato, any chance we had to investigate a gang angle without tipping them off is gone."

"Maybe not," Ron said with exaggerated optimism. "We can hope the gangbangers are too busy committing crimes to watch the news."

Brick pondered that possibility for a minute. "Be careful what you wish for."

# CHAPTER SEVENTEEN

*He'd been surviving on four hours sleep and energy drinks for over a week now and it was taking its toll. All he needed was another hour or so; then he'd turn off the computer. He picked up his can of Red Bull and drained what was left. He thought an energy drink was supposed to give him energy, but nothing was kicking in. Had he built up a tolerance? Maybe, and that could be a problem. He'd have to find something stronger if he had to keep up this kind of schedule.*

*It was driving him crazy. She was out there somewhere, he knew it. He thought he'd found her, really found her this time, but he was wrong. No, she was wrong and what she did was wrong. Deceitful bitch. Just thinking about how she lured him in looking sweet and innocent made him angry all over again. How could he know she'd have tattoos up and down her arms and angel wings across her back? How ironic was that— angel wings on a whore. That's what she was, a whore. No different than the ones sitting in front of a camera with their big tits hanging out and legs spread apart.*

*He pulled up a new website and entered his credit card number. He scrolled through page after page of pictures before it occurred to him. As disgusting as these women were, at least they were being honest. What you see is what you get; wasn't that the message they were sending? No one could accuse them of pretending to be something they weren't.*

*He was calmer now. Finally, he turned off the laptop and set it on his nightstand. A few hours of sleep would do him some good. Then he'd be ready to start searching again. He told himself it was okay if he didn't find her this very minute. He needed to be patient. Maybe it would happen tomorrow or the next day. She was out there, and all he had to do was keep searching. He would find her.*

# CHAPTER EIGHTEEN

NORMALLY, A DAY spent in court was a source of frustration for Brick, but on this morning, he was looking forward to it. He was still trying to keep his distance from Blancato, and testifying before the grand jury would take most of the morning. It was easy compared to being grilled on the witness stand by an overzealous defense attorney who liked nothing better than to trip up cops. After entering the H. Carl Moultrie Courthouse, Brick stopped by the cafeteria for a bagel and cup of tea. For the next half hour he refreshed his memory by studying a file from a two-year-old case. The crime scene photos of a partially charred body brought back the grisly details. All that was missing was the smell of burnt flesh. For that, Brick was grateful. Compartmentalizing was a skill he had mastered over the years, and for now, thoughts of Maria and Jose had to be pushed aside, at least for a few hours.

Brick checked his phone before leaving the cafeteria. No messages. He dumped his trash in the recycle bin and headed to the escalator. Unlike the formal atmosphere of the Federal Courthouse less than a block away, Superior Court was a beehive of activity. Adjudicating all local trial matters from small claims to landlord-tenant to civil and criminal cases contributed to a circus-like environment where bizarre things could happen and often did. The morning was particularly frenzied as lawyers, litigants, witnesses, and jurors all rushed to their designated locations. A judge's threat of contempt was incentive for being punctual.

As he rode the escalator to the third-floor office of the Assistant U.S. Attorney responsible for presenting the case to the grand jury, Brick glanced around. On more than one occasion he had found himself face-to-face with someone he had arrested. It was times like that when his red hair was a liability, but unlike his days undercover, he wasn't willing to dye it or shave his head. On some men, bald looked good—he wasn't one of those guys. The encounters were sometimes awkward, but so far none of his arrestees had jeopardized their bond status by doing something stupid. One more look around. With the exception of Lily Nguyen, an attractive attorney known around the squad room as the Dragon Lady, he didn't recognize anyone else sharing the escalator.

"Excuse me."

Brick stepped to the left as Nguyen rushed past and hurried toward one of the courtrooms. In her wake, Brick picked up a whiff of perfume, a welcomed contrast to the odors he usually associated with the place. He often thought if a deodorant manufacturer ever wanted to test a new product, this was an ideal proving ground. The stress of being in court would generate enough sweat to challenge its effectiveness.

Brick proceeded past the vacant secretary's desk to the small corner office occupied by AUSA Kyle Thibodeaux. He was about to knock on the door just as Thibodeaux exited. Given his rolled-up sleeves and missing necktie, it was apparent he wasn't headed to the Grand Jury Room.

"Aw, geez, Brick. I'll be back in a minute." He ran his hand through his thick curly hair. "I'm up to my ass in alligators."

Coming from anyone else, the expression would have sounded contrived, but Thibodeaux was born and raised on the Louisiana bayou.

It was his unconventional background that made him one of Brick's favorite prosecutors. Unlike so many Ivy League Law Review types with the right political connections who filled the ranks of the office, Thibodeaux had taken a different path. He'd dropped out of school at sixteen, went to work on the oil rigs in the Gulf of Mexico, eventually got his GED, graduated with honors from LSU, and went to law school at Tulane when he turned thirty. His work in post-Katrina New Orleans caught the attention of a group of volunteer attorneys from D.C. who encouraged him to make the move north.

Boxes of archived case files made passage into the usually neat office difficult, but Brick managed to make his way to the only chair that wasn't piled high with stuff. Even Thibodeaux's desk was cluttered with what appeared to be evidence envelopes. Brick had no idea what was going on, but he was sure that whatever it was, it was big.

"I look like a candidate for one of those hoarder shows, don't you think?"

Brick glanced up as Thibodeaux reappeared carrying a can of Diet Pepsi and two bags of chips.

"Breakfast of champions?" Brick asked.

"I wish." Thibodeaux tore open one of the bags and stuffed a couple of chips in his mouth. "Time will tell if that's how I'm thought of when this is said and done."

"What is all this stuff?"

"Can't say." Thibodeaux took a swig of soda then looked for a clear space on his desk where he could place the can. "But if it is what it seems, you'll know. Trust me, everyone will know unless they're living under a rock. In the meantime, I owe you an apology. I had to postpone the grand jury and forgot to call you."

"No problem." Brick appreciated his honesty rather than blaming the oversight on a subordinate. "Although if I had known, I would have chosen more appetizing reading material this morning."

"I hear ya—don't want to be chowing down on some crispy bacon and looking at pictures of what was left of that poor barbequed bastard. I know he had a rap sheet longer than my arm but he didn't deserve that. Nobody does." Thibodeaux took another sip of soda and tried unsuccessfully to keep from belching. "Pardon me. I hate postponing the case, but it's not my decision."

"I understand." Brick reached over and caught a thick file as it was about to topple to the floor. "By any chance, did you see Blancato's news conference yesterday?"

Thibodeaux nodded.

"For the record, the whole task force thing—not my idea."

"I didn't think so. A little premature, if you ask me."

"Absolutely. Sometimes I think Blancato's watched too many reruns of *Law and Order*. If the case isn't wrapped up in an hour, he starts to panic."

"And then he blabs something he shouldn't. At least that was the general consensus around here when we watched that train wreck. And he thinks he's ready for a big-time fancy fed title? I've heard he's got his sights on everything from heading up the Secret Service to Homeland Security." Thibodeaux munched a couple of potato chips. "Who knows, there might just be another vacancy he hasn't considered."

Brick figured the reference related to whatever it was Thibodeaux was working on. "I thought his ambition was a well-kept secret within the department."

"C'mon, Brick, you know better than that. Secrets in this town are as rare as an honest politician in Louisiana."

*   *   *

"Back so soon?" Ron asked as he glanced down at his watch. "That might be a new record. What'd they do, return an indictment before you had a chance to sit down and introduce yourself?"

"The grand jury was postponed."

"Why?"

Brick shook his head. "Don't know, but I do know Thibodeaux is working on something big."

Ron seemed to think about what Brick had just said. "A scandal of some sort?"

"I don't know, but it does seem like the city is overdue."

"Yeah, kind of like Florida's overdue for a hurricane. Wonder what it will be this time, sex, drugs, or rock and roll?"

"We're way too sophisticated for rock and roll—more like sex, drugs, and the symphony." Brick took off his suit jacket and draped it over his chair. Time to shift his focus back to the Delgado cases. "Any new developments?"

"The A-Team finally got copies of Jose's cellphone records. Looks like there hasn't been any activity since the multiple calls Rory made. Last I heard, the Dynamic Duo were tracking down the other numbers. They left about an hour ago."

"Good, that should keep them out of here for a while."

"For the sake of the carpet, I hope that's true. I've noticed Allen has been wearing a path between his cubicle and Blancato's office." Ron headed back toward his desk then turned around. "The whole missing cellphone thing bothers me."

"The A-Team said they scoured the apartment looking for it," Brick said.

"I know, but it doesn't make sense. Why would someone leave the money in Jose's wallet and steal a cheap cellphone?"

Brick was about to say something else but got distracted by a flyer someone had placed in his inbox. He was troubled by what he saw. He picked it up and handed it to Ron. "Have you seen this?"

"No, where's it from?"

"Arlington County PD."

"What, did someone swim the moat?"

The Potomac River, separating Arlington County from the District of Columbia, seemed to provide the same protection moats once afforded medieval castles. Arlington usually had fewer homicides in a whole year than D.C. did on a quiet weekend.

"Says she's missing from Arlington." Ron studied the flyer closely. "Either I need glasses or Fernanda Lopez looks a lot like Maria Delgado. Long dark hair, brown eyes, slight build—am I right or wrong?"

"Right, as far as I'm concerned." Brick thought about what he should do with this information. "Let's go see what Blancato thinks."

*   *   *

Blancato studied the flyer before handing it back to Brick. "I'll take your word for it since you two are the ones who know what the Delgado girl looked like." He shrugged his shoulders. "But I don't see what this disappearance has to do with anything."

Brick weighed his words carefully. "It may be totally unrelated and, frankly, I hope it is, but I think we need to consider the possibility that someone could be targeting young women meeting a specific profile – petite, long dark hair—"

"Stop!" Blancato held up his hand as if he were directing traffic. "I see what you're doing and we're not going there. Everything is pointing to this being a gang-related killing and now you're thinking serial killer."

Brick struggled to keep his composure. He reminded himself to respect the lieutenant's rank even though Blancato didn't deserve to be where he was. Political connections catapulted him to the position, not intelligence or even paying his dues like most detectives. "All I'm saying—"

Blancato didn't give him a chance to finish. "I'm sure it's hard for you to accept that this Jose that everyone thought was a great kid was involved in something he shouldn't have been. Well, you need to get over that. Going off on a wild goose chase is a waste of time and re-sources." Blancato ran his fingers around the inside of his shirt collar. "Jesus, that's all we need right now is for the public to think there's a crazed serial killer running around."

Brick saw no reason to remind Blancato that, according to FBI sta-tistics, serial killers were always operating within the United States, mostly under the radar. "I thought since this is now a task force effort, you might want to involve the surrounding jurisdictions."

"Fairfax County, Loudon, and then in Maryland—Montgomery and Prince Georges—where does it stop, Brick? Where? I'm satisfied that keeping our interaction on a federal level is the appropriate thing to do." Blancato looked first at Brick, then at Ron. "Is there anything else?" Brick shook his head, as did Ron. "Okay, then—time for you to get to work."

"As if we weren't working before?" It was the only comment Ron made as he and Brick headed back to their cubicles.

"I've got to get out of here for a while." Brick snatched his jacket from the back of his chair. "Wanna go for a ride?"

"Got a destination in mind?" Ron asked.

Brick nodded. "One I should have thought of before now."

# CHAPTER NINETEEN

"LOOKS LIKE OUR timing is good."

Brick pulled the Crown Vic into a parking space across from the entrance to Our Lady of Sorrows. It appeared noon Mass had recently ended since a small group of parishioners was gathered at the door talking with the priest. Even though he and Ron kept a respectful distance, Brick could see it was an eclectic group. An elderly woman leaning on a three-prong cane stood next to a young woman carrying an infant wrapped in a blue blanket. Behind them was a construction worker in a dusty Carhartt, a hard hat in one hand. Brick watched as he and the priest exchanged a few words. Instead of a handshake, a fist bump marked the end of the conversation.

Father Miguel Sanchez was very different than the priests Brick remembered from his youth. In fact, his altar boy days were something he tried hard to forget. But even as a fallen-away Catholic, he recognized and respected the positive impact Sanchez had on the neighborhood.

"Father Mike," Brick called out as the priest was about to go back inside the church.

The priest turned slowly and squinted in the sun. Then he smiled broadly. "Brick Kavanagh—official business or would you like me to hear your confession?"

Brick laughed. "How much time do you have?"

"How much do you need?" the priest asked.

"To confess my sins—a lot. But it's police business; we won't need much." Brick introduced Ron who extended his hand in the priest's direction.

"In that case, let me go hang up my robe, and we can head over to Dunkin' Donuts. Don't know about you guys, but I need caffeine."

The two-block walk was interrupted three times as Father Mike stopped to chat with someone they passed on the street. Whether parishioners or not, it didn't seem to matter. He made time for everyone, and it was that quality Brick relied on. The priest had been a useful resource in the past, and if anything, he was more active in the community now than ever before.

With coffee and donuts in hand, the three men settled down at a window table looking out on Calvert Street. Outside, a road crew worked filling several potholes, which had made the intersection resemble a giant slice of Swiss cheese.

"Looks like this winter has left its mark on the streets. Seems every season challenges the city in one way or another." Father Mike took a sip of coffee. "Although I prefer warm temperatures, I wouldn't be disappointed if we could skip over summer entirely."

"You're not talking humidity, are you, Father?" Brick asked.

"No, but it does seem to be a contributing factor."

Brick nodded. "Most of the homicides I've investigated up here have happened in the four months between June and September."

"But the past two summers, I've noticed a shift." Father Mike popped a glazed Munchkin into his mouth. "We're still losing too many, Brick, but it seems to be from different causes. It used to be the gang violence, but now it's heroin overdoses and PTSD-related suicides among returning vets." He took another sip of coffee. "What brings you to the 'hood today?"

"The Delgado murders."

Father Mike set down his cup. He closed his eyes as he shook his head from side to side. He opened them and took a deep breath. "I know I'm supposed to accept God's will and not question why things happen because there is a plan for each and every one of us, but the death of Jose and his sister . . ." His voice trailed off, leaving his thoughts incomplete.

"How well did you know them?" Brick asked.

"I can't say I knew Jose well, but he reminded me of when I was his age—a quiet, hardworking kid hoping to find a better life. That was my goal when I sneaked across the border at El Paso thirty-some years ago." A fleeting smile crossed the priest's lips. "My understanding is he had a green card. But it's not easy being in a new country, even if you're here legally."

Brick nodded as the priest continued. "Jose usually attended an early Mass on Sundays. I encouraged him to take advantage of some of our outreach programs. I figured it would improve his language skills and he'd meet others his age, but he seemed to spend most of his waking hours at work. As for his sister, I met her only once when he brought her to Mass. Now that I think of it, that was just a few days before she died."

"Did you ever sense that he was in some kind of trouble?"

"No."

"How about gang involvement?"

"Nothing that I'm aware of. And like I said, the gang violence has diminished over the years, mainly because gangs don't have the stronghold on this area that they once did. They've moved on—suburbs like Arlington and Wheaton. Those places are seeing problems they probably thought were confined to the District."

"Thanks, Father. I think we're finished unless Ron has any questions for you."

Ron shook his head.

"Afraid I haven't been very helpful." Father Mike pushed his chair back and got to his feet. "I'll keep my ear to the ground. It's always possible I may hear something, and provided I'm free to share that information with you, I'll do so."

Brick knew the priest had to honor what was told to him in confession, but other things were fair game. "I appreciate that." Brick handed one of his cards to Father Mike. "It's been a while; I have a new number."

The priest slipped the card into his pocket. "One thing just occurred to me. Have the bodies been sent back to Guatemala?"

"Not yet. We're working with the embassy, but there's some red tape that's been holding it up. Plus, there's the matter of the expense. We're trying to get some help from the Victims Fund."

"Perhaps there's something the parish can do in that regard. I'll let you know. In the meantime, I'll pray for Jose and Maria." Father Mike shook hands with Ron and Brick. "And I'll pray you find whoever did this."

* * *

"So much for that idea," Brick said.

"Hey, it was worth a try. I'm not Catholic, but I've spent enough time at the Ebenezer Baptist Church to believe in the power of prayer. I've seen it work, man."

"Well, given how little we really know about the victims, solving this one just might take divine intervention."

"Could happen," Ron said with conviction. "And we've got an advantage. The Super Bowl and March Madness are over."

"What has that got to do with anything?"

"God doesn't have to listen to all those crazy fans praying for a win."

Brick rolled his eyes. "I never would have thought of that."

"Mark my words, partner, when the Nats make it to the World Series, there'll be plenty of fans on their knees. You might be lighting a candle or two yourself."

A quick look in both directions, then Brick and Ron jaywalked across Columbia Road to where the Crown Vic was parked. It was just as they had left it except for the parking ticket slipped under the windshield wiper.

"Are you kidding me? Everybody in town knows this is a cop car except the genius writing tickets." Brick retrieved the ticket then unlocked the doors. Before starting the car, he checked his phone. A voicemail was waiting. He entered his passcode and listened to a message from the liaison at the Guatemalan Embassy. He listened a second time before disconnecting.

"Apparently, one problem's been solved." Brick pulled away from the curb. "An anonymous donor has fronted the money to get Jose and Maria sent back home."

"Seriously?" Ron looked over in Brick's direction. "Did someone drop a big chunk of change into the donation jar?"

"Maybe, and I have a pretty good idea who it was." Brick drove east on Calvert Street then turned north on Connecticut Avenue. "As long as we're in the neighborhood, let's check it out."

Boland's Mill was a popular spot for Sunday brunch, but during the week the lunch hour was quiet. A couple of regulars sitting at the bar were the only customers at the moment. Brick and Ron walked past them to the end of the bar where Eamonn was reading the *Washington Post*. He looked up and smiled as he tossed the paper aside.

"Don't know why I still subscribe—the paper keeps getting thinner and thinner."

"You can always read it online," Brick said.

"It's not the same. What am I supposed to do, carry the computer into the loo? All this technology that's supposed to make life easier—"

Eamonn seemed frustrated. "Ah, I'm sounding like a grumpy old man and that's probably not what you came to hear, is it now?"

"Actually, I wanted to let you know what I heard from the liaison at the embassy. It looks like there's progress in getting Jose and Maria flown home. A donor, who wishes to remain anonymous, is paying the cost."

"That's grand." Eamonn seemed genuinely surprised. "It's important they be buried in their country. God rest their souls."

Brick noticed a catch in Eamonn's voice as he said those words. He had often heard him mention that, despite having spent so many good years in America, when his time came, he wanted to be buried in Ireland.

Eamonn cleared his throat. "Can I get you lads something? I'm guessing you're working, but a Coke or iced tea?"

"I'll take a Coke," Ron said.

"Make it two."

Eamonn filled two glasses with ice and Coke. He set them on the bar.

Brick picked up his and took a sip. "Thanks, Anonymous."

Eamonn sighed and looked embarrassed. Brick wasn't surprised. Throughout the years he was aware of several examples of Eamonn's generosity. All were done quietly so with the exception of the recipients, very few people knew about his largesse.

"For now, let's just keep it between ourselves. I haven't told Rory yet."

That did surprise Brick. "Knowing Rory, I'm sure he won't object."

"He may. You see, when I went to the embassy to make the arrangements, I applied for a visa. The processing takes a while, but once it's done, I'm going to escort the bodies back to Guatemala."

"With all due respect, Eamonn, that's a long trip for you to make, and given some of your health issues—"

Eamonn didn't let Brick finish. "I've always taken care of those who worked for me. It's a terrible thing that happened to those kids. The least I can do is let the family know people cared. And I intend to give them the money we collected. Last count it was over five hundred dollars." Eamonn poured a shot of Jameson into his cup of tea. "I'll be fine . . . and if I'm not, I won't be around to worry about it."

Brick knew better than to try to dissuade Eamonn. Truth be told, he admired the old man's determination to do what he felt was his responsibility even though there might be a cost far greater than that of a plane ticket. It was a trait that seemed as much an inherent part of Irish DNA as red hair and freckles.

"Brick, are you watching this?"

Ron's voice interrupted Brick's thoughts. "What?"

Ron pointed to the TV over the bar. A "Breaking News" banner scrolled across the local midday news broadcast. "Arlington County police confirm their first homicide of the year," the anchor announced. "The nude body of a woman was discovered this morning by a jogger in the Four Mile Run section of South Arlington. Identification is pending, but a source close to the case indicated it may be that of a young Hispanic woman who went missing earlier this week. We hope to have more details on our broadcast starting at four. In other news . . ."

"Damn!" Ron talked over the news anchor's next story. "Wonder if Blancato might sit up and take notice now."

Brick didn't respond immediately. He finished the rest of his Coke and wiped the back of his hand across his mouth. He gave his empty glass to Eamonn. "He might, Ron, but it doesn't matter. If it turns out the cases are connected, there's no satisfaction in being right. That only comes from a conviction."

# CHAPTER TWENTY

SLEEPING LATE FOLLOWED by a hearty breakfast had been Brick's first choice for his Wednesday/Thursday weekend, but that would have to wait for another day. At Metro Center, he dodged commuters as he transferred from the Red Line to the Orange Line. Four stops later, he got off at the Courthouse Station in Arlington. Riding the escalator to street level, he tried to recall the last time he made the trek to northern Virginia.

Even though he'd only spent about fifteen minutes on the Orange Line, he felt like a tourist. The business conducted within the county buildings was equivalent to that of the District's Judiciary Square, but that's where the similarities ended. This was a neighborhood with high-end condos and luxury apartment buildings. Inviting ethnic restaurants and cafés lined the intersecting boulevards. And on Saturdays, the courthouse parking lot was home to a farmers market. As Brick headed toward Wilson Boulevard, he heard what sounded like a basketball game in progress. He realized the noise wasn't coming from a school playground; it was coming from the jail located in the high-rise across the street.

Brick crossed Wilson Boulevard, walked half a block, then turned onto Franklin Road. He easily spotted Detective Tracy Collins at a small corner table on the patio in front of The Java Shack. They had met two years ago at the FBI Academy in Quantico when both attended a class in hostage negotiation. So far, neither had been called upon to put to use what they had learned.

"Brick, good to see you." Slowly, Tracy got to her feet. She and Brick exchanged a quick hug before she eased herself back into her chair. "Hope you still drink your tea unsweetened. I ordered you a large."

"Good memory. Are you okay?" Brick asked.

"Yeah, I pulled a muscle a couple of days ago. I'm training for another triathlon."

"Well, thanks for making me feel like a total slacker."

Tracy laughed. "I doubt that; more like you're working too much."

"It's hard not to, given our caseload." Brick was about to continue when the barista announced their drinks were ready. "Stay where you are, I'll get them." Brick went up to the counter, got the drinks and a couple of napkins and returned to the table. He handed Tracy a large cappuccino.

"Are you working the brother/sister murder?" Tracy asked.

"Yes, my partner and I are privileged to be part of the task force."

"From the way you said that, sounds to me like it's anything but a privilege."

Brick nodded. "I hope I'm wrong, but I've got a bad feeling about the way it's being handled."

Tracy took a sip of her drink. "It's gang-related, right?"

"That's the general consensus but I'm not convinced." He went on to tell her about the physical similarities between Maria Delgado and the missing person's case in Arlington.

"Oh, jeez, I see where this may be going."

"The body at Four Mile Run—where was it actually found?" Brick asked.

"Just north of Columbia Pike. The jogger spotted her floating where the creek is at its deepest point."

"Does the jogger check out?"

"Yeah, a law student at Georgetown, jogging with his girlfriend."

"Any sus—excuse me, persons of interest?" Brick asked.

Tracy laughed. "Oh yes, gotta be politically correct. God forbid we offend some asshole who just killed an innocent woman." She lowered her voice even though the other tables were empty. "We've got nothing."

Brick nodded. "Have they positively identified her?"

"Officially, no, but I can tell you the missing girl had some major ink—angel wings across her back, butterflies up and down one arm, something else on the other arm, I don't remember what it was. Anyway, our homicide victim's tattoos match up. What are the odds?"

"Slim and none?" Brick guessed.

For a minute, neither Brick nor Tracy said anything. Then they both spoke at the same time before each deferred to the other. Brick motioned for her to go ahead.

"It's early and I shouldn't be impatient, but let's face it, on this side of the River, we don't have a lot of homicides. I'd like to say I'm confident the Major Crimes guys assigned to the case are up to the challenge, but—" She stopped and brushed a strand of blond hair off her forehead and out of her eye. "I didn't mean to criticize my colleagues, but it's frustrating because the stakes are so high. If you're right, my guess is—this guy's not going to stop at two."

There was nothing else to say, but as far as Brick was concerned, the meeting had been productive. Plus, it was good seeing Tracy. He liked her and was glad he had a chance to hear about what was happening in her life outside of work. Before leaving, he marked his calendar for the second Saturday in October. Tracy assured him he would get a formal invitation, but she wanted to be sure he saved the date for her wedding. Now that Virginia had passed same-sex marriage, she and her partner planned to make it official.

*   *   *

Once again, the weather forecast was wrong, not that Brick minded. Instead of overcast and threatening, the sky was a brilliant shade of blue. Still, he wondered how meteorologists could be wrong so often and not get fired. A pretty good gig—maybe he should have paid a little more attention to science when he was in school.

Already the temperature was in the high sixties and would probably climb several more degrees. It was a perfect day for baseball and today's game was Brick's personal rain check for having to miss the Nationals' Opening Day. He checked his watch. Good, it was still early. The park wouldn't open for at least an hour. He considered his options and decided to grab some lunch at the Hawk and Dove on Pennsylvania Avenue. He took a seat at the bar and ordered a cheeseburger and fries. While he waited, he flipped through the latest edition of *The City Paper*. The annual reader poll named winners in several categories, most of which didn't interest him. But Food and Drink caught his eye. He made a mental note to check out the Lebanese Taverna, which had won for best Middle Eastern restaurant.

Brick tried not to obsess about checking email on his days off, but when his phone vibrated, he couldn't ignore it. He recognized Blancato's number and let it go to voicemail. For all of Blancato's faults, he was respectful of a guy's days off, and Brick could count on one hand the times he had been disturbed. Still, he didn't want to get in a conversation. Instead, he checked his voicemail as soon as the icon indicated he had a message. He felt his pulse quickening as he listened to Blancato's voice.

"This morning, ICE rounded up several illegals during a raid. One indicated he had knowledge about a recent homicide. Not sure it's ours, but they're bringing him in for questioning. I know it's your day off, but figured you and Ron would want to know."

So much for spending the afternoon watching the Nats. Brick signaled to the bartender. "Make that order to go."

# CHAPTER TWENTY-ONE

THE DOOR TO the observation room was ajar. Before entering, Brick stopped and listened. He heard Blancato's and Allen's voices. He knocked once then stepped inside. It took a minute for his eyes to adjust to the dimly lit room. Once they did, he saw Blancato leaning against the wall opposite the two-way mirror. Paul Adkins stood next to him. Allen straddled a wooden chair missing a couple of slats.

"Lieutenant." Brick nodded in Blancato's direction. "Thanks for letting me know. Ron texted me; he's on his way."

"All right. I'll wait 'til he's here then we'll fill both of you in on the latest developments."

Brick walked past Adkins and grabbed a chair. He pulled it up to the table and sat facing the mirror so he could get a good look into the interrogation room while he ate his lunch. At about ten-by-twelve feet, the room was only slightly larger than a prison cell. With its drab gray walls, floor, and ceiling, the nondescript room looked like every other interrogation room Brick had ever observed. The only distinguishing feature was an overhead fluorescent light that emitted a low hum. The sound was annoying, but the room wasn't designed with comfort in mind. At the moment, a Hispanic male who looked to be in his mid-twenties was seated in an armless metal chair. His elbows rested on the table in front of him. Brick wondered if the subject was aware of the microphone hidden under the table or the camera secreted in the fake thermostat.

"Is he under arrest?" Brick asked.

"No, but he belongs to ICE"

"Civil detention?"

"Oh yeah, they've got him as long as they want him. And there's nothing he can do about that." Allen turned away from the mirror. The chair creaked ominously as he shifted his weight. "Hey, are you going to share what's in the bag?"

"Have some fries." Brick shoved the bag within Allen's reach.

Allen shook his head. "Nah . . . the old ball-and-chain's been complaining lately about my love handles." With his thumb and forefinger, he pinched an ample amount of flesh beneath his shirt. "On second thought, the way she's packed on the pounds, she's got no room to bitch." He reached across the table and grabbed a couple of fries.

Brick guessed the reference was to Allen's wife, not one of his girlfriends. "If I had known, I would have brought you a salad or a stir fry with tofu." Brick unwrapped his cheeseburger and took a bite.

"I'd rather eat cardboard." Allen stuffed a few more fries into his mouth. "What do you think, Paul, have we let him sweat long enough?"

Adkins checked his watch. "I don't think he's sweating."

"He's gotta be, he's still wearing that hoodie and it's over eighty degrees in there."

"Give it a few more minutes."

Brick knew the drill and sometimes it worked. Leave a suspect or witness alone for a while and there's no telling what you might see, including some things you'd rather not. But it wasn't always effective and it appeared that might be the case this time. From what he could see, the subject didn't look nervous or agitated. If anything, he just looked bored, which diminished the effectiveness of focusing on body language. At least for Brick, he was more interested in what the subject said rather than how many times he licked his lips or crossed his arms.

"Lieutenant, guys." Ron Hayes closed the door behind him. "Would have been here sooner, but I was at the gym when I got the message and I needed to take a shower."

"Glad you did," Allen said. "'Cause I don't have any Vicks to shove up my nose."

Blancato turned toward Adkins. "Paul, go ahead and bring Brick and Ron up to speed."

Adkins nodded. "We got the call early this morning. ICE raided a house on Georgia Avenue. Our boy in there—Guadalupe Cruz, goes by the name Lupe—"

"They're all fucking loopy, if you ask me," Allen added.

Adkins laughed at his partner's observation before continuing. "At first, it looked like a typical raid—a bunch of illegals living together, but it turned out Cruz was the only one with an expired visa. Before ICE slapped the cuffs on him, they patted him down. Seems he had another visa in his pocket—one that didn't belong to him. That got the agent's attention. He alerted his supervisor who called the task force and we . . ." Adkins stopped mid-sentence as he approached the mirror. "Hey, check this out." The subject had finally removed his hoodie. He was wearing a short-sleeved black t-shirt, which left his forearms exposed. Adkins pointed to Cruz's left arm.

The tattoo looked home grown as though it had been done by an amateur or even by the subject himself. Nevertheless, the symbol was familiar. The last time Brick had seen it, it was drawn in blood on the edge of Jose's bathtub. More and more, Brick had to consider the possibility that Jose's murder had a gang connection.

"It's time," Adkins said. "He's all yours, Travis."

Allen picked up a file folder marked "Confidential." He wrote Guadalupe's name across the top.

"What's in the file?" Ron asked.

"Nothing having anything to do with him. Just some old case notes I was going to shred but numb nuts doesn't know that." He smiled smugly as he headed for the door. "Showtime."

Adkins laughed as did Blancato. Brick failed to see the humor.

Allen entered the interrogation room and closed the door behind him. He pulled up a chair opposite the subject and introduced himself. The audio transmitted to the observation room crackled with static like a cheap transistor radio from the 1960s. While still standing, Allen dropped the file on the table out of Cruz's reach but close enough for him to see his name printed in bold letters.

"You speak English, don't you?"

"Yes."

"Good. I've been reading this file—some interesting stuff in there." Allen sat down and stared in Cruz's direction. Cruz looked away. "So, I understand from the ICE agent who brought you in here that you know something about a double homicide—the murders of Maria and Jose Delgado."

Cruz didn't respond.

"Okay, well, I'm anxious to hear what it is and I'd appreciate it if you don't screw around, wasting my time. How about if you just cut to the chase." Allen glanced toward the mirror then back toward Cruz. "You understand what I mean by 'cut to the chase'?"

"Yeah."

"Then let's hear it."

Cruz leaned forward and locked eyes with Allen. "I want a lawyer. You understand what I mean by that?"

Travis Allen reentered the observation room and slammed the door. "Son of a bitch!" He paced back and forth in front of the mirror then kicked the chair he had sat in earlier. "He's just fucking with me."

"Take it easy, Travis. I've never seen anyone want to lawyer-up that fast who wasn't guilty." Blancato looked pleased. "I think we've got our man, and he's not going anywhere, thanks to ICE. And civil detention means he won't be getting a lawyer anytime soon. That buys us time to build our case." Blancato glared at Brick. "That's exactly why this needed to be a task force, even though not everyone saw it that way."

Brick got the message, loud and clear. He stood up, nodded to Blancato and the A-Team, and headed for the door. It was still his day off and he wasn't about to stick around any longer. Apparently, Ron felt the same way. Together, they left.

"Well, that's forty-five minutes of my life I'll never get back." Brick stopped in front of the elevator bank. "Elevator or stairs?"

Ron didn't hesitate. "Stairs. The way things are going we'd probably get stuck and waste what's left of our weekend. Still going to the game?"

Brick checked his watch. "No, it'd be like walking into a movie after it's already started. I want to be there for the first pitch and the last out or not at all. What do you have planned?"

"Tomorrow is Jasmine's birthday so we're celebrating tonight."

"Nice. Going someplace special?"

"No, she's really uncomfortable right now so we're staying in and I'm cooking dinner. Shrimp and grits, one of her favorites."

"Sounds good. I'll see you in about sixteen hours."

# CHAPTER TWENTY-TWO

BRICK EXITED THE Metro at Judiciary Square and made a beeline for Starbucks. He wanted to get in and out before the morning crush of caffeine junkies overran the place. He made it with little time to spare. He checked to see the lid on his tall green tea was secure, grabbed a couple of napkins, and headed across the street. His morning was going well until he heard Travis Allen call his name. Brick stopped short of the entrance to Headquarters. When he turned around, he saw Allen was smiling broadly.

"Too bad you and Ron didn't stick around yesterday."

"Why?"

"You missed the best part. ICE executed a search warrant on the place where Cruz was living and guess what they found?" Allen seemed to be enjoying the suspense but Brick wasn't.

"Better yet, just tell me."

"Jose's cellphone and your girl . . . what was her name?"

"Maria."

"Oh yeah, Maria. Found her passport. Both of them were in Cruz's underwear drawer." Allen was beaming like someone holding a winning lottery ticket. "Paul and I got the honor of arresting the bottom feeder."

"Congratulations." Brick didn't offer a handshake or high five but he meant what he said.

"Yeah, that's one more the A-Team can add to the win column. The lieutenant is really pleased."

"I'm sure he is." Brick didn't even attempt to sound sincere, but he doubted Allen noticed.

"In fact, he wants us all to attend the arraignment this morning." Allen started to walk away but turned back in Brick's direction. "I got to go get something to eat. Be sure to tell your partner, it's at nine thirty."

Cruz's arrest really wasn't a surprise. Brick just didn't expect it to happen so quickly. He took a sip of tea then headed up the stairs to the revolving door. Once inside, Brick took the stairs to the third floor and stopped at Ron's cubicle before going to his own.

"So the A-Team is getting the credit for the arrest?" Ron asked.

"That's what he said."

"But we're all part of the task force—that doesn't seem fair."

Brick laughed. Ron's short tenure in the squad was showing. "Welcome to Homicide. Oh, and Blancato wants us all to attend the arraignment."

"Because we were such good props at the press conference?"

"Now you're catching on. Nine thirty, Courtroom C-10." Brick headed across the room to his own cubicle. As he drank his tea, he could hear Allen. Wherever he went to get breakfast, he was back and letting everyone know about the latest notch on his belt.

\* \* \*

Brick and Ron arrived at C-10 shortly before nine thirty. They took a seat on a bench in the back. Lieutenant Blancato was in the front row. Next to him were Travis Allen and Paul Adkins.

Ron leaned over and whispered to Brick. "I see the butt boys are present and accounted for."

Brick managed to keep from laughing as he pointed to an older woman sitting toward the front of the courtroom on the opposite side of the aisle. "She's from the *Washington Post*, been covering the courthouse forever."

"See any others?" Ron asked.

Brick looked around. "No. Not exactly the media presence Blancato was probably hoping for."

"They're all probably over at Landlord-Tenant. It's a lot more interesting."

Ron's observation was pretty accurate. For defendants, Arraignment Court is a lot like standing in line at the deli waiting for their number to be called. The difference being the defendants are shackled and under the watchful eyes of marshals guarding them. It looked as though Cruz drew number one—he was already seated at the defense table. Next to him was a female attorney. Just seeing her from the back, Brick wasn't sure who it was. Nor did he recognize the assistant U.S. attorney seated at the prosecutor's table.

"All rise." The bailiff's booming voice bounced off the walls of the nearly empty courtroom. Even the court reporter jumped at the sound. The door leading to the judge's anteroom opened and a robed figure emerged along with his law clerk carrying a carafe of ice water. "The Honorable Stephen R. Newton presiding." The bailiff had turned down the volume. "Be seated and come to order."

Brick was amused as he watched Newton settle into what Brick knew was a chair custom designed to make the judge look taller. The robe helped conceal that the man was nearly as round as he was tall. He patted the thinning hair combed over the top of his head as if making sure each hair was in place.

"Call the first case."

The bailiff picked up a manila file folder. "The United States of America versus Guadalupe Cruz."

"Who's representing the government?"

"I am, Your Honor."

"State your name for the record."

"Jonathan Eliot."

"And for the defense?" Newton appeared to look over his glasses and smile slightly.

The attorney seated next to Cruz stood. "Lily Nguyen, Your Honor."

"Oh, good morning, Ms. Nguyen."

"Good morning, Your Honor."

Brick knew the judge wasn't showing partiality to the defense. He had a reputation for being pro-prosecution, but he also had a reputation for paying attention to the female attorneys who appeared in his courtroom.

Newton appeared to shuffle some papers before addressing the defendant directly. "Mr. Cruz, the purpose of this hearing is to advise you of the charges you are facing and the maximum penalty those charges carry. Do you understand?" Cruz nodded his head. "You have to speak up so the court reporter can record your answer. I'll ask again, do you understand?"

"Yes."

"All right. According to the indictment filed by the Government, you are being charged with felony murder as to the death of Jose Delgado and Maria Delgado. If convicted, felony murder carries a mandatory penalty of twenty years to life for each count. Do you wish to enter a plea at this time?"

It sounded to Brick like Newton was just phoning it in. He had recited those lines so many times and the only thing that changed was the crime and the victim's name. It even looked like he had to stifle a yawn as he waited for Cruz to respond.

"Guilty."

For a second Brick thought he had hallucinated, but then he saw the stunned look on several faces in the courtroom—including the judge.

"Counselors, approach the bench."

AUSA Eliot and Ms. Nguyen quickly complied. It was killing Brick not to be able to hear the discussion between the judge and the lawyers. From what he could see, the prosecutor was saying little, but Lily Nguyen was very animated. When she returned to the defense table, she did not look pleased. She pulled her chair close to Cruz and spoke to him in a hushed tone. After letting Nguyen confer with her client for a few minutes, the judge spoke again.

"Ms. Nguyen, are we ready to proceed?"

"Yes, Your Honor."

"All right then. Mr. Cruz, do you wish to change your plea?"

"No."

All that was left was for Cruz and his attorney to sign the paperwork and be given a sentencing date. There was no need for Brick and Ron to stick around. Blancato and the A-Team had already left, nearly colliding with the *Post* reporter as they all bolted for the door. She had the scoop; Blancato wanted to tell the mayor before he heard it from another source.

"Have you ever seen that happen before?" Ron asked as he and Brick headed to the escalator.

"No, not on a felony murder charge. And, I might be wrong, but I don't think Cruz's attorney knew what was coming."

"She did seem shaken." Ron hesitated for a second. "Isn't she the one the guys call the Dragon Lady?"

Brick nodded. "One and the same."

# CHAPTER TWENTY-THREE

"What do you say, partner? The party should be in full swing by now."

Brick looked up from the keyboard, nostalgic for the days when clerks typed the handwritten police reports cops turned in. His hunt-and-peck technique was slow and error-prone but at least for now it gave him an excuse to stay behind. "Go ahead, Ron. I'll meet you over there."

Post-conviction or guilty plea celebrations were customary but Brick wasn't in a hurry to join in. Still, he felt obligated to make an appearance, have a drink, and leave. Let everyone see he was a player even though he hoped he'd never again have to work that closely with the A-Team. Given a choice, directing traffic at Connecticut and K during rush hour in a blizzard would be preferable.

Brick glanced up at the clock—about fifteen minutes had passed. He reread the report he had written, corrected a couple of typos, and hit close. As he waited for the computer to shut down, he called Tracy Collins. He got her voicemail.

"Hey Tracy, it's Brick. Just wanted to give you a heads-up. Our perp shocked everyone by pleading guilty at his arraignment. That puts our double in the closed column. Anything new on your case? Hope you're enjoying your day off." He hung up, locked his desk, and headed toward the elevators.

On this April day, which felt more like August, beads of sweat rolled down Brick's back as he walked the six blocks to the FOP. *Go along to get along*, he reminded himself as he approached the unmarked front door. He hesitated. Access required entering a code into the cypher lock. For a minute he was stumped, then he remembered. Routinely, on the first of January it got reset to the current year. He entered the four digits and stepped inside, grateful the AC was cranked up. As Brick made his way to the bar, he passed one of three pool tables. He nodded to a deputy marshal he recognized. Cue stick in hand, she appeared to be planning her next shot.

"Hey, Brick, long time no see." Hank Murphy wiped his hand on his bar rag before extending it in Brick's direction. "How have you been?"

"Okay, how about you?"

Hank's hand gesture indicated so-so.

"You look good, like you've gained some weight."

"Can't complain. I'm thankful for every day above ground."

Murphy had reason to be. Three years earlier, while assigned to the Robbery Squad, he had responded to a silent bank alarm and walked into a robbery in progress. Wearing a vest saved his life, but one of the three bullets he took shattered his knee and ended his career. While in the hospital, he contracted an infection that nearly killed him. Bartending left him in pain, but as he liked to say, he'd still be in pain sitting in front of the TV so he might as well supplement his disability pension. Brick suspected it really wasn't about the money; Hank missed being a cop and working at the FOP allowed him to be around his buddies.

"Go ahead, Brick, name your poison." Hank was kidding but not by much. Some of the bottles lining the bar wouldn't even be used for rail drinks in most places.

"How's the gin?"

"Good if you're painting and run out of turpentine." Hank gave Brick a knowing look. "Go for the whiskey."

"If you say so." Brick was skeptical but trusted the guy he was often paired with when they were cadets at the Academy.

Hank reached behind the bottles of whiskey on the counter and retrieved a hidden bottle of Bushmills 1608. He poured a generous shot into a glass and slid it across the bar. "Try this."

Brick took a sip and smiled. "That's definitely the good stuff."

Hank nodded. "According to my doctor, the old liver can tolerate an occasional drink. No sense wasting it on the rot gut I serve in this place." He returned the bottle to its hiding place.

Brick looked around the room. "Have you seen Ron?"

"Your partner, Ron? Yeah, he was here a minute ago. Think he stepped out to take a phone call." Hank motioned toward the table where Travis Allen was holding court. "Kind of hard to hear yourself think with your man over there telling the same friggin' joke he tells every time he's in here—which is way too often, if you ask me."

Brick laughed. "Don't hold back, Hank, say what you think."

"Oh Christ, here he comes."

Allen bumped into a chair as he made his way to the bar. He tapped the two empty pitchers up and down on it.

"Hey, bartender, looks like we need refills." Allen's speech was just this side of slurring.

Without saying a word, Hank obliged and slid the full pitchers across the bar. As Allen picked them up, he noticed Brick.

"Grab your ass, I mean glass, and join us. We got reason to celebrate."

Brick followed him to the table but not before turning and rolling his eyes in Hank's direction.

Allen set the pitchers of beer down, sloshing some onto the table and narrowly missing a crime lab tech still in uniform. Brick pulled up a chair and sat across the table from Allen. He recognized most of the guys at the table as having been assigned to the task force. He was about to introduce himself to the two he hadn't met but didn't get a chance. Allen's voice filled the room.

"A priest, a rabbi, and a hooker—" The table erupted in laughter. Allen swallowed a hiccup. "What?"

"You just told us that one. Last call for you." Adkins playfully reached for his partner's glass, but Allen grabbed it first.

"I don't think so." Allen tipped up his glass and drained the contents before refilling it. "Gotta have a toast." He took a swig of beer then stood and held up his glass. "Come on, raise your glass." One by one, except for Brick, the guys followed suit.

"Here's to . . . I forgot what it's called." He lowered his glass. "You know, in hockey."

"Hockey?" Adkins asked. "What's that got to do with anything?"

"Come on . . . when a guy scores three times." Allen took another drink. "Know what I call it when I score three times?" He raised one eyebrow and waited. "A slow night." Even Brick laughed at that.

"A hat trick," two guys at the table responded at the same time.

"What?"

"In hockey, it's called a hat trick."

"Oh, right." Once again Allen raised his glass. He cleared his throat and swayed slightly. "Here's to a Mexican hat trick—one in jail and two in boxes."

It only took a nanosecond for Brick to wrap his head around what he had heard. The image of Maria floating in the Tidal Basin and Jose dead on his bathroom floor flashed in front of his eyes. Instantly, he jumped up, lunged across the table, and grabbed the front of Allen's shirt. The beer glass Allen had been holding flew out of his hand. Budweiser rained down on the two cops seated next to him before the glass hit the floor and shattered. Suddenly, the room was silent and everyone seemed frozen in place.

"HEY! HEY! HEY! Let him go!" As Ron grabbed Brick's arm in a viselike grip, Brick's fingers relaxed, releasing the fist aimed at Allen's jaw. He and Allen glared at each other but said nothing. If looks could kill, they'd both be dead. Brick shook free of Ron's hold and headed for the back door leading to the alley. He kicked it open and heard it slam shut behind him.

As if reflecting his mood, the sky had turned gray and overcast. Huge drops of rain splattered on the dirty pavement. Brick took a couple of deep breaths. What just happened felt like an out-of-body experience. The adrenaline, which had surged through his veins, now slowed. His heart still beat so fast, it felt like it might crash against his rib cage.

Brick could count on one hand the times he had lost control like that. He hated letting Travis Allen, a shit-faced Allen no less, get to him, but he couldn't stand by and let him disparage Jose and Maria. He had ignored plenty of remarks in the past—not this time. All cops used gallows humor, but as far as Brick was concerned, there was a line you didn't cross. Blatant disrespect for victims crossed that line.

It was raining harder. A striped awning over the service entrance to the restaurant across the alley provided shelter, but it was already occupied. A guy wearing an ICE windbreaker taking a smoking break leaned against the wooden exterior. The last thing Brick wanted was company, but he craved a cigarette, and a whiff of secondhand smoke made it worse. It had been at least a year since he had actually bought a pack and almost that long since his last smoke. One lousy cigarette was just that. It wasn't a relapse, he told himself.

Out of the corner of his eye, Brick watched the guy take one last drag before dropping the butt on the pavement. With his heel, he ground out the glowing ember. He stepped out from under the awning and nodded in Brick's direction as he crossed the alley.

"Can I bum a cigarette?"

"Sure." The guy reached inside his pocket and retrieved a pack of Marlboros. He handed them to Brick along with a lighter.

"Thanks." Brick took one, lit up, and inhaled deeply. He held the smoke in his lungs as long as he could before exhaling, then handed the half-empty pack and lighter back to their owner. The guy took a step toward the door of the FOP but stopped and looked back in Brick's direction.

"For what it's worth, if you ask me, Allen's an asshole. He had it coming."

Brick didn't respond. The vote of confidence was unexpected, but it didn't make him feel better. Already, he regretted making a scene. It wasn't his style.

The Marlboro Man left it at that. He reached for the doorknob then stepped back as the door swung wide. He and Ron brushed shoulders as one man exited and the other reentered the FOP.

For a moment, Ron didn't say anything. Thunder rumbled in the distance and a jagged streak of lightning lit up the western sky. "You okay?"

Brick nodded.

"C'mon, I'll drive you home."

Brick took another drag on his cigarette. "I'll walk."

Ron shook his head. "In case you haven't noticed, we're about to get a mother of a storm. You need to beat feet to my car before those Cole Haans are waterlogged."

One more look skyward, and Brick knew Ron was right. They made it to the car just as the skies opened up.

"That was close." Ron exhaled and started the car. Hip-hop music blared from the radio. "Sorry about that." He quickly turned down the volume and changed stations. As Ron backed out of the parking space, the sound of WJZW's smooth jazz competed with hailstones pelting the roof of his car.

# CHAPTER TWENTY-FOUR

"THE LIEUTENANT WILL see you now."

Blancato's secretary was clearly back to her prim and proper self. Brick couldn't resist. "What . . . no f-bombs this morning?" He smiled as he rose to his feet.

His half-hour wait had been reminiscent of his youth sitting outside the principal's office. At least the upholstered leather chair was more comfortable than the wooden bench where his younger self sat waiting for his punishment. Usually this had meant a detention, which he didn't mind all that much. He managed to read several of Ed McBain's novels cleverly hidden inside his calculus or chemistry folders. Had it not been for the cops of the 87th Precinct, he might have pursued an entirely different career.

"Shut the door and have a seat."

Brick complied.

Blancato tossed a toothpick in the direction of the wastebasket. He missed. The toothpick landed next to a couple of others scattered on the floor. "I heard about the incident at the FOP."

"It was off-duty."

"Not to my way of thinking. As long as you're within the District of Columbia, technically, you're never off-duty. This is the kind of conversation I'd expect to have with a rookie, not someone who's been on the job as long as you have." Blancato leaned forward across his desk. "Jesus Christ, just when we close a big case and are getting some positive press for a change. What were you thinking?" Brick was about to tell him but Blancato only paused long enough to take a breath. He held up a copy of the *Washington Post*. "They'd love a story about a couple of detectives punching each other out."

"Especially when the reason was an ethnic slur about two homicide victims." Brick locked eyes with Blancato, willing himself not to blink.

"Okay, you have a point and I've spoken to Allen." Blancato smirked while shaking his head. "You know how he is—sometimes his mouth opens before his brain engages. Besides, he admits he'd had a couple of beers."

"So, *technically*, he was drinking on duty." Brick couldn't resist throwing the lieutenant's screwed-up, you're-never-off-duty logic back in his face.

"I'm not going to get in a pissing contest with you. Like it or not, I'm in charge here, and all I need to do is pick up the phone, and you'll be back in uniform patrolling Anacostia." He cracked the knuckles on his right hand. "I don't want to do that. I'm going to cut you some slack. I should have taken you off the case right from the start. I know you said you could handle it, and I thought you could, but looking back, it was a bad idea. You were never on board with the task force; you just went through the motions." Blancato opened a manila folder and pulled out a sheet of paper. He scanned it before continuing. "Do you even know how much vacation time you've got built up?"

Brick shrugged his shoulders. "No."

"Enough that you're in the use-or-lose category. Take some of it and get a little R and R. Go to Lauderdale and lay on the beach. Better yet, go to the beach and get laid." He flashed a self-satisfied smile. "That's what I would do." Blancato slid the form across the desk. "I need you to sign this leave slip."

Brick glanced down and saw the dates had already been filled in—two weeks, effective immediately. It wasn't vacation, it was a suspension. Without hesitating, he picked up the leave slip and tore it in half.

*   *   *

Brick exited the revolving door and walked down the steps of Headquarters like he had done thousands of times over the past twenty years. But this time was different; he was a civilian. He knew the day would come when he would turn in his badge and gun, he just didn't think it would be today. For the second time in less than twenty-four hours, he had acted impulsively. It was totally out of character for him, but there was no denying it felt right. It also felt surreal. It was nine o'clock in the morning and there was nowhere he had to be.

It had been years since Brick frequented the FOP—now he was walking through the door for the second time in two days. He was relieved to see the place was empty except for Hank.

"Better be careful, Brick, this could become a habit."

"I don't think so." He settled onto one of the mismatched stools lining the bar. "I owe you an apology."

"For what?"

"The incident yesterday."

"Oh that." Hank laughed. "If you need to apologize for anything—it's for not knocking Allen on his ass. That motherfucker's been a thorn in my side for as long as I can remember."

"You're not alone," Brick said. "He's a decent detective, I'll give him that. But if he weren't so connected, he'd never get away with the stuff he says and does."

"Yeah, it definitely helps when your daddy's been a congressman for the past twenty years or so." Hank rinsed a couple of glasses and set them aside to dry. "Where's Ron?"

"Last I heard, he's at Georgetown with his wife—you know she's about to have twins."

"Well, God bless him. I'd offer you a shot of whiskey, but I'm guessing you're on duty."

"Not anymore." Brick managed a half-hearted smile.

Hank did a double take. "What the hell does that mean?"

Brick told Hank about his meeting with Blancato.

"Jesus, Brick, what are you going to do?"

"I don't know. Buy season tickets for the Nats?"

"C'mon, I'm serious. I know you well enough to know being a cop is in your DNA. Take it from me, you're going to miss it more than you could ever imagine. I'd give my left nut—hell, my right one, too— just to be back in uniform. Don't end your career this way. Go back and talk to Blancato. Do it now before the word gets around."

Brick shook his head. "I hear what you're saying, but I'm done. I'm tired of the politics and bullshit that get in the way of doing the job."

"That's always been the case. It's the way this town operates."

"It's worse now. Blancato's so far up the mayor's ass he could be checking for polyps."

Hank had just taken a drink of water and almost did a spit-take. "Thanks a lot—that's an image I won't be able to get out of my head. Guess he's laying the groundwork to be Chief of Police. Right?"

"I'm hearing he's got ambitions beyond chief. That's why he created the task force with ICE almost before the bodies were cold. There was a time when calling in the Feds would have been the last resort."

"I don't mean to play devil's advocate, but it's hard to argue with success. A guilty plea at arraignment—doesn't get much sweeter than that."

"You're right." It was easier to agree with Hank than to get into a debate. What he said was true, but a plea isn't sweet if the guy isn't guilty and something about Cruz's plea just didn't make sense. "I need to get going; take care of yourself."

"You do the same." Hank reached across the bar and the two former cops shook hands. "Don't be a stranger."

Brick couldn't get out of there fast enough, yet he wasn't ready to go home. It was just after ten, which meant Boland's Mill would be open. A few hours ago, he never would have imagined turning this morning into a pub crawl. Then again, he hadn't seen himself pulling the plug on a twenty-year career.

*   *   *

"The cat's freaking me out." Rory eased off the Guinness tap and waited for the pint to settle. "I bought her one of those scratching posts with a perch on top so that she'd have a nice place to sleep. She'll crawl up there during the day but at night she sits and stares at my bathtub. And sometimes she makes a sound that's not a meow—it's more like a cry." He set the glass in front of Brick. "I don't know, it's like she misses Jose and remembers seeing him by the bathtub. It's kind of weird, don't you think?"

"What's weird?"

"The cat."

"What about the cat?"

"Jaysus, have I been talking to myself here? I was telling you about Elvis."

"What about him . . . her?"

"Never mind, I'm probably imagining things." Rory yawned, practically exposing his tonsils. "I haven't had a decent night's sleep since Jose died."

Brick didn't respond. He picked up his glass and set it back down without taking a drink. Rory watched as he did it again.

"Something wrong with your glass?"

"No, why?"

"You keep picking it up and putting it down."

"Really?" Brick shook his head. "Guess I'm a little preoccupied."

"A new case?" Rory refilled a couple of salt shakers then went to work on the pepper shakers. "Sad to say, but in this crazy feckin' world, cops and grave diggers will never have to worry about being unemployed."

Brick stared at his own reflection in the mirror behind the bar. He exhaled slowly. "I quit, Rory."

"Quit what?"

"The job."

Rory gave Brick a quizzical look. "Are you serious?"

Brick nodded. "I'm done—no badge, no gun, it's over."

Rory poured himself a Coke and took a drink. "Man, talk about left field. I didn't see this coming."

Brick laughed. "That makes two of us." He gave Rory an abbreviated version of his encounter with Blancato.

"And just like that, you quit?"

"Yeah, just like that."

"What are you going to do?"

Brick shrugged. "I'll figure it out." To his ears, the words sounded confident, but Brick felt numb. What would he do? He'd always liked being a cop, but he loved being a homicide detective. It was going to be a tough act to follow, no matter what he decided.

"I don't know what to say." Rory shook his head. "Congratulations doesn't sound right."

Brick took a sip of his Guinness. "Sounds right to me."

"Then, congratulations it is." Rory raised his glass of Coke. "*Slàinte!*"

Brick tapped his glass against Rory's. "Is Eamonn in his office?"

"No. He's running a few errands, getting ready for his trip."

"When's he leaving?" Brick asked.

"Day after tomorrow." Rory shook his head. "Just between you and me, I'm worried about him, Brick. I tried everything I could think of to talk him out of it, but I may as well have saved my breath. He's made up his mind and that's that. He's so feckin' stubborn." Rory yawned again and Brick wondered if worrying about Eamonn was also contributing to his insomnia. "By the way, Jose's landlord, what's his name?"

"Carlos."

"Right, Carlos. He stopped by and dropped off some stuff from Jose's apartment. Their clothes and the bigger stuff Eamonn's storing for now, but he figured he could take a few small things the family may want. That's what's in those bags over there." Rory finished his Coke. "Want to make yourself useful? You could help me pack it up."

"Not like there's anywhere I need to be." Brick pulled off his tie and stuck it in the pocket of his suit coat. It took a second for him to remember he no longer was walking around with a gun and handcuffs on his belt. He took off his jacket and hung it over the back of a chair, rolled up his sleeves, and followed Rory to the corner where the bags were stacked. Scissors, tape, and bubble wrap were set out on a nearby table along with a sturdy cardboard box bearing the logo of Captain Morgan White Rum.

Rory opened one of the bags and retrieved the contents. He handed some framed photos, a couple of religious statues, a strand of rosary beads, and a crucifix to Brick. "Guess all this stuff should be wrapped up before it's put in the box."

"Okay." Brick went to work encasing the items in bubble wrap while Rory emptied the next bag.

"This must have belonged to Maria."

"What is it?" Brick asked.

Rory held an ornate wooden box in his hands. "Looks like a jewelry box." He flipped it open. "Yeah, a bunch of earrings, some bracelets and necklaces. I don't know much about jewelry, but it doesn't look like anything all that valuable."

Brick peered over Rory's shoulder. "Stuff probably has sentimental value."

"Maybe, I wouldn't know about that. Just looks like cheap jewelry to me." Rory reached into the bag again. "Hey, this looks like a photo album." He flipped through a few of the pages. "Aw, jaysus, there's one of me and Jose doing karaoke." Rory closed the album and dropped it in the box. "I can't look at those. Hand me the scissors." Brick complied and watched as Rory cut the string securing the top of another bag. "Oh man, this was the soccer jersey I brought back for Jose the last time I was in Ireland." Brick heard Rory sniffle a couple of times. "He was so excited when I gave it to him. He told me he was going to hang it on the wall instead of wearing it."

"Now that you mention it, I remember seeing it in his bedroom," Brick said. "It was hanging on the wall over his bed."

Rory removed the jersey from the bag and set it on the table. "Looks like he wore it at least once to some kind of party. There's confetti stuck to the sleeve."

Brick set down the jewelry box he was wrapping. "Where?"

"Right there." Rory pointed to the right sleeve of the soccer jersey just as his cellphone squawked. He pulled the phone out of his shirt pocket and checked the display. "Gotta take this." Rory ducked into Eamonn's office and closed the door.

Brick bent down to get a better look. Immediately he saw what Rory was talking about and understood how he could have thought it was confetti. Brick knew better. He was 99 percent sure he was looking at taser dots. He grabbed a piece of tissue paper, and using his ballpoint pen, knocked the dots onto the paper, folded it into a square, and slipped it into his pocket. Brick walked over by the window looking out on Connecticut Avenue. He thought for a moment. In order for taser dots to attach to Jose's soccer jersey, a taser must have been discharged near where the jersey was hanging. The bruise on Maria's hip . . . the Medical Examiner couldn't determine the cause, but could it be the result of a taser? That was just one of the questions swirling around in Brick's head. How could the Mobile Crime Unit miss something that could prove to be critical evidence? With encoded serial numbers, taser dots are as identifiable as a fingerprint. Sloppy police work. Given all the budget cuts, Brick had seen plenty of examples lately. But even for cops working a double-shift, they're supposed to be professionals and overlooking evidence was inexcusable.

Brick was angry and frustrated. Frustrated that guys who are paid to find evidence didn't. He turned away from the window. And angry, that as a civilian, there was nothing he could do about it.

Then again, maybe there was.

# CHAPTER TWENTY-FIVE

BRICK GRABBED HIS phone the instant it rang. He was relieved to see Ron's number pop up. "How's Jasmine?"

"She's fine, we're back home." Ron exhaled loudly. "A false alarm, but the doctor says she's going to need bed rest until she delivers. Her mother and sister are moving in as we speak." He lowered his voice to a whisper. "Just shoot me now."

Brick laughed. "Any chance you can get away for about an hour? There's a couple of things I need to talk to you about and I'd rather it be in person."

"Only an hour?" Ron sounded disappointed. "How about Ike's in forty-five minutes?"

"Works for me." It'd been a while since he'd had a chili dog. Might as well have the best D.C. has to offer.

It was just after sunset when Brick exited the U Street/Cardozo Station along with a crowd of dressed-for-success young men and women. He guessed that most of them heading to their luxury condos or apartments were too young to appreciate how the neighborhood had evolved. Like the mythical phoenix, it had risen from the ashes of burned-out shells that remained after the '68 riots following the assassination of Martin Luther King Jr. But it was a long time coming. For many years drug dealers sold heroin in open-air markets.

Then construction of the Metro's Green Line turned the area into a sixty-foot hole. Most of the business in the area closed, some overnight, but through it all, Ike's Chili Dog not only survived, it thrived.

Brick arrived first. It was always comforting to see that Ike's hadn't changed much over the years despite the recent influx of boutiques, high-end home furnishing stores, and trendy restaurants. He nodded to a young man behind the counter before heading to one of the booths in the back. The photos on the wall were an eclectic mix of familiar faces—politicians, local celebrities, musicians, and athletes. Brick was happy to see a couple of Nats players had earned a spot. With the team wrapping up a six-game road trip to Milwaukee and Chicago, they'd be back home by the end of the week. Brick figured he owed it to himself to finally take in a couple of games.

"Sorry I'm late—had to pick up a prescription for Jasmine."

Brick looked up as Ron eased into the opposite side of the booth. "No problem. I've been checking out some of the new photos over there."

"Cool." Ron got up, walked over, and took a look, then returned to the table. "Did I ever point out my father's picture?"

"No."

"That's him next to Roberta Flack. He was good. Some critics even compared him to Thelonious Monk." Ron shook his head. "Probably could have been great if the drugs hadn't killed him first." He sat down again. "Guess I'll have to bring the twins in here when they're old enough to understand. So, what's up?"

"I quit, Ron."

"Smoking . . . that's good."

A sad smile crossed Brick's lips. "I turned in my badge this morning."

"Why . . . what . . . is this a joke?"

"No."

Ron slumped against the back of the booth. "Damn, this is the last thing I expected to hear." Ron was silent for a minute, but when he spoke again, he sounded angry. "You been planning this for a while and didn't even bother to tell me?"

Brick shook his head. "No, it wasn't like that at all." Over chili half-smokes and fries, he recounted his earlier meeting with Blancato.

"Fucking Blancato." Ron picked up a fry then threw it back on his plate. He wiped a blob of chili off his hands and dropped the crumpled paper napkin next to his plate. "Why quit? He could be gone in six months or a year."

"It's not just about Blancato."

"Travis Allen? Oh man, please don't tell me—"

"No, it's not one person or one thing. It's the culture—the only thing more outdated than the computers is the mind-set of the White Shirts in charge. You know what I'm talking about."

Ron nodded. "Yeah, I do. I get that and it's frustrating as hell, but walking away like this, it's so sudden."

"Not really. You might say I just 'know when to hold 'em, know when to fold 'em.'" Brick waited, expecting Ron to identify the movie line, but he didn't. "Come on, even I know that was Kenny Rogers in *The Gambler*. Maybe I'll catch up on all those movies I've missed and challenge you to a trivia smackdown."

That elicited a smile from Ron, but it faded quickly. "It was a hit song before it was a movie, so it doesn't count. Seriously, what are you going to do?"

"Until a couple of hours ago I didn't know, but now I do." Brick glanced around, making sure no one was within earshot. "What would you say if told you I found some overlooked evidence from Jose's apartment?"

Ron didn't respond immediately. "Guess it would depend on the evidence."

"Taser dots."

"Say what?"

Ron listened intently as Brick recapped the discovery he'd made. "Remember the bruise on Maria's hip—the one the ME said was inconclusive?" Ron nodded as Brick continued. "If she was hit with a taser—"

"That's a big *if*, man."

"Maybe, maybe not. If she was the target and Jose interrupted an abduction in progress—"

"You mentioned something like that back in the brainstorming session with Blancato and the A-Team. Seemed far-fetched then, and I gotta say, it still does."

"You've worked Homicide long enough now to know stranger things have happened."

Ron didn't respond immediately. "True, but are you sure this isn't a you-versus-them kind of thing?"

"No, it's never been about that. I don't have a vendetta against Blancato or the A-Team. I don't like working with them, but that's not breaking news. This is about one thing—finding the truth. Whatever that truth is. If you've learned nothing else from me, I hope you've learned that."

"Rest assured, I got that message loud and clear on day one." Ron shook his head. "I'm going to miss you, man. We've only been together a year, but every day I've learned something from you." The emotion in Ron's voice was palpable. "Because of you, I know I'm a better cop and a better man. If ever there's anything I can do . . ." Ron's voice trailed off, leaving his offer open-ended.

Brick didn't hesitate. "As a matter of fact, there is."

# CHAPTER TWENTY-SIX

FOR THE FIRST time in as long as Brick could remember, he hadn't been jarred awake by an alarm clock. Eight hours of sleep had felt good, so good it could easily become a habit. Before zipping his leather bomber jacket, Brick reached inside his pocket and retrieved his sunglasses. It was close to noon and he was going to need them. Time for the first big decision of the day—where to have lunch.

From fast-food franchises to family-owned ethnic establishments to upscale, Michelin-rated restaurants, the neighborhood provided something for everyone. Over the years, Brick had tried most, if not all, of them. He started walking south toward the intersection of Calvert Street and Connecticut Avenue. Around the corner and up a flight of stairs was one of his favorites, Pho-75. "Pho" referred to the traditional Vietnamese soup that was the mainstay of the menu and "75" represented the year the family who owned the place fled Saigon. Just as he expected, most of the tables were full and a line extended from the cash register back to the door.

At first Brick didn't recognize Lily Nguyen as she approached the counter where orders were placed. Her hair was pulled back into a ponytail and she was wearing faded jeans and a sweatshirt imprinted with a sketch of the Golden Gate Bridge. It was a sharp contrast to her usual, no-nonsense court attire but didn't diminish her ability to turn heads. Brick saw two young Asian guys elbow each other as she walked past them to a small table in the back.

With a menu limited to pho, the line moved quickly. Brick grabbed a tray and a couple of paper napkins in anticipation of his turn.

"Next!" Dong Minh had taken over the restaurant since his father had been diagnosed with Parkinson's. He looked up and tipped his Nationals cap in Brick's direction. "The usual?"

Brick nodded. For him, the "usual" meant beef brisket as his choice of meat.

"Sure you don't want tripe?" Dong asked.

It was a running joke between the two. Brick shook his head. "Next time."

"That's what you said last time." Dong placed the steaming bowl on Brick's tray. "Been to a game?"

"Not yet." Brick spared him the details of his two aborted attempts.

Dong patted his shirt pocket. "Two tickets for this afternoon. I'm taking my boy—his first game."

"Strasburg's pitching so it should be a good one." Brick managed a smile despite a wave of sadness that unexpectedly washed over him as he thought about taking Jose to his first game. The kid had been so eager to embrace all things American. And unwittingly he had, although Brick was sure becoming a homicide victim wasn't something Jose considered a possibility. Brick carried his tray to Dong's mother at the cash register.

"*Bạn khỏe khộng?*" Brick asked.

The woman smiled, revealing a few missing teeth. "I good. How are you?" She counted out Brick's change and handed it to him.

"*Cảm ơn bạn.*" Brick dropped the change in the tip jar.

"Thank you, too." The woman smiled again and bowed her head in Brick's direction.

There were a couple of empty tables near the window, but Brick walked past them to where Lily Nguyen was seated.

"Mind if I join you?"

Lily looked up from the crossword puzzle she was working on. "Detective Kavanagh, right?" Brick nodded. "It may be seen as consorting with the enemy."

"I like to live on the edge."

She responded with a smile that was more polite than welcoming before motioning to the chair across from her.

Brick set his tray on the table and sat down.

"Help yourself." Lily pointed to the bowl of bean sprouts and herbs that were traditionally added to the chopped scallions and cilantro already sprinkled on the broth. She watched as Brick added the ingredients before squeezing a wedge of lime over the top. A couple of drops of Sriracha added the final touch. "Looks like you've been here before."

Brick tasted the soup. "Guess you could say I'm a pho-natic."

Lily groaned but she also laughed. "Next time, have the tripe."

"I don't think so." Brick added a few more bean sprouts to the broth.

"You're the one who said you like to live on the edge."

"I lied."

"Guess that's okay since you're not under oath." Lily took a sip of water. "I have to say this is a bit awkward. Usually when I talk to cops, it's on cross-examination."

"And that's preferable?"

"Let's just say, I'm better at that than small talk since I don't see things the way most cops do."

"Well, I can make it easier for you—I'm not a cop anymore."

Lily's spoon was poised in midair. "What . . . what do you mean?"

"I retired."

"Congratulations." She put her spoon down. "And what great tim-ing—a quick arrest and a defendant who pled, against my advice, I might add. Doesn't get any better than that, does it?"

"That depends. If the defendant is guilty—yeah, that's as good as it gets. But if the defendant isn't guilty even though—"

"Stop right there. Are you speaking hypothetically or specifically about one of my cases?"

Brick hadn't planned to have this conversation, at least not now, but he couldn't recant what he had said. "I'm talking about Guadalupe Cruz."

"Are you implying he may not be guilty?"

Brick nodded. "I think that's a possibility."

Lily pushed back from the table. "You may be retired, but that doesn't matter one bit. I'm an officer of the court, and if you have any proof, I need to know about it. I'm obligated to bring it to the atten-tion of the presiding judge." She stared across the table. "Why are you telling me this?"

Brick stared back. "I want justice for Jose and his sister."

Lily shook her head. "That sounds a bit rehearsed. My gut tells me there's more to it than that."

"There isn't, but if the truth ultimately wins out, what difference does it make?"

Lily crumpled her crossword puzzle and threw it next to the napkin on her tray. She stood up, reached into her purse, and extracted a silver card case. She dropped one of her business cards on Brick's tray. "I don't have time to play games. If you're serious, be at my office at 8:00 a.m. on Monday. If you don't show—we never had this conversation."

Brick watched as Lily Nguyen turned and walked away. He picked up her card and slipped it into his pocket.

# CHAPTER TWENTY-SEVEN

BRICK CHECKED HIS watch. Just over an hour had passed since he'd left home. The rest of the day was his for the taking, but he wasn't sure what to do with it. In the past, with only a finite amount of personal time, the days always seemed to be in fast forward. Now it sometimes felt as if time was standing still. He headed back toward his condo but made a spur-of-the-moment decision, turned, and headed in the opposite direction.

Although Brick lived close enough to the National Zoo to regularly hear the lions roar, he couldn't remember the last time he had been there other than on police business. Given it was a beautiful Saturday spring afternoon, he knew it would be crowded, but that didn't deter him. He dodged strollers, obliged a Chinese couple by taking their picture in front of the panda house, and watched the frenzied activity of the prairie dogs. Just as he made his way to the Great Cats enclosure, his phone rang.

"I can hardly hear you. Where are you, man?" Ron asked.

"The zoo."

"Seriously?"

"Yeah, meet me on Tiger Hill." Despite the poor connection, Brick heard Ron sigh.

"If you say so."

For the next fifteen or twenty minutes, Brick watched as a trio of Sumatran tiger cubs played under the watchful eye of their mother. Although they were bigger than most domestic cats, their flexibility when they stretched reminded Brick of the contortions he had seen Elvis perform. The thought of Jose's cat conjured up images of the bloody paw prints leading to Jose's battered body. Brick gripped the hand rail on the security fence and closed his eyes, hoping to clear his head. It worked and he started to relax but only for a moment. He jerked and looked to his right as he felt a tap on his shoulder.

"Sorry, didn't mean to startle you," Ron said.

Brick brushed it off. "I didn't expect you so soon. Lights and sirens?"

"No, I was at Connecticut and K when I called. Figured it was better to make these copies at Kinko's. Most likely all this file's going to do is gather dust but I figured no one needs to know I was making a duplicate."

Ron handed Brick a thick, sealed envelope.

"Feel a little like Deep Throat?"

Ron looked surprised. "You saw that movie . . . oh, I get it; the FBI guy from Watergate. No, wouldn't we have to be meeting in an underground parking garage in Rosslyn?"

"Too late. According to the *Post*, it's being torn down to make way for a high-rise." Ron shook his head. "I'll never get it. Nixon was going to win reelection anyway. Why'd he do it?"

"As long as you work Homicide, you'll ask that question a lot. Sometimes it's obvious and sometimes it's so convoluted, you'll just shake your head."

"Guess as long as I figure out who and lock up their sorry ass, I won't worry about why."

"That works." Brick tapped the envelope. "Thanks for getting this for me."

"Sure." Ron looked over at his former partner. "You okay, man? You seem a little, I don't know, uptight."

Brick told Ron about his unexpected encounter with Lily Nguyen.

"Whoa, no wonder they call her the Dragon Lady." Ron glanced down at his watch. "Much as I'd like to knock off the rest of the day watching the pandas eating bamboo, I need to get back. For now, I'm still working solo, and it looks like I'm finally making some progress on the Southeast Freeway road-rage case."

"Really?"

"Yeah, seems a Crime Stoppers reward jogged someone's memory. Imagine that?"

"It'd be nice to put that one in the closed column." It had been one of the first cases the two detectives had worked together, and for a moment, Brick regretted he wouldn't be a part of how the investigation progressed. He shook it off. "Where did you park?"

"I found a spot near the entrance."

"Must be living right."

"I try, man. And a certain Official MPDC Business placard on the dash helps."

Together they made their way back to the zoo's entrance on Connecticut Avenue.

"Take it easy, man," Ron said as the two shook hands. "Let me know what you find."

"Will do. And just for future reference, when the twins are old enough, Uncle Brick will be happy to take them to the zoo."

The offer brought a smile to Ron's face. "You got it, man."

The two former partners headed in opposite directions; Ron to his car and Brick toward his condo. The meeting had yielded what Brick needed, but Ron's departure sparked an emotional response Brick hadn't anticipated. In the year they had worked together, they had bonded in a way Brick hadn't experienced before even though he had previously worked with guys he liked and respected. Maybe it had been the teacher/student roles that had made the difference. Or maybe in Ron, Brick saw a younger version of himself. He still remembered how it felt that first year. He was thrilled to be working Homicide, eager to learn everything he could, and never gave a thought to the day it would be over.

Hopefully, he and Ron would keep in touch, but Brick knew that, even if they did, it would never be the same.

Before going home, Brick made one more stop. He walked into Boland's just as Rory high-fived a young woman at the end of the bar.

"Hey, Brick, our boy Strasburg is on his game today. Six up, six down." Rory picked up a glass and reached for the Guinness tap.

Brick stood at the bar. "Did Eamonn's flight get off okay?"

"Yeah, right on schedule." Rory handed his iPhone to Brick. "Got this app tracking it—he's about two hours out from Guatemala City." Rory stepped back to the tap and retrieved the Guinness he had left there to settle. He set it in front of Brick. "Gotta say I felt awful watching him walk through security at BWI, but there was nothing I could do."

"He'll be fine." Brick tried to sound confident but, like Rory, he was worried the trip would prove to be too much for Eamonn.

"I have my doubts, but I guess it's better to do what you believe you need to do than regret not doing it." Rory moved down the bar to where a guy had been looking over the menu. "Decide on anything?"

"I'll have a corned beef sandwich."

"Something to drink?"

"Harp, but hold off on that. I'm going outside for a smoke."

As the guy walked past the end of the bar, Brick thought he looked familiar but couldn't place him. It wasn't until he returned that Brick remembered. He moved to the vacant barstool next to the guy and sat down.

"Unless I'm mistaken, you're with ICE."

The guy nodded but didn't say anything.

"Brick Kavanagh. I bummed a cigarette from you outside the FOP after . . . well, not one of my prouder moments."

"Oh yeah, I remember." He put down his glass and wiped his hand on a napkin before extending it in Brick's direction. "Eric Monroe." He reached into his pocket and retrieved a pack of Marlboros. "Help yourself."

Brick waved him off. "Thanks, but I quit over a year ago except for that one slip. It was just—"

"Hey, like I said then, I'll say again now. The guy, what's his name—Alden?"

"Allen, Travis Allen."

"Oh yeah, he's an asshole. I don't envy you having to work with him."

Brick took a sip of Guinness. "That's not going to be an issue anymore." He had no intentions of sharing the details of his abrupt retirement; instead he explained it away as a decision to pursue other interests after twenty years on the job.

"That's cool. Congratulations. Twenty years, seems like a long time, but I'm almost halfway there, five years with ICE and four in the Army—military police."

"Iraq or Afghanistan?"

"One of the lucky ones—both." Eric shook his head. "There was a time I thought I'd be a lifer, but after that second tour in Afghanistan, I wouldn't have re-upped if they paid me what the Nats are paying Strasburg."

"That bad?"

"Unless you've been there, you have no idea."

Brick thought it best to change the subject. "How do you like working for ICE?"

"It's a job." His sandwich arrived and Eric took a big bite before continuing. "Until a week ago, I was living up near Baltimore and the commute was killing me. Now that I've moved into the city, my job attitude might improve."

"Guess it's hard to love your job, any job, when you're spending all that time on the Parkway sitting in traffic."

"You're right about that. Whole different lifestyle now. Taking the Metro to work, walking to a neighborhood bar—the SUV's been parked all week." He took another bite of his sandwich and washed it down with a swallow of Harp. "Maybe I should get rid of it."

"Reduce your carbon footprint?"

Eric shrugged. "Screw that. More like reducing my monthly expenses. No car payment or insurance—it's tempting but I don't know, I've had a car since I was sixteen."

"Rent one when you need to. That's what I do since mine got torched by the local pyromaniac."

"Seriously?"

Brick nodded. "Turned out to be the teenage son of a Superior Court judge."

"Nothing like making your parents proud." Eric finished his beer. "Good sandwich. I can see myself becoming a regular."

"Boland's has kept me from starving."

"Or dying of thirst?"

"That, too."

"This is where Jose Delgado worked, right?"

"Yes." Brick took a drink before continuing. "And as we speak, the owner is escorting the bodies back home to Guatemala."

"You mean . . ." Eric paused and seemed to consider what Brick had just said. "Wow, I'd say that goes above and beyond what you'd expect from an employer. He must have thought a lot of him."

"He did." Brick set his empty glass on the bar. "It seems everyone who knew Jose did."

Brick didn't stay to watch the end of the game. The Nats tacked on a couple of insurance runs in the eighth inning so victory was all but assured. Normally the game and a Guinness were all Brick needed to relax and temporarily forget about whatever was weighing heavily on his mind. Not today. By running into Eric Monroe, he was reminded of the ugly incident with Travis Allen. And he couldn't escape the nagging thought that, had he just gone along with Blancato, sucked up the two-week suspension, he'd be in a better position to follow up the new evidence he discovered.

Brick collected his mail before climbing the stairs to his third-floor walk-up. At the time he bought the place, the price was right and a no-elevator building meant less maintenance and lower condo fees than a mid- or high-rise one. Although high-rise in D.C. doesn't mean the same as it does in other cities like New York or Chicago. Height restrictions keep buildings from exceeding that of the Washington Monument. With each flight his knees questioned his no-elevator strategy, but given the area's inflated real estate prices and taxes, he knew a move was not in his future. Besides, the place suited him. It was small enough to keep clean but large enough to not feel claustrophobic. That was important especially now that he'd probably be spending more time there. Granted, it could use some sprucing up. Maybe he'd finally get around to painting the walls and replacing the carpet. Might even consider having wood floors installed. And the TV with the broken remote—its days were numbered. Once inside, Brick sorted through his mail. He opened his Visa statement and scanned the charges. Nothing he didn't recognize so he set it aside, along with his Pepco bill. He'd write the checks later. For now, he was eager to get started reviewing the files Ron had copied.

As much as Brick would miss his days working Homicide, he wouldn't miss attending autopsies. Just looking at the photo of Maria lying on the slab conjured up the sound of the Stryker saw. He flipped through the copies. The quality wasn't great, kind of grainy, but he could still see what looked like a bruise on her left hip. On the written report, a contusion was noted, its cause undetermined.

Had she been tased? Brick knew he might never know for sure. The remote possibility of a second autopsy disappeared when Maria's body was loaded on a plane bound for Guatemala. Brick set the autopsy report aside and read through the investigative files for Jose and Maria. Both were still fresh in his memory, but he needed to satisfy himself that he hadn't missed something. Even something that seemed insignificant before could be important now, but nothing struck him as overlooked. He closed the files and thought about something Ron had said. At the time, Brick adamantly denied that pursuing this case wasn't about discrediting Blancato. But was that part of his motivation on a subconscious level? How honest was he being with himself?

Brick decided to take a break from his self-analysis. Given the empty shelves in his refrigerator, a trip to the Safeway was long overdue. He picked up his keys and headed toward the door but only made it halfway when his cellphone rang. Answer or ignore? Seeing who was calling made the decision easy.

"Tracy, how's it going?"

"Got a minute?" she asked.

Brick raised his voice so he could compete with the traffic noise at her end. "For you, I've got two."

"You didn't hear this from me, our girl had . . . hang on . . . fire trucks."

For a several seconds, Brick held the phone away from his ear, impatiently waiting for the sirens to fade. Whatever Tracy had to say, he was anxious to hear.

"Okay, according to the ME, our girl had bruises consistent with being tased. It didn't kill her—cause of death was asphyxiation. It's probably how the perp subdued her. Anyway, we're deliberately keeping it quiet, but I thought you should know."

"I appreciate it and I understand. And something for your ears only, our crack evidence guys missed something." Brick went on to tell her about the recovered taser dots.

"Holy shit. What do you plan to do with them?"

"I've already called in a favor and just waiting to get the serial number off the dots. Then I can track down the make and model of the taser, find out where they're sold . . ."

"Maybe get a lead on where Jimmy Hoffa's buried."

Brick chuckled. "Thanks for the vote of confidence."

"Sorry, didn't mean to bust your chops. That's not going to be easy, but if anyone can do it—"

"That's more like it."

This time Tracy laughed. "If I hear anything else, I'll let you know."

"Thanks," Brick said. "I'll do the same."

# CHAPTER TWENTY-EIGHT

ON MONDAY AT 7:55 a.m., Brick stood outside the Dupont Circle building where Lily Nguyen's law office was located on the second floor. He pressed the button on the intercom next to Nguyen's name. No response. Brick wasn't surprised. Her office, like that of the CPA on the first floor, was dark. No signs of life. Brick shook his head. Had he always thought in terms of life and death or was that an occupational hazard from too many years on the job. But wouldn't a normal person just see the office as being closed? Maybe in time Brick would think more along those lines, but he doubted he'd ever describe himself as normal. Then again, what is normal? Abnormal—that was easy. He saw evidence of it every day. No longer from the front-row seat most cops occupy; but all he had to do was watch the news or step outside his door. Normal, who the hell knows? Although since he wasn't expressing these thoughts out loud, lacing them with expletives and shouting at passersby, he took that as a good sign.

Brick glanced at his watch; ten minutes had passed. It wasn't as if he had an actual appointment. Maybe Lily had gone directly to court. He'd give her a few more minutes. At 8:25 a.m., just as he was ready to walk away, Brick saw her turn the corner onto M Street. She stopped to get a newspaper before continuing down the street.

"This is a surprise. I really didn't expect you'd show up, Detec—or I guess it's Mr. Kavanagh now." She made no apologies for having kept him waiting.

"Just call me Brick."

"How's life as a civilian?"

Brick picked up a hint of sarcasm in Lily's question. "I'm adjusting."

She unlocked the outer door to the building, entered a code into the keypad on the wall, then proceeded up a flight of stairs to her office. Brick followed, enjoying the view.

Lily's IKEA-furnished office contrasted sharply with the no-expense-spared high-powered law firms located a few blocks away. Proof there's a whole lot more money in lobbying than in representing indigent clients. But the District's Criminal Justice Act ensured court-appointed attorneys would be assigned to take on overflow cases from the Public Defender Service. CJA attorneys, as they were commonly called, weren't likely to get rich, but they could count on steady work. Lily sat down at her desk and motioned for Brick to take a seat in one of the chairs across from her.

"Okay, so tell me, why are you here?"

To say she was direct was an understatement, but Brick liked her no-nonsense style. He responded in kind. "Taser dots."

Lily knitted her brow. "Excuse me?"

Brick briefly explained what happens when a taser is discharged before telling her about the discovery of dots attached to Jose's soccer jersey. He had more to say, but Lily didn't give him a chance.

"Those could have been there for a long time." Lily exhaled somewhat dramatically. "I don't see any relevance."

It was the type of response Brick expected from an experienced defense attorney. "Maria's autopsy showed she sustained an injury, which, I believe, was consistent with being tased."

"What does the Medical Examiner believe?"

"He determined it was inconclusive."

Lily smirked. "But you know better."

"It wouldn't be the first time." He deliberately let her think about that for a moment. "There are things about this case that just don't make sense."

"That could be said about a lot of cases." Lily glanced at her watch. "Go on."

"Up until now, Lupe had a few minor run-ins with the law but no felony arrests."

"I'm aware of my client's record. What's your point?"

"Supposedly, he went to the apartment to collect a debt. If Lupe wanted to intimidate Jose, why not tase him rather than beat him to death. With him dead, there was no way he'd collect whatever Jose owed. If, in fact, Jose owed him anything."

"You question that, too."

"Jose had saved a substantial amount of money."

"You know that for a fact?"

"Yes. His employer was holding it for him. He didn't need to borrow money from a gang member."

Lily pushed her chair back from her desk and started to get up. "Do I need to remind you my client pled guilty?"

Brick sensed she was about to end their meeting. "Do I need to remind you, not every defendant who pleads guilty is guilty? It doesn't happen often but it does happen."

"Did I really hear a cop—excuse me—ex-cop say that?" Lily rolled her eyes. "All right, do you have a theory as to what may have happened?"

"Thoughts, yes . . . theory, no."

Lily laughed, but her expression told him she wasn't amused. "What's the deal—you're retired a week or so and you become the caped crusader for the wrongly accused. If you have time on your hands, google the Centurion Ministries or some other innocents' project. I'm sure they could use a volunteer."

Brick wasn't sure how to respond. He didn't have to.

"That was uncalled for." Lily tried to stifle a yawn. "Guess I'm a little burned out at the moment."

Brick waited but she didn't elaborate. Still, he figured it was the Dragon Lady's version of an apology. "Let me clarify my motivation—this isn't about your client as much as it is about making sure justice has been served and the right person is behind bars for killing Jose and his sister. Lupe is the only person who can answer the questions I have."

"And I'm the gate keeper?"

"Afraid so."

Lily picked up her calendar book and flipped a few pages. "High tech, right? I learned my lesson the hard way after my laptop was stolen . . . by one of my clients." She stopped on a page and appeared to be studying the notations written next to specific dates and times. "I'm free until two this afternoon."

Brick wasn't about to let this opportunity slip away. "I'd check my calendar, but I don't have one."

Lily almost smiled. "All right then, next stop—D.C. Jail."

*   *   *

All it took was approaching the Visitor's Control Entrance and Brick was immediately reminded of his new former-cop status. He was subjected to the screening required of all civilians entering the jail. Although Lily simplified the process somewhat by listing Brick as her investigator on the access request form.

"I'll need your ID," Lily said.

Reluctantly Brick gave her his driver's license. He felt self-conscious doing so and almost made a comment about it looking like a mug shot, but that would have only called more attention to the unflattering photo. He watched as Lily completed the form and turned it over along with his license to the guard on duty. The guard glanced at the paperwork and handed it back to Lily. Either he was adept at speed reading or he hadn't bothered to read it at all. Brick suspected the latter.

"Your ID and D.C. Bar card." Lily handed them over. "Purpose of your visit?" he asked in the same rote monotone he'd used previously.

"My investigator, Brian Kavanagh, and I are here to meet with my client, Guadalupe Cruz."

"Sign in. Put the date and time." Lily signed first then handed the pen to Brick. As Brick signed his name, he wondered if the guard was competing for Bored Employee of the Month. If so, he probably stood a good chance of winning. "Give me your cellphones. Put your watches, keys, coins, other metal in the plastic bowl." He pointed at Lily. "Briefcase goes on the conveyor belt. Walk through the metal detector." She did as directed. The guard motioned for Brick to step through. A buzzer sounded.

"You wearing a belt?"

Brick nodded.

The guard looked annoyed. "Take it off and walk through again."

This time Brick made it without tripping an alarm.

Simultaneous pat-downs followed before they were each issued a numbered visitor pass by a female guard. "Make sure this is displayed at all times." She pointed to a bench against the wall. "Take a seat over there. The next available officer will escort you to the inmate's housing unit."

Brick sat down next to Lily and spoke softly. "I think I liked it better when I used to flash my badge and waltzed on through. No signing in, no questions asked."

Lily rolled her eyes. "Welcome to my world. One improvement though, same-sex guards conducting the pat-downs. Only took several complaints from female attorneys and threats to sue."

"Killjoy." From the look on Lily's face, Brick knew she wasn't amused. He raised his hands in mock surrender. "Just kidding." After that, Brick didn't attempt to engage Lily in conversation as they waited to be escorted to the visiting hall of Southwest-2, the high-security block where Cruz was being held. Unlike family and friends restricted to video visitation, attorneys were permitted to meet face-to-face with inmates in a glass enclosure. Conversations were, for the most part, confidential unless the guard stationed outside was skilled in lip reading. After taking a seat, Brick checked under the table. He was pleased to find a panic button. Hopefully, they wouldn't need it, but Brick always preferred working with a net.

From his seat at the table Brick observed two guards escorting Guadalupe Cruz down the narrow hallway. Cruz was wearing an ill-fitting orange jumpsuit; his hands cuffed in front and secured to a waist chain. His legs weren't shackled, but even so, his gait was uneven, favoring his left side.

Lily stood as Cruz was brought into the confined area. "Thank you." She nodded toward the guard just before he left, closing the door on his way out. "Good morning, Mr. Cruz."

The formality Lily used in addressing her client seemed dated given our casual culture, but Brick understood her reasoning. Familiarity, especially from an attractive female, could easily be misinterpreted.

Cruz responded with a scowl before he spoke. "Who's he?"

Lily sat down and folded her hands on the table. "That's Mr. Kavanagh. He works for me."

"He looks like a cop."

Brick laughed. "That's very observant. I was a cop, but I'm not anymore. What happened to your leg?" It wasn't the first question Brick planned to ask, but depending on Cruz's response, it could be the only answer he needed.

Cruz stared across the table at Brick. "You'd limp too if you got shot in the hip."

"I'm sure I would. When did that happen?"

"I dunno, two or three years ago."

"Who shot you?"

Cruz shrugged his shoulders.

"You don't know or you're not saying?"

"Yeah."

"Sure you didn't shoot yourself?"

"No, man, are you crazy?"

"Hey, it happens all the time, even to cops. I had a partner who got up one morning, put his gun in its holster, and BAM, just like that, shot himself in the leg."

"The guy must have been stupid."

"Come to think of it, he wasn't the sharpest knife in the drawer." Brick smiled and leaned back in his chair. "Instead of a gun, they probably should have just issued him a taser, kind of like your weapon of choice."

"What?" Cruz looked confused, as if Brick had slipped from English into a foreign language.

"A taser . . . oh, my mistake, you MS-13 guys are more inclined to use a machete, right?"

Cruz looked over at Lily. "Why'd you bring this guy here?"

"I think it's in your best interest—"

Cruz didn't let Lily finish. He jumped to his feet. So did the guard seated outside the door. "I know what's in my best interests—and it's not talking to him."

"Guadalupe, please—"

Cruz shook his head. "No, I'm done."

Lily gestured for the guard to enter. She waited until he escorted Cruz into the hallway before turning and glaring at Brick. "That's it?" She sounded incredulous. "We spent a half hour getting into this place—"

"Let's talk outside," Brick said.

Lily picked up her briefcase and headed for the door. "I don't think we have much to talk about."

"Trust me," Brick implored even though he was sure that was the last thing she'd be willing to do.

Brick and Lily turned in their visitor passes, collected their cellphones, and exited through the security checkpoint where they had entered. Outside the skies had turned gray, but even the heavy humid air was preferable to the stagnation inside the jail. A couple of cabs idled at the curb. Brick approached the first one in the queue and held the door for Lily. He slid in next to her and closed the door.

"Where to?" The cabdriver interrupted the animated conversation he was having on his cellphone just long enough to hear their destination.

"Dupont Circle," Lily replied then glanced over at Brick. "So . . ."

"If Cruz did it, which I don't think he did, he didn't act alone."

Lily sighed dramatically. "And you came to that conclusion—"

"The minute I saw him limp."

"Why did that surprise you? Weren't you at his arraignment?"

"I was, but he was already seated at the defense table, and I left before the marshals stepped him back." Brick lowered his voice, as the cabbie had concluded his call. "Lily, the guy who dumped Maria's body was caught on a security tape. He's taller than Cruz and didn't walk with a limp."

"Are you sure?" Lily's sarcasm had morphed into skepticism.

"Positive. I watched it several times."

"Cruz could be faking."

"Even if he's faking the limp, he can't fake his height."

"You're right." Lily seemed embarrassed. "Guess I was thinking out loud. Still, he could have been involved."

Brick shook his head. "You saw his reaction when I mentioned the taser."

"Clients lie all the time claiming they're innocent, I'm used to that. But lying about being guilty, I don't know." Lily glanced at her watch before continuing. "It doesn't make sense."

"Maybe not to you or me, but for whatever reason, it must make sense to Cruz."

Traffic was unusually heavy on Massachusetts Avenue. The second the light turned green, the cabbie laid on the horn. Several other drivers did the same. When the cacophony subsided, Lily instructed the cabbie to pull over at the next intersection. She turned in Brick's direction.

"I think we need do a little brainstorming, and we might as well walk from here; it'll be faster." Lily tucked a stand of hair behind her ear. "Besides, I need a cup of coffee. I feel a lack-of-caffeine headache brewing, no pun intended. There's a Caribou on the corner of M Street." Lily opened her briefcase and retrieved her wallet.

When the cabdriver pulled over to the curb, Brick got out and held the door for Lily. He watched as she handed the driver a ten. He heard him ask if she wanted change.

"No." She got out and Brick closed the door. "I'm so glad the powers-that-be finally got smart and went to a metered cab system. Remember the old zone system? I never knew if I was overly generous or a cheapskate."

"No one did, but at the end of the day, I'm sure the universe gave the cabbies exactly what they deserve."

Lily didn't look convinced. She slung the strap of her briefcase over her shoulder. "Next thing you'll be telling me is you believe in karma."

"Actually, I do. It's far more reliable than the criminal justice system."

The morning rush at Caribou appeared to have slowed. Lily found a table in the corner and appeared to be checking her phone while Brick waited in line. He thought about the brief meeting with Cruz and what it had revealed as the barista repeated the complicated order of the two customers ahead of him. Brick felt energized even though now there were more questions than answers.

"Next . . . next in line, please."

Unlike the previous order of the coffee connoisseurs, his was simple, a medium coffee with cream and a large green tea. He grabbed a couple of napkins and joined Lily.

"Looks like my two o'clock status hearing has been postponed until tomorrow, which, of course, conflicts with a preliminary hearing before Judge Newton." Lily set her phone aside. "I'm sure you know his reputation."

"Inflexible, tends to be pro-prosecution."

"And patronizing to women." Lily lifted the lid on her coffee. "Oh, that's hot."

*So are you. A guy would have to be blind not to see that.* The thought flashed through Brick's head, and for a moment, he was afraid he had spoken the words aloud. It was just that, sitting across from Lily here in a coffeehouse, she didn't seem like the formidable defense attorney with the Dragon Lady reputation. So much for a little fantasizing—a defense attorney and a cop, even a retired one, gave a whole new meaning to the term *odd couple*. It took a moment for Brick to realize Lily had said something.

"Sorry, I didn't hear what you said."

"I said, I'm impressed. Believes in karma and drinks green tea."

"I'm atoning for all the years on the coffee and doughnut diet."

"Doughnuts I can do without, but giving up coffee—no way." As if to prove her point, Lily picked up the still steaming cup and took a sip. "What do you suggest we do about Cruz?"

"We?" Even though at the jail Lily had introduced Brick as her investigator, they hadn't formally agreed to his working in that capacity. "Does that mean you're hiring me as your investigator?"

"I guess it does, but it will have to be on a pro bono basis. It's only April and I've already spent my CJA allotment for investigative services."

"I'm okay with that." Brick put down his cup. "The first thing I want to know is more about the incident in which Cruz says he was shot."

Lily took another sip of coffee before snapping the lid back on the cup. "Well, good luck with that. In the meantime, I'd better go back to my office and call Judge Newton's law clerk and beg for a continuance." She stood up and so did Brick even though he wasn't ready to leave. "One other question—the partner you mentioned to Cruz, what happened after he shot himself?"

"Nothing. I made up that story."

"So you lied?" Lily seemed to think about that for a moment and for the first time all morning, she laughed. "Sounds like you have something else to atone for."

# CHAPTER TWENTY-NINE

"HOMICIDE, DETECTIVE HAYES."

"Ron, it's Brick."

"Hey, man, how's it going?"

Brick filled Ron in on his meeting with Guadalupe Cruz. He heard a familiar sound, a faint whistle, as his former partner exhaled through the gap between his front teeth.

"I'm telling you, Ron, when I saw him walk up the hall—"

"In other words, 'he had you at hello.'"

Same old Ron, Brick thought. "Okay, that one I know. Renee Russo in *Jerry McGuire*." Brick wished Ron could see how pleased he was with himself for scoring a movie trivia quote.

"Close, bro. It was Renee Zellweger."

"Okay, whatever. I need you—"

"Damn! Gotta say I had my doubts, but I think you're on to something now. Man, if we had just seen him walk into the courtroom, everything could have been different. Limping . . . damn."

"I need you to do a little digging for me. I've got to confirm that Cruz really did take a bullet in the leg and the circumstances surrounding it."

"No problem—I should have something later today."

"Thanks. How's Jasmine?"

"Big as a house—just don't ever let her know I said that. Her doctor is giving her until Friday. If nothing happens by then, she'll have a C-section on Saturday morning."

"How are you doing?"

"I'm fine." Ron answered quickly but not convincingly.

Brick laughed. "No, you're not."

"Yeah, you're right. My heart rate doubles every time my cellphone rings. It's like a giant shot of adrenaline. I don't know how women do it. I thought police work could be stressful, but, man, this is something else . . . oh, that's my other line, gotta go."

\*　\*　\*

After grabbing a quick lunch, Brick took the Metro to the Tenleytown section of Northwest D.C. Unlike a lot of guys, shopping for clothes excited him, electronics not so much. Actually, not at all. He wandered up and down the aisles where all the flat-screened TVs were displayed. Some of the brand names were recognizable, and except for the size of the TV, that seemed to be the only thing distinguishing one from the other.

"Can I help you?" The sales clerk flashed a mouthful of braces and looked like he should be in fourth period American history class rather than working at Best Buy.

"Yeah, I'm looking for—" Just then Brick's cellphone rang. He recognized Ron's number on the caller ID. "I need to take this."

"Ron, hang on while I step outside." Brick walked out of the store. "Okay, go ahead."

"I'm still checking, but I figured you'd want to hear what I've got. Our boy did take one in the hip about two and a half years ago. According to the report, it was a drive-by on Columbia Road in Adams Morgan. Hard to tell whether he was the target or just in the wrong place, but either way, it was probably gang-related."

"Any arrests?"

"Not that I've been able to find so far. According to the report, Cruz claimed he didn't recognize the car or anyone in it. Big surprise, right?"

"Exactly, thanks, Ron. I owe you."

"Later, man."

Brick slipped his cellphone back into his pocket and headed toward the Metro. Getting home and rereading the Delgado files was a lot more important than buying a TV.

# CHAPTER THIRTY

BRICK CHECKED THE clock. It was nine a.m., a respectable time to give Alma Gonzales a call. She answered on the third ring.

"Hold on just a minute." In the background, Brick heard a baby cry. "I had to go to another room. Are you still there?"

"Yes, I'm guessing your sister had her baby."

"She did."

"Congratulations. I understand this might not be a convenient time, but I'd like to stop by and talk to you this morning."

"Is this about Roberto?"

"Yes."

"Can you give me about two hours? I haven't had time to take a shower or wash my hair in two days."

"How about if I come by around eleven thirty?"

"That would be good."

The next thing Brick heard was a dial tone. He wished all people he dealt with were as straightforward as Alma.

It had been a while since Brick had cooked breakfast for himself, but he had time to kill. He checked the contents of his recently stocked refrigerator and considered his options. Despite his limited culinary skills, a ham and cheese omelet he could manage.

Brick cracked a couple of eggs into a bowl and beat them with a fork. He adjusted the flame under the frying pan and waited for the butter to melt before pouring the eggs into the pan. He added pieces of ham and sprinkled shredded cheddar over the eggs. While the omelet cooked, he thought about Roberto's attitude when he and Ron talked to him. When Cruz pled guilty, he did Roberto and Carlos a huge favor by eliminating them from the suspect list. That was no longer the case. In some ways Brick felt like he was back to square one, but there were worse places to be. Better to be starting over than to let the real killer get away. He turned off the burner, slid the omelet onto a plate, grabbed some ketchup, and sat down to eat.

*　*　*

Brick double-checked the address. Just after eleven thirty, he knocked on the door of the modest single-family home. He heard a female voice yell, "I've got it." Alma opened the door wearing a sweatshirt and black yoga pants, a towel wrapped around her head.

"Come on in, Detective." She proceeded to unwrap the towel and let her damp hair fall onto her shoulders. A few drops of water spotted her top.

"Thanks for your time. I can see things are hectic for you."

"Yeah, but it will get better. It was a rough delivery so it's going to take my sister a while to regain her strength, but she's okay and the baby's beautiful. Thank God, they're both sleeping right now."

"Boy or girl?" Brick asked.

"Boy. Looks just like his father. Roberto's an asshole, but even I have to admit he's a good-looking guy." She brushed back some strands of wet hair sticking to her face before pointing to a chair next to the sofa. "Have a seat. You said this is about him, but I don't understand. I saw on the news a guy confessed to the murders, right?"

"Yes, but before we get to that, I want you to know I'm no longer with the police department."

"You got fired?"

Brick smiled. "Retired. I'm doing some related investigative work." He turned abruptly as a buzzer sounded.

"Sorry about that, it's the dryer. Excuse me while I go see if the stuff is dry." Alma got up from the sofa and walked down a narrow hallway. She returned carrying an armload of baby clothes. "I've been washing more clothes than a Chinese laundry. Do you want some coffee?"

"No thanks."

"Don't mind me, I just need to fold these before they wrinkle."

"No problem." Brick leaned forward. "Has Roberto seen the baby?"

Alma sighed loudly as she folded a blue-and-green-striped onesie. "I don't know what to think. It's like he's done a three-sixty. No, that's not right—what is it, a one-eighty. Anyway, what I'm trying to say is for the first time in his life, at least since I've known him, he's acting like a responsible adult."

"How so?" Brick asked.

"Well, before the baby came, he kept calling and wanting to see Lourdes. Finally, she said okay and he was supposed to come over after work, but it turned out Lourdes went into labor before he got here. And you know how usually first babies take a while—not this one. The contractions were coming so fast I had to call 9-1-1. The EMTs got her to the hospital and it's a good thing because there were some complications that could have killed her and the baby." Alma made the sign of the cross before continuing. "Thank God, I don't even want to think about what could have happened." She took a deep breath. "Sorry, I got a little sidetracked. I'm operating on about three hours of sleep."

Brick smiled. "You're doing fine."

"Thanks, even if it isn't true. Anyway, I figured I should let Roberto know when we got to the hospital. He was there in about fifteen minutes and ever since it's like he's a different person. Do you think people are capable of changing that fast?"

"Yes, especially if they think someone they care about almost died. It can put things in perspective."

"Well I'm not convinced, but I guess I'm willing to give him the benefit of the doubt . . . for now. From the time he got to the hospital, he stayed by her side until she came home."

"What days were those?" Brick asked.

When Alma responded, he realized Roberto had an alibi for the homicide in Arlington. If both cases were committed by the same guy, it wasn't Roberto.

"I gotta get a cup of coffee. Sure you don't want one?"

"I'm sure, but thanks."

Alma put a tiny t-shirt on top of the stack of clothes she had folded. She disappeared for a couple of minutes and returned with a coffee mug in her hand. She sat back down on the sofa.

"You know the other thing that's given me some hope Roberto has cleaned up his act, he's been meeting with Father Mike. You're Catholic, aren't you?"

Brick deliberately sidestepped the question. "I know Father Mike. He does a lot of good work in the Hispanic community."

"Yeah, especially counseling guys about beating up women. It's a big problem, although from what I've seen on shows like *Dr. Phil*, it's not just Hispanics."

Brick nodded. "Some things are universal, and unfortunately, that's one of them. I hope for your sister's sake and the baby's, it works out."

"Yeah, I'll never understand what she sees in him, but he is the baby's father. As long as he takes care of them, my opinion doesn't matter. But if he ever mistreats either one of them, he's going to have to answer to me."

"Your nephew may not know it yet, but I think he and his mom are in real good hands."

Alma smiled, but at the same time her chin quivered. "Oh, I'm so emotional. You'd think I was the one who just gave birth."

Brick smiled as he stood up. "Thanks for seeing me on short notice. Before I go, is there anything else?"

Alma thought for a moment. "It was just something that happened before Lourdes moved . . . it's probably not important."

"You never know, it might be," Brick said.

"I didn't think much about it at the time, but when she and I were packing up her stuff, Carlos, you know the building manager, stopped by to see if he could help. I thought it was nice, but Lourdes didn't want him around. She was kind of rude and that's not like her. Anyway, after he left, she said the guy gave her the creeps. Always made her feel like he was . . . undressing her with his eyes."

"Did he ever say anything inappropriate or try to touch her?"

"I asked her about that, but she changed the subject. She didn't want to talk about it, and I let it drop." Alma shrugged. "*Undressing her with his eyes* is not a crime, is it?"

"No and if it were, we'd have to have a lot more prisons."

Alma laughed. "I probably shouldn't have even—"

"Don't apologize. I'm glad you mentioned it. If you think of anything else, give me a call." Brick automatically reached for one of his business cards before remembering he no longer had them. He asked Alma for a slip of paper, wrote down his cellphone number, and handed it to her. After he left, the thought occurred to him he should order new business cards, but he quickly dismissed the idea. What would be the point of having business cards when he didn't have a job.

*  *  *

Brick had hoped to find Father Mike in his office but was directed instead to the sanctuary. He saw the priest kneeling near the altar. Brick stood by the door and waited. A few minutes passed. For a split second he saw a younger version of himself in his altar boy garb. Then, as now, he found the cloying smell of incense oppressive. He was relieved to see Father Mike turn and walk toward him.

"Second time in as many weeks. I have time to hear your confession if you're so inclined. I'm guessing it's been a while."

Brick laughed as he shook hands with Father Mike. "You should know by now, guilt doesn't work on me."

The priest nodded. "And I should also know insanity is doing the same thing and expecting different results." Father Mike shook his head. "Honestly, Brick, sometimes this place is enough to make me crazy. We talk ad nauseam about ending the violence and twice this week I've administered last rites to teenagers . . . teenagers, both stabbing victims. All because of a cellphone—they were fighting over a cellphone. To have so little regard for life, I don't know how we can change that mind-set. And the next day, I accompanied an Army chaplain while he delivered the news to a parishioner that her husband was killed in Afghanistan. What words of comfort can one provide to a young widow with a baby in her arms?"

The priest continued to talk, but Brick had tuned out. He was thinking back to a time he was too young to remember but had often imagined. He reached out for the back of the pew in order to steady himself.

"Brick, are you okay?" The sound of Father Mike's voice pulled Brick into the moment.

"I'm fine. It's just when you mentioned accompanying the chaplain, I kind of got an image of what it must have been like for my own mother when she got the news about my father."

"I'm not sure I follow," Father Mike said.

"That's because I've never mentioned it." Brick cleared his throat. "My father was an Army captain—a Green Beret stationed with the 82nd Airborne out of Fort Bragg. Two months after I was born, he was declared missing-in-action in Vietnam. Of course, I was too young to remember when she got the news, but every so often, that scene plays out in my head."

"I'm so sorry, Brick, I had no idea. And your father—"

"Officially, his status is still MIA." Brick had surprised himself by revealing something he seldom talked about. He shook his head. "The not-knowing took a terrible toll on my mother. She died when I was seventeen. And after her funeral, I quit going to Mass. Just didn't see the point."

"I understand." The priest laid his hand on Brick's shoulder. "If ever you decide to come back, you'll always be welcomed."

"Thanks." Brick sat silently for a minute or two. "So why am I here? It wasn't supposed to be about me, actually it's about the Delgado case."

"Oh yes, you and your partner must be pleased the case is closed. I saw that on the news."

"Don't believe everything you see. It's complicated, but if you have the time—"

"I do."

The priest listened as Brick brought him up-to-date on all that had transpired since Guadalupe Cruz pled guilty. "And you have your doubts that he actually committed the crime?"

"More than doubts, evidence. For whatever reason, he prefers being in jail, even for something he didn't do, than to be on the street."

"And in the meantime, the real perpetrator is free. That has to concern you even though you're no longer a cop. I know you want justice for Jose and Maria."

"Are you hearing anything that would be relevant?"

"No, in fact, at the moment things seem to be calmer than they've been for a while."

"Any thoughts as to why?"

"It's hard to say, but sometimes I think rival gang members help each other to stay one step ahead of ICE."

"The 'enemy of my enemy is my friend' theory?"

"Exactly. It's not surprising; every ethnic group has always looked out for its own although it's a different world now. They're all Hispanic, but even within the culture there are differences that sometimes cause conflict. Some community leaders and I are doing what we can to teach alternative means for handling disputes. We've got some counselors donating time for anger management group therapy. Plus, we have a couple of twelve-step programs for alcohol and drug addiction."

"And the gang bangers are receptive to that?"

Father Mike smiled. "We can't help them if we can't get them in the door so we lure them here to watch soccer or play basketball then work in a counseling session."

Brick smiled. "That's sneaky, Father."

"But it's cheaper than pizza. That's our backup plan."

"Whatever works. Are you familiar with Roberto Morales?"

"I am, although it's only recently that he's started attending our program. Why do you ask?"

"Jose and Maria lived across the hall from Roberto."

"Really—that put him on your radar screen, didn't it."

Brick nodded. "It did. Especially since I know he abused his pregnant wife."

"My understanding is he's cleaned up his act since his son was born," Father Mike said. "I don't know if you're familiar with his sister-in-law, but I'm confident she'll make him accountable if he steps out of line."

"I think you're right about that, but I wonder if Roberto knows more than he's letting on."

"It's possible. Bodegas have always served a purpose beyond selling what's on the shelves."

Brick thanked the priest and left the church with a blessing from Father Mike to "go in peace." He wondered if that would ever be possible.

# CHAPTER THIRTY-ONE

BRICK WALKED BY the El Mercado Bodega where Roberto worked and for a moment considered going in before he thought of a better resource. He pulled out his cellphone and scrolled through his contacts list.

It was just after six p.m. when Brick arrived at Boland's Mill. Most of the seats, even Brick's favorite, were taken with the happy hour crowd. It was an eclectic mix of suits, business casual, and a couple of dusty Carhartts. Eamonn would be pleased if he were here. Brick waved to Rory before settling in at a table for two in the corner near the fireplace. On this unseasonably chilly spring day, the heat was welcomed. While he waited, Brick checked his email. Had he been so inclined, he could have purchased recommended books from Amazon, a jacket from Territory Ahead, and Viagra from Online Pharmacy. He sent all three messages to trash and checked the sports section of the *Washington Post*. He scrolled through the National League scores. It was early in the season, but wins in April counted just as much as wins in September.

About fifteen minutes later, Eric arrived. "Fucking Red Line." The two shook hands before Eric sat down. "Not sure what caused the delay because I couldn't understand a word the announcer was saying. I'm not even sure it was English. And just to make my day, the escalator was out of service. So I had the privilege of walking up that sucker, which has got to be the longest one in the system."

Brick was pretty sure the Rosslyn escalator was slightly longer but saw no need to point that out. "Won't have to do the Stairmaster at the gym, at least for today."

"Yeah and it's still better than being stuck in traffic twice a day." Eric picked up the menu. "How's the fish and chips?"

"Good, especially if you're hungry. It's a big portion." Brick glanced over to the bar and saw Rory was looking a little frazzled. "Might be better if I place our order at the bar."

"Okay." Eric handed Brick the menu. "I'll take the fish and chips and a Harp."

Brick went up to the bar and waited until Rory seemed to have things under control.

"Bet you'll be glad when Eamonn is back."

"Yeah, but it looks like he's going to be there for another week or so. Not that many flights and something got hosed . . . I don't know." Rory set a glass under the Harp tap. "And I screwed up the work schedule today so I'm a one-man show."

"You're running the kitchen, too?"

Rory managed a laugh. "No, that's the only feckin' thing I didn't mess up." He wiped the back of his hand across his forehead. "What can I get ya?"

Brick placed the order and returned to the table, drinks in hand. "Your day might not have been great, but at least it's over. Rory's is worse and it won't end until last call."

"What happened?"

"Scheduling mix-up. I know he'll be glad when his uncle is back from Guatemala."

Eric looked confused. "So the owner here is Rory's uncle?"

"Yes."

"So despite messing up, I'm thinking his job is secure." Eric raised his glass and took a long swallow. "Kind of like working for the government."

"Something like that, I guess."

"Well, speaking of working, or not, how's retirement?" Eric asked.

"Different." Brick took a sip of Guinness.

"Different good or different bad?" Eric asked.

"A combination of both." Brick could have elaborated but he chose not to.

"I've always heard retired cops, especially homicide detectives, are often haunted by cold cases. Any keeping you awake at night?"

Brick thought for a moment. "No. Over the past couple of years several cold cases were closed through DNA. I'm confident others will be, too. If anything keeps me awake, it's the Delgado case."

"Really? A guilty plea . . . how sweet is that." Eric picked up his beer and drank. "Why would it bother you?"

"Not sure, maybe because Cruz wasn't even on our radar so his guilty plea seemed to come out of left field."

"I get that, but it's like my grandfather used to say, don't look a gift horse in the mouth." Eric took another swig of beer. "At the time, I didn't have a clue what he was talking about, but as far as I'm concerned now, Cruz could be renamed Seabiscuit. He saved us a lot of work but I'm kind of surprised he didn't make a run for the border. It would have been easy for him to get out of the country."

"How so?" Brick asked even though he was sure he knew the answer. Still, it would be interesting to hear Eric's perspective.

"Money, weapons, vehicles, places to stay—you name it—it's out there and easy to get. Here in the city and close-in suburbs, there's a very well-organized network. All too often, the illegals are one step ahead of us."

Eric confirmed Father Mike's take on the situation. "Sounds like a modern-day underground railroad," Brick said.

"Exactly. And I'll clue you in—the apartment building where Jose and his sister lived, we call that Union Station. You questioned Carlos, right?"

"The building manager?"

"Yeah, that Carlos." Eric laughed. "Don't let the 'I just the caretaker and my English no so good' routine fool you. Carlos is smart and running a lucrative operation. The guys on my team refer to him as the ticket agent. For the right price, he'll arrange transportation complete with a fake passport, if needed." Eric picked up his beer but set it back down without drinking. "I don't get it," Eric said. "If Carlos applied his know-how to a legitimate business, good chance he'd be successful. As it is, all his hard work will probably land him in federal prison for a long time."

What Brick was hearing reminded him of a legendary D.C. drug case he first learned about when he was a rookie. "Have you ever heard of Slippery Jackson?"

Eric hesitated before answering. "No, can't say that I have."

"Back in the late '70s and early '80s, Jackson ran an international drug operation that brought heroin to the streets of D.C. and other East Coast cities. Eventually, he got caught; but reading some of his testimony about his complicated dealings was mind-boggling. I think the guy dropped out of school in the eighth grade, but his business savvy would have put a team of Wharton MBAs to shame."

"Maybe Carlos studied Slippery's business model." Eric shook his head. "They're a pain in the ass but a whole lot more interesting than the average mopes we usually deal with."

"Yeah, it's the clever criminals that keeps . . . kept me in the game." Brick took another swig of Guinness.

"Hey, I almost flunked Psych 101, but it sounds to me like you miss working Homicide. Probably more than you're willing to admit to yourself."

Brick laughed. "Maybe you should have gotten an A. So what's in store for Carlos . . . plans to shut him down?"

"We will when he stops being useful. Even though he doesn't know it, because of Carlos we've nabbed several illegals. Surveillance on him and the building is easy since he's a registered sex offender." Eric smiled. "Go in front of a judge and say those three magic words and a wiretap or search warrant is as good as signed."

"Here you go." Brick looked up as Rory set two orders of fish and chips on the table. "Eric, another Harp?"

"Sure." He handed his empty glass to Rory.

"Either of you want some malt vinegar?"

Brick shook his head and laughed. "Rory, I ordered shepherd's pie."

"Are you feckin' kidding me?" Rory reached for Brick's plate, but Brick waved him off.

"It's okay, I'll have the fish."

Rory nodded. "Aw, it's better for you anyway."

"Yeah . . . especially beer-battered and deep-fried." Brick picked up his fork. "My arteries thank you."

*　*　*

Brick waited until he got home before he called Lily. He got her voice-mail and felt a twinge of disappointment. He considered hanging up and calling back in an hour or so but instead left a message letting her know Cruz's leg injury checked out. Brick dropped his phone on the distressed steamer trunk doubling as a coffee table. Before sprawling on the sofa, he grabbed a Coke Zero from the fridge and turned on the radio. The familiar sound of WJFK's Charlie Slowes filled the room with play-by-play action. Somehow, he felt more engaged in the action by visualizing what was happening so maybe a dead TV wasn't such a bad thing. The Nats were leading the Braves by two runs, but it was only the bottom of the third. He stretched out, adjusted a pillow behind his head, and closed his eyes. Hopefully, he'd hear Charlie's signature call of "Going, going, gone, goodbye!" several times before the game was over.

# CHAPTER THIRTY-TWO

AT FIRST BRICK thought it was the alarm on his clock radio. He reached across his nightstand fumbling to find the off switch. A couple of books crashed to the floor before he realized his cellphone was ringing. He hit "accept" without checking the caller ID and managed a groggy "hello."

"Did I wake you?"

He immediately recognized Lily's voice. "No." In his not-fully-awake state he felt compelled to lie as if sleeping revealed a character flaw he wanted to hide from Lily.

"Sounds like I did."

Brick sat up in bed and glanced at his clock. It was just after six. Sleeping was justified, but he struggled to stifle a yawn. "You did."

"My bad. I assumed you're a morning person."

"Too many years of shift work to know if I am or not."

"Anyway, I got your message and wanted to get back to you before I leave for court. Guess we should confront Cruz?"

"I think it would be better if I talk to him by myself . . . the sooner, the better."

"Today?"

"That's my plan."

"I should be out of court by eleven, noon at the latest. Let me know how it goes."

"Will do."

"Carpe diem." Lily paused and Brick sensed she was smiling. "Just for the record, I've been up since four thirty."

Before Brick could respond, Lily hung up. He threw back the covers and headed to the bathroom. A hot, steamy shower was his usual morning ritual but with thoughts of Lily, a cold one might be necessary.

\* \* \*

It had been a couple of weeks since Brick turned in his badge and gun, but he still had the feeling he was forgetting something when he left home. As he headed south on Connecticut Avenue, he noticed the air was fragrant with the scent of spring flowers even though the cherry blossoms had come and gone. Too bad the same couldn't be said about the tourists. Instead of crowding on to the Metro, he decided to walk to Farragut West to catch the train to Stadium/Armory. Walking also gave him a chance to think about his interview with Cruz. Unlike Lily, over the years, he had encountered plenty of false confessors. Most were garden-variety nutjobs, but Cruz didn't seem to fall into that category. It was possible he was covering for another gang member, but that seemed unlikely. "Honor among thieves" has its limits, especially when it means life without the possibility of parole.

Brick passed the Hilton Hotel where Ronald Reagan was shot. Although it was arguably the most well-known crime scene in the Dupont Circle neighborhood, it was just one of many. For Brick, some of the details had become sketchy over the years, but he could still recall every building where he had worked a scene. The names of the victims were engraved on his psyche like those of distant relatives he hadn't seen in years. He crossed K Street and walked a half block to the entrance of Farragut West. Before entering the station, he bought a copy of the *Washington Post*. He still preferred reading the news on paper rather than online, but he wondered how much longer he'd have that option.

*   *   *

Once again, Brick went through the required security procedures for admission to the jail. He collected his change, keys, and belt and waited to be escorted to Cruz's unit. At least he could take comfort in knowing that, unlike Cruz, he wouldn't be subjected to a strip search when their meeting was over.

Brick's escort arrived and motioned for him to follow. Standing next to the burly guard, Brick noticed he bore a striking resemblance to Dexter Manley. As they made their way down the hall, it occurred to Brick he knew the names of most of the Washington Redskins from the '80s but would be hard-pressed to name more than a handful from the current roster. They got to the interview fishbowl at the same time as Cruz.

"What the fuck . . . they said it was my lawyer."

"Good morning to you, too, Guadalupe."

"You're wasting your time. I'm not talking to you."

The guard directed Cruz to take a seat. Reluctantly, he complied and glared across the table at Brick. The guard left, closing the door to the glass enclosure, but didn't go far.

"I can understand why you're pissed," Brick said. "If I were you, I'd much rather get a visit from Ms. Nguyen."

Cruz continued to glare. He shifted in his chair as if trying to find a comfortable position that probably didn't exist.

"I'm going to get right to the point. I was a homicide detective for over ten years, and during that time, lots of guys confessed to crimes they didn't commit. Most of them were crazy, a few were taking the rap for someone else, and a couple just wanted to make a name for themselves." Brick paused, giving Cruz a chance to think about what he said before continuing. "The crazies were easy to spot, the others a little more challenging. I'm trying to figure out where you fit in."

Cruz stared at the floor. "I pled guilty because I'm guilty."

"I don't believe you."

"Who gives a shit? The judge believed me."

"Only because he hasn't seen the videotape . . . yet."

"Videotape?" Cruz raised his voice as he looked up but still avoided making eye contact. "What the fuck are you talking about?"

"Guadalupe, I know for a fact, you didn't dump Maria's body in the Tidal Basin. We've got the person on tape. He or she is taller than you and doesn't walk with a limp."

"What are you, some kind of do-gooder fag, getting off on springing guys from jail?" Cruz slumped against the back of his chair.

The accusation caught Brick off-guard, but he didn't react. He'd been called plenty of inappropriate names over the years, but to the best of his recollection, this was a first. He continued to force himself to keep a straight face. Brick sensed he was making progress breaking through Cruz's façade and waited for him to continue.

"Why do you care?" Whether Cruz realized it or not, he had dialed down the attitude.

"I care because I knew Jose. For me, this is about him, not you." Brick paused and took a deep breath. "He was a good kid, a hard worker just trying to better himself and give his sister a safe place to live. I owe it to him to find the bastard who killed them." Brick got to his feet. "It's hard to imagine why you pled to something you didn't do, but you must have your own reasons. Of course, you'd have been smarter pleading to a federal offense."

"What's that supposed to mean?" Cruz asked.

"Much better accommodations. Talk to a couple of your cellmates here, then ask some guy whose done time with the Feds, he'll know what I'm talking about." Brick picked up his notebook and headed toward the door. "If you ever decide you have something to say, call your lawyer. She'll know how to get in touch with me." Brick was about two steps from the door. He reached for the handle.

"Wait."

Brick wasn't sure, but it sounded like Cruz was sniffling. He turned around and saw him using the sleeve of his jumpsuit to wipe his nose and swipe at a tear rolling down the side of his face. This was the reaction Brick had been hoping for. He returned to the table, and once again, sat down opposite Cruz.

For the better part of a half hour, Brick sat and waited for Cruz to open up. It was tempting to prod him, but Brick felt that wouldn't accomplish anything. Instead he waited and watched. Occasionally, Cruz seemed deep in thought, but at other times, he seemed agitated, rocking back and forth and pounding his fist against his thighs.

"So I didn't dump the body . . . okay?"

Brick nodded. "Now tell me something I don't know." The wait began anew. After several minutes, Brick asked Cruz what should have been an easy question for him to answer. "What was Jose's apartment number?"

Cruz didn't respond immediately. "It was—" he shrugged his shoulders. "I forget."

"Guadalupe, you can't forget what you never knew." Brick sounded like an exasperated parent addressing a child caught in a lie. "You weren't there when Jose was killed, were you?"

Cruz didn't respond. He sat motionless.

Brick leaned forward and spoke softly. "Guadalupe, have you ever been in Jose's apartment?"

Cruz moved his head slowly from side to side. For the first time, he made eye contact with Brick. "No."

* * *

When Brick arrived at Lily's office, she was seated at her conference table surrounded by law books, a half-eaten club sandwich, and a glass of ice water. She pointed to a seat across from her. "Hold on just a second."

Brick pulled out the chair and sat down. He watched while she wrote notes on a yellow legal pad. She was left-handed, her fingers long and thin like those of a pianist. On her right hand she wore a ring that Brick recognized as a scarab. It appeared to be carved out of jade. She closed one of the law books and set it aside before looking up. "Done." She took off her glasses and rubbed her eyes. "How was your meeting?"

"Validating." Brick summed up what he had learned from Cruz.

Lily tapped her pen against the legal pad. "But we still don't know why he pled to something he didn't do."

"Right, but we can rule out two possibilities. I'm convinced Cruz isn't crazy or craving attention."

"What does that leave? Taking the rap for someone else?"

"That's what I would put my money on."

Lily shook her head. "My client, the altruist . . . sorry to burst your bubble, but I'm not buying it."

"I wouldn't expect you to. I've seen his rap sheet. He's MS-13 and someone scrawled the gang's signature on the side of the tub using Jose's blood." Brick saw Lily grimace even though the blood on the tub evidence wasn't something she hadn't heard before. Thanks to

Blancato, the immediate world heard it. "I don't think he's acting out of selflessness. I think he's being coerced. He may come across as a thug, but from what I saw, he's scared. Does he have family here?"

"No, they're in Mexico. His wife and baby daughter live with his mother." Lily reached up and massaged her temple with the fingertips of her right hand. "I guess it's possible he's taking the heat in order to buy his family's safety."

"Only Cruz can answer that, and I'm not sure he will."

"Great . . . he may be okay with rotting in jail, but now that I know this, if I want to hold on to my license, I have a responsibility to notify the court." Lily fished an ice cube out of her glass and pressed it against her forehead. "This case is giving me a migraine."

She seemed to be in pain, but Brick couldn't relate. If he took three Tylenol a year, it was a lot. "Is there anything you can take?"

"I already did—just hasn't kicked in." Lily closed her eyes. "It hurts my head to think—what do you suggest?"

"If protecting his family is his motivation, Mexico is hardly a safe haven." Brick thought for a moment. "I know a guy, an ICE agent. I'll talk to him and hopefully get a better idea of how the subculture works. No guarantees but—"

"Okay . . . whatever." Lily didn't sound very enthusiastic, but Brick figured the headache might be to blame.

"Need anything before I leave?" Brick asked.

"No." Despite her obvious discomfort, Lily managed a smile. "But thanks anyway."

# CHAPTER THIRTY-THREE

Brick studied the Old Ebbitt Grill menu while Ron checked in with his wife on the baby front.

Ron shook his head as he set his phone down on the table and picked up his menu. "Kind of like waiting for a jury to come back; you know it's going to happen sooner or later, but the waiting is killing me. I don't know how much more I can take." He picked up his water glass and took a drink.

"I'm guessing it's not a walk in the park for Jasmine, either."

"You're right." Ron unfolded his napkin and laid it across his lap. "Listen to me bitchin' like I'm the one who's gained seventy-five pounds and hasn't slept in three days. Her doc is surprised she's gone this long, but he said it could be today. I hope he's right."

"Then maybe we'd better go ahead and order in case it is."

"Good thinking." Ron scanned the menu then set it aside. "I've probably packed on ten pounds in the last two weeks. I should just get oatmeal, but I can tell you, that ain't happening. I mean, Jasmine's got an excuse, she's eating for three. The problem is, she gets these cravings for Big Macs and fries, milkshakes, cheesecake. She never used to eat stuff like that and she doesn't want to eat alone so I keep her company." Ron patted his midsection. "I gotta get working on this before it gets out of control."

"You can start after breakfast. Go for the bacon and eggs." Brick caught the eye of the waiter who immediately approached the table and took their order.

"Anything from the bar . . . I recommend a Bloody Mary."

"No, thanks," Brick said.

Ron simply shook his head. He waited until the waiter walked away. "Given where I just spent the last four hours, a Bloody Mary is the last thing I want."

"Medical Examiner's Office?"

"No, a double murder-suicide on Georgia Avenue, up near Howard. Unless something bigger goes down, it will lead the news at four."

"What happened?"

"Seems a professor was, let's say, 'tutoring' one of his students, and his wife walked in on the lesson. Popped both of them before she turned the gun on herself."

"Hell hath no fury . . ."

"You got that right." Ron blinked a couple of times in quick succession. "Just trying to get that image out of my mind."

Brick could relate. Over the years he found the best eraser was a crime scene that was even worse. If Ron stayed in Homicide, sooner or later, it would happen, but now wasn't the time to mention it. Brick pointed toward the back of the restaurant. "The bar over there, the one named for Ulysses S. Grant, was used in a scene from a well-known movie. Name the movie and the actors who sat at the bar."

Ron sat quietly for a minute or two. *"All the President's Men?"*

"Wrong."

Ron looked around the room, trying to spot a clue. He shrugged his shoulders. "I got nothing." He reached for his cellphone, but Brick slid it out of his reach.

"No fair looking it up."

"Okay then, what's the answer?"

"Think about it. In the meantime, I'll tell you about my second meeting with Guadalupe Cruz." As they waited for their food to arrive, Brick brought Ron up-to-speed.

Ron waited until Brick was finished, then a wry smile crossed his lips. "I'm still kind of new to this, but I've been around long enough to know the shit's going to hit the fan. Kind of gives new meaning to 'Houston, we have a problem.'"

"I think that's fair. There's an innocent guy, at least innocent as far as the Delgado case, sitting in jail and the killer is out there somewhere. Yeah, I'd say that's a problem. Cruz's attorney is planning to petition the arraignment judge to revoke the guilty plea."

"Then we're right back where we started."

"Except we've—or I should say you've—lost a lot of valuable time."

"It sucks." Ron leaned back in his chair. "What's your gut telling you?"

"Carlos has moved up a couple of rungs on the suspect ladder. Someone needs to take a closer look at him." Brick went on to tell Ron what he had learned from Eric about the operation Carlos was running out of his apartment.

"Seriously? I mean, I'm not surprised there's a network. I just wouldn't have guessed Carlos is the brains behind the whole shebang." Ron shrugged. "But what do I know? I'm sure Eric knows what he's talking about. I've asked around, and from what I hear, Eric is a stand-up guy."

"Here we are." The waiter set a buttermilk waffle and side of sausage in front of Ron, and turned to retrieve a tray held by another waiter. "And for you, sir, the eggs Benedict." He set the plate in front of Brick. "Enjoy."

For a few minutes, conversation stopped while both men ate. They didn't wolf down the food but polished it off quickly. In time, Brick may learn to slow down, but for now, he remembered too many meals interrupted by a dispatcher's call. Dropping money on the table and rushing out of a restaurant was a common occurrence.

Ron broke their silence by speaking first. "Okay, man—it's driving me crazy—what was the movie?"

Brick put down his fork. *"In the Line of Fire."*

"No way." Ron reached across the table and grabbed his phone. His thumbs went to work. Immediately, he laughed as he looked toward Grant's Bar. "You're right, bro. John Mahoney and Clint Eastwood sat at that very bar. Too bad it wasn't *Dirty Harry*, but knowing my man Clint was there—that 'makes my day.'"

"I thought it would."

Over Ron's objection, Brick picked up the check. It was a small gesture to repay the favors Ron had done for him recently.

"Here you go." The waiter handed Brick the credit card slip to sign just as a cellphone rang.

Ron jumped up, startling a couple passing by their table. "Sorry." He sat back down.

"Relax, Ron. My phone." Brick ignored the call, signed the receipt, and handed it to their waiter. "He's on baby watch—twins."

"Wow, congratulations." The waiter extended his hand.

"Thanks." Ron smiled sheepishly as he shook his hand.

Brick slipped his credit card back into his wallet. "Hang on while I check this voicemail." The message was brief, but it made him laugh.

"What?" Ron asked.

"That was Lil . . . Cruz's attorney. She's headed to the jail because it seems our boy wants to talk. Wondered what method I used to get him to open up." Brick stopped and chuckled. "She guessed waterboarding."

"So the Dragon Lady has a sense of humor—who knew?"

"Well, she doesn't get much chance to show that side in court."

"But it sounds like you're getting to see it."

Brick shook his head. "It's not like that."

"Really? Think again, Brick. If you had been looking in a mirror when you listened to that voicemail you'd have seen your face light up like a Christmas tree."

"C'mon, that's not true."

"Hey, you're the one who taught me to read body language and I know what I saw." Ron checked his phone again. "Nothing yet, but I need to go." He pushed back his chair and stood. Brick did, too.

"Give Jasmine my best," Brick said as he embraced his former partner in a quick bro hug.

"Will do. And let me know how things go with Cruz and his attorney. Especially with his attorney, if you know what I mean."

"Get out of here."

"Just sayin'."

Brick smiled to himself as he sat at the table and finished his cup of tea. He always thought of himself as a decent poker player, able to conceal his feelings, but he may have overestimated his abilities. Although comparing a poker hand reaction to the sound of Lily's voice was probably equivalent to the proverbial apples and oranges. Still, he couldn't discount what Ron had said. He might as well admit it, he was eager to hear back from Lily and not just for an update on Cruz.

# CHAPTER THIRTY-FOUR

"I CAN FIT you in if you can be here in a half hour."

It was the response Brick was hoping to hear. "Great, I'll be there." Brick waited for the walk light then crossed 15th Street. As he headed west on Pennsylvania Avenue, he noticed the tulips in bloom on the north lawn of the White House. He maneuvered around photo-taking tourists and continued past the Old Executive Office Building. His destination was Adil's Salon on Wisconsin Avenue. As picky as Brick was about his clothes, he was even more so about his hair. A former girlfriend recommended her stylist, and all these years later, Brick was still seeing Adil on a regular basis. The same couldn't be said for the girlfriend. The last he heard, she had gotten married and moved to Atlanta.

An ambulance, sirens blaring, sped by and pulled into the emergency entrance at George Washington University Hospital as Brick rounded Washington Circle. It occurred to him if he had invested a dollar for every time he'd been summoned to an emergency room to interview a victim, his retirement fund would be a lot more impressive. But now, if he never saw the inside of a hospital again, that would be compensation enough.

When Brick walked into the salon, Adil was removing the hair cutting drape from the shoulders of a distinguished silver-haired man who looked to be in his early sixties. The two spoke in French although Adil quickly switched to English to greet Brick before switching back to his native tongue. There were few things Brick envied, but being bilingual was at the top of his list, and he was impressed with the way Adil's English had improved over the years. It reminded him of the way Jose's language skills were getting better. Brick had no doubt that, in time, Jose would have achieved his American dream just as Adil had done. The thought triggered a feeling of sadness that morphed into anger as a vision of Jose's lifeless body flashed in front of his eyes. He sat down and picked up a copy of *People*, flipping through the pages trying to find a story to distract him from the thoughts dominating his brain. He set the magazine aside. It would take more than the latest news on the Kardashians or who was still competing on *Dancing with the Stars* to do the trick. Thankfully, Adil was ready for him.

"How's retirement?" Adil asked as he adjusted the black vinyl drape to cover Brick's shoulders.

"I'm keeping busy."

"Hanging out at Nats Park, right?"

Brick laughed. "Not exactly."

"So, is this the year the Nats are going to the World Series?" Adil snipped some hair around Brick's right ear. "My boys want to see a Nats-Orioles Series."

"Don't think that's likely to happen. Tell them to keep their eyes on the Royals."

Adil went to work on the hair over Brick's left ear. "Oh my God, I almost forgot." He put down his scissors and grabbed an envelope from the counter in front of the mirror. He handed it to Brick. "Go ahead, open it."

Brick scanned the first paragraph of the letter inside. He looked up and saw Adil's beaming reflection in the mirror. Brick smiled, too. "Congratulations."

"Just two weeks I'll officially be an American citizen."

"Where's the ceremony going to be?"

"Baltimore." Adil hesitated for a moment. "If you could attend, it would mean a lot to me and my family."

Brick reached in his pocket to retrieve his phone. "I'll put the date in my calendar right now." Before doing so, he noticed he had a text from Lily.

"Heading back to office. Meet me there ASAP."

\* \* \*

Lily was already at her office when Brick arrived. She greeted him with a quizzical smile. "Got to hand it to you—Cruz was more cooperative than he's ever been since I've had the pleasure of representing him." Lily pointed to a chair at the conference table. "Have a seat."

Lily hung up her raincoat and closed the closet door. "Would you like anything to drink: water, orange juice, cranberry juice?"

"No thanks."

Despite Brick's response, Lily continued. "Almond milk, coconut water."

"Coconut water—you actually drink that stuff?"

Lily returned to the table with a bottle of water in hand. "No. I had a paralegal student working here for a semester. She left a couple of containers and it seems wasteful to throw them out."

"Give it to one of the street people."

"Tried that, didn't work."

Brick laughed. "Why am I not surprised?"

"Maybe you could talk them into it—given your magic touch."

"I think that would require more than I'm capable of."

"Don't sell yourself short; you got Cruz to respond. What did you say to him to break through that façade?"

"I don't think it was as much what I said as how I said it." Brick leaned back in his chair and thought for a minute. How best he could respond without sounding sanctimonious. "Lily, I learned early in my career that treating someone with respect, even someone who turned my stomach just by being in the same room, was the most efficient way to get to the truth."

"So you took the good cop role?"

"That's not what I'm saying. As far as I'm concerned, the whole good cop/bad cop routine is bullshit. You may hear what you want to hear, but too often it turns out the suspect is lying out of fear or exhaustion. All that does is screw up the investigation. For the most part, with Cruz, I didn't say anything. I just sat and waited until he was ready to talk. I figured the silence would eventually get to him and it did."

Lily nodded. "For what it's worth, he said you didn't act like other cops."

Brick smiled. "I used to hear that a lot. Most times it wasn't a compliment."

"Well, this time I think it was," Lily said. "And you were right; Cruz is worried about his family in Mexico. He was convinced the only way he could ensure they won't be harmed was for him to take the rap." Lily tried unsuccessfully to twist the cap on her bottle of water.

"Can I help you with that?"

"I hope so or I may die of thirst." Lily handed the bottle to Brick. A quick twist and the seal on the cap was broken. He handed it back to Lily.

"Thanks. What was I saying . . . oh yeah, the question needing an answer is: Who is Cruz covering for? And without a guarantee of protection for him and his family, he's probably not going to tell." Lily took a sip of water. "I know it's complicated, but there is precedent for a non-citizen to be placed in the Witness Protection Program."

"How long ago?" Brick asked.

"Not sure, why?"

"Budget cuts—WITSEC isn't what it once was, just like a lot of other programs."

"That's not encouraging."

"It is what it is." Brick shrugged. "I don't mean to be flippant, but that's the reality we're facing. A lot is going to depend on how big the fish is we're reeling in."

Lily popped a pill of some kind into her mouth and washed it down. "Okay, I'm sure you have better contacts at the U.S. Attorney's Office than I do. Who should I call?"

Brick didn't have to think twice. "Kyle Thibodeaux."

"Name doesn't sound familiar."

"He may not be the person you'll need to deal with, but I would trust him to point you in the right direction." Brick reached in his pocket and retrieved his wallet. He pulled out a tattered business card and handed it to Lily. "Haven't gotten around to cleaning out my wallet since I retired, but even if I had, I would have hung on to Kyle's card."

Lily picked up her phone and started tapping in numbers. She stopped short. "Maybe it would be better if you called."

*   *   *

The call to Kyle Thibodeaux resulted in a late afternoon meeting. It was just after four when Brick and Lily exited the Judiciary Square Metro Station. They crossed Indiana Avenue and headed toward Superior Court, going against the eclectic tide of humanity exiting the courthouse. Conservatively dressed attorneys and jurors still wearing their badges mingled with young guys in low-riding baggy jeans and a couple of scantily-clad women.

"Do you think it occurred to those women that it's hard to convince a judge you're not a hooker when you're dressed just like a hooker?" Lily didn't wait for Brick to respond. "Maybe I should give up this defense gig and do a fashion police show, *What Not to Wear...* *to Court*."

"That's probably just one of many shows you could do. I've always said this place has more drama than the Kennedy Center."

Lily nodded. "Except if someone says 'break a leg' here, they might take it literally."

Brick laughed. "Which reminds me, the last time I was in Thibodeaux's office it would have been easy to get injured. I don't know what he's working on, but stuff was piled everywhere. Getting to his desk was like navigating an obstacle course."

Lily pointed at her feet. "No worries, I'm wearing sensible shoes these days."

"Retiring the heels?"

"Maybe. At least when I'm walking around D.C. The sidewalks are so uneven; I've lost my balance a couple of times." Lily checked her watch. "We're about fifteen minutes early. I need to stop by the law library."

"Okay. I'll meet you at Thibodeaux's office."

For a minute, Brick considered stopping by the Police Liaison Office, but he quickly dismissed that thought. He would be required to check in if he were testifying in his former official capacity, but to do so now would only raise questions as to why he was here. Instead, he went down to the cafeteria and got a can of Coke from the vending machine. He popped the top and took a couple of swigs. It had only been a few weeks since he had turned in his badge, but already the courthouse seemed like an unfamiliar place. A place where he didn't belong anymore in the same way kids don't belong hanging around their high school after they've graduated. And if they continue to hang around, they're looked upon suspiciously. So where does a retired cop *really* belong? Brick gave that question some thought as he finished his soda. He didn't have an answer, at least not yet. He dropped the empty Coke can in the recycle bin and headed toward the escalator.

The door to Kyle Thibodeaux's office was closed when Brick arrived. He knocked twice, waited, and knocked again. No response. He was about to go back to the receptionist's office when he spotted Thibodeaux leaving the men's room. He stopped briefly to speak with a colleague, then headed in Brick's direction.

"So how's the life of leisure?" Thibodeaux asked as he unlocked his office door. "I know, stupid question, but the standard one you get when you retire. Am I right?"

Brick nodded. "Thanks for seeing us on short notice. Lily stopped by the library; she should be here any minute."

"Gotta say, I was surprised. You working with a defense attorney . . . what's up with that?"

"They're not the enemy—well, not all of them."

"Not sure many around here would agree with that, but I don't have a personal opinion about Lily Nguyen since I haven't gone up against her in court. Hell, I've been stuck in my office so long I barely see the light of day. But I do know her reputation; I hear she's tough. Guess that's why a few of my colleagues call her the Dragon Lady."

Brick felt defensive. "Would they slap that label on her if she wasn't Asian?"

"Probably not but I'm confident they'd come up with something equally politically incorrect. Didn't take long for me to hear what I was being called behind my back."

"The Crazy Cajun?"

Thibodeaux laughed. "I'm kind of proud of that. Otherwise, they'd probably just call me crazy." Thibodeaux opened the door. "Let me grab something to write on and we'll use the conference room. I'm not sure all three of us can fit in my office with all the crap piled up in there."

When the door opened, Brick could see the tiny office was even more cluttered than the last time he had been there. Thibodeaux reached across his desk and grabbed a legal pad. Upon exiting, he locked the door. That seemed a little odd to Brick given that only authorized personnel were allowed in this corridor. Whatever Thibodeaux was working on must be highly sensitive.

"Thank God we're close to going to the grand jury, and I'll be able to reclaim my piece of real estate. As small as my office is, it's going to seem huge when all this stuff gets out of here." Thibodeaux turned the door handle, making sure it was locked. "I'm telling ya, Brick, when I was assigned this case, I had no idea what a can of worms I was opening up."

Brick was curious but knew there was no point in asking what the case was about. He figured information was shared only with those on a need-to-know basis and he didn't fall within that category. But he could also see it was taking a toll on Thibodeaux. He looked thinner than usual and the dark circles under his eyes were probably a result of sleep deprivation. It was even more reason Brick appreciated Thibodeaux meeting with them. He was glad to see Lily step off the elevator so they could get started.

Brick introduced the two attorneys who shook hands. A quick exchange of pleasantries then Thibodeaux led the way to the conference room. Upon entering the room, he switched on the lights and motioned for Brick and Lily to take a seat. Thibodeaux sat at the head of the table and turned in Lily's direction.

"So what's the deal with Guadalupe Cruz?"

"I have reason to believe he was coerced and I plan to file a motion to vacate his guilty plea. Before I do that, I wanted to get some feedback from someone familiar with this kind of situation. Brick suggested we talk to you."

"Thanks, Brick, you owe me one." Thibodeaux leaned back in his chair and stretched his long legs out in front of him. "It's not uncommon for a defendant to have second thoughts and want to withdraw his guilty plea. But it's very uncommon for a judge to rule in the defendant's favor."

"I figured as much," Lily said. "But given what I now know, as an officer of the court, I have no choice."

"Girl's gotta do what a girl's gotta do."

Brick stole a quick glance in Lily's direction. Her eyes were focused on Thibodeaux and if looks could kill, the prosecutor would have keeled over right then and there.

"Didn't mean to sound sexist. In case you don't know, I'm from Louisiana. We tend to say things like that. Of course, you need to do what's right." Thibodeaux picked up his pen and tapped it against his palm. "So who coerced your client?"

"I don't know."

Thibodeaux dropped his pen. He leaned forward, resting his elbows on the table and gesturing with his hands. "Whoa, whoa, whoa. I'm not telling you how to do your job, but personally I don't have the balls to file a motion to vacate claiming coercion without knowing who's responsible. Judge Newton will eat you alive."

"I know it's risky, but Cruz refuses to identify who he's taking the rap for unless he's guaranteed protection. Once the judge hears the evidence we have exonerating Cruz, I plan to petition the court to have him placed in protective custody as a material witness."

"Good luck with that." Thibodeaux got up and stretched. "My back is killing me." He paced back and forth before sitting down. "Protection just for him?"

"And his family—his wife and baby daughter."

"Where are they now?"

"Mexico."

"Seriously? What's their immigration status?"

"Cruz and his wife have green cards. The baby was born here."

"You're not going to like what I'm about to say." Thibodeaux shrugged his shoulders. "You're between a rock and a hard place. These days with all the budget cuts, getting someone into WITSEC almost takes an act of Congress. I'm not saying it's impossible, especially if the person threatening him is, let's say, the big enchilada in a drug cartel. Then it's a possibility, but if he's just your typical lowlife, it ain't happening."

"But even if the person responsible is a typical lowlife, he's killed two people."

"I'm just telling you like it is, I'm not saying it's fair." Thibodeaux raked his fingers through his bushy hair badly in need of a trim. "Has Cruz given any hint as to who he's covering for?"

"No, but my client's involvement in MS-13 leads me to think it could be someone within the gang."

Thibodeaux chewed on the end of his ballpoint. "You know there was a time when just saying 'involvement in MS-13' would open the door, but gang activity isn't the threat it once was so it's lost its cachet. Do you think Cruz is linked to terrorism in any way?"

"No." Lily shook her head. "Definitely not."

Thibodeaux turned toward Brick. "Do you agree?"

"Yes."

"Well, that's a bummer," Thibodeaux said. "Used to be if you had dirt on the Mafia, you were in. Then it was the Columbian drug lords. Now it's Middle East terrorists. It's the world we live in today."

"Unbelievable." Lily's brief laugh had a sardonic edge. "I'm not sure Cruz could identify the Middle East on a map of the . . . Middle East."

"I'm just saying if he had some insight it would be to his advantage." Thibodeaux interlaced his fingers and stretched his arms forward.

"But you know the old saying, gotta dance with the one who brung ya."

Lily looked over the top of her glasses at Thibodeaux. "Afraid I don't know that one."

Thibodeaux smiled. "What I'm saying is, you don't have a choice. You have to go with what you got. Maybe he does know something that's a missing link to bigger things than a double homicide. If that's the case, it could be the bargaining chip you need to make your case to get him into WITSEC. But your first hurdle is to win the motion to vacate."

"All right then." Lily smiled politely. "I think we're done." She pushed back her chair and stood. "Thank you for your time."

"My pleasure," Thibodeaux said. "Let me know what happens with that motion."

"I will," Lily said.

"Hopefully, you'll catch Newton on a good day. Might help if you wear a short skirt." Thibodaux looked around as if checking to see if anyone else was in the room. "Did I really say that?"

"No," Brick said. "Must have been the other Crazy Cajun."

# CHAPTER THIRTY-FIVE

THE SUN WAS setting and Indiana Avenue was all but deserted when Brick and Lily left the courthouse. She had said little since their meeting with Kyle Thibodeaux, leaving Brick to wonder what she was thinking

"So are you going to do it?" Brick finally asked as he and Lily entered the Metro Station.

"File the vacate motion—absolutely."

"No," Brick smiled. "Wear a short skirt?"

Lily rolled her eyes. "Not exactly breaking news that Newton is a sexist pig."

"But at least, as far as I know, he's not having the marshals pimp for him. I could name three judges who are."

Lily shook her head as she slipped her fare card into the turnstile slot. "Not going to ask; I'd rather not know."

Brick understood. Sometimes ignorance is bliss. Together they rode the short escalator down to the platform where the flashing indicator light signaled a train's approach.

"Good timing," Brick said.

Lily nodded. "I don't know about you, but I'm starving and all I can think about is—"

"'Pho?"

Lily shook her head. "No, pizza . . . Luciano's." She shrugged her shoulders. "What can I say, I'm a pizza snob."

"Nothing wrong with that; besides it's probably the best in the city."

"Want to get one?" Lily asked.

"Okay." Brick could have responded a little more enthusiastically, but he still wasn't sure where he stood. Lily was hard to figure out. She did seem less formal around him, even a little flirty at times, or maybe that was just wishful thinking on his part. An invitation for pizza— he needed to take it at face value. It wasn't a date, but then again, it could be a good start.

The doors on the subway car opened. Brick and Lily stepped on board and moved away from the door. At this hour, the train was still crowded but not packed. Lily sat next to an elderly man while Brick stood, holding on to a strap with one hand. With the other, he checked his phone—no messages. Apparently Jasmine still hadn't had the babies. He slipped it back into his pocket. At Gallery Place, the elderly man got up and headed toward the door. Brick sat down next to Lily.

"You were right about WITSEC and also about Thibodeaux."

"What do you mean?" Brick asked.

"I never expect someone from the U.S. Attorney's Office to be receptive to what I present because I'm always in an adversarial position, but Thibodeaux seems like a good guy . . . for a prosecutor."

Brick glanced to his right, seeing Lily in profile. Her delicate features reminded him of a cameo his mother often wore. "Next thing I might hear is some cops aren't so bad either."

Lily turned toward Brick. "Don't count on it."

To Brick's relief, she smiled when she said it.

* * *

At Luciano's, Brick and Lily snaked their way past a throng of pizza enthusiasts to the hostess stand. They could see all the tables in the small restaurant were filled.

"The wait time is about an hour," the hostess said.

"Really? Why is it so crowded tonight?" Lily asked.

"We got reviewed in the *Post* last weekend. It's not just the locals now that the secret is out. Should I add your name to the list?"

Brick deferred to Lily to make the decision.

"How about carry-out? It will be faster and my place is practically around the corner."

Again, Brick kept his enthusiasm in check. "That's okay with me."

"Actually, if you don't mind waiting for the pizza, I'll go pick up some beer or wine. Any preference?"

"Red wine."

Lily opened her wallet and offered Brick a twenty. "This should cover it."

Brick appreciated the offer but had no intention of letting Lily pay. "You're getting the wine, I'll take care of this."

"Thanks." Lily hesitated for a moment. "Rather than backtrack from the liquor store, makes more sense for me to head home from there. I'm in the red brick five-story building at the corner of 17th and R. Just press the button next to 3-S."

"Sounds good." Brick was thinking it sounded better than good, maybe even great, but continued to keep things in perspective by reining in his enthusiasm.

"See you there." With that, Lily was gone but a hint of her perfume lingered, mixing with the aroma of garlic and oregano.

"What'll it be?" The pizza man's apron was stained with tomato sauce. At least, Brick hoped it was tomato sauce.

Brick's mind went blank for a second. He glanced at the list of ingredients to remind himself of what they had agreed on. A large thin-crust with mushrooms, sausage, green peppers, and Kalamata olives.

The cashier, sporting a Nationals cap, rang up the order and quoted a price just under twenty dollars. "It will take about forty-five minutes to an hour."

Brick handed him two twenties. "Think you might be able to speed that up?"

The cashier smiled broadly. "Looks like your pie's going into the oven next."

"Thanks. You're from New York, aren't you?"

"Yeah, moved here from Queens a month ago." He looked surprised. "How'd you know?"

"When you said 'pie,' that's what gave you away."

"Really?" The cashier laughed. "Guess it'll take more than a baseball cap for me to fit in around here."

"But that's a good start."

*　　*　　*

Twenty-two minutes later, Brick left Luciano's with the large pizza. When he got to Lily's building, he pressed the button next to 3-S.

"Who is it?'

He shifted the pizza to his left hand and reached for the door. "Pizza man."

The next sound he heard was a deafening drone. He felt as though he had announced his arrival not only to Lily but everyone else in the neighborhood. He pulled the door open as quickly as he could to silence the buzzer. He stepped inside, making sure the door locked behind him before starting up the stairs. His heart rate accelerated but climbing three steep flights was only partly responsible.

Lily waited in the doorway to her apartment. She had changed her clothes. The court-appropriate suit had been replaced by jeans and a long-sleeved black blouse with white polka dots. As she took the pizza box from Brick, he noticed she was barefoot, her toenails painted red.

"That was fast. What'd you do, bribe the pizza guy?"

"No, the cashier."

"Whatever works." Lily closed her eyes and inhaled deeply. "This smells so good and I'm starving. Make yourself comfortable," she called over her shoulder as she disappeared around the corner of the living room into a small galley-style kitchen.

Brick looked down at the white wall-to-wall carpet and slipped his feet out of his loafers. He set his shoes by the door next to the ones Lily had worn earlier. He glanced around the combination living and dining room. It was very much like he expected—an artsy mix of contemporary furnishings and antiques, feminine without being frilly. He took off his jacket and draped it over the back of a dining room chair before pulling off his tie and loosening the collar of his shirt.

"Need any help?" Brick asked.

"Yes." Lily emerged from the kitchen and handed Brick a bottle of Oregon Pinot Noir and a corkscrew.

Brick hesitated before opening the wine. "Maybe I should do this in the kitchen. Red wine and a white carpet, I don't want to be responsible for making your place look like a crime scene."

Lily laughed. "You really need to stop thinking like a cop." She moved out of the doorway so Brick could enter the kitchen. He opened the wine over the sink, poured two glasses without spilling a drop, and handed one to Lily.

She set the glass down as she removed the flowered cloth covering the table. She placed the pizza box in the middle. "I'll get a couple of plates. Go ahead and sit down."

Brick was opening the pizza box as Lily returned. She handed him a plate as she took a deep breath.

"Smell the basil. That's by far my favorite herb." She picked up a slice and took a healthy bite even before sitting down. "Luciano's has ruined me for every other pizza place in D.C., and, believe me, I've tried most."

Brick laughed as he helped himself. He liked sharing a meal with a woman who obviously enjoyed food, even something as basic as pizza, without obsessing about calories and fat grams.

Lily raised her glass of wine in Brick's direction. "Cheers!"

"*Sláinte.*"

"Excuse me?" Lily said.

"That's the Irish equivalent."

Lily picked up her second slice and took a bite. She chewed and swallowed before continuing. "You're proud of your Irish roots, aren't you?"

"Yes."

"A lot of Irish-Americans are—maybe more so than other ethnic groups."

Brick thought about that for a moment. "I'm not sure that's true. It may seem that way because there's a lot of us. And, of course, everyone wants to be Irish on St. Patrick's Day. It's actually kind of annoying." Brick separated two slices, putting one on his plate. "What about you, I'm sure you're proud to be Vietnamese."

"I am, but sometimes I feel as though I'm denying my heritage."

"How so?" he asked.

Lily took a sip of wine. "My birth parents died when our village was bombed. I was one of the lucky ones. I survived and was adopted and raised with an appreciation of everything America had to offer. It's just that there weren't many Asians where I grew up in Wisconsin. I'm not complaining, but I wasn't exposed to much ethnic culture."

"But what about at home?" Brick asked.

"Especially at home. Can you believe it, I never tasted pho until I moved here to D.C." Lily laughed. "Don't let the name fool you. From the time I was adopted up until I went to law school, I was Lily Nguyen Adams. Somehow on my law school application to University of Chicago, my name got transposed to Lily Adams Nguyen. Not only did I get accepted, I got some very generous minority scholarships. So with my parents' blessing, I legally changed my name and graduated from law school with a lot less debt than I would have otherwise."

"Well, Midwesterners are known for being practical."

"True. And, my parents are . . . were. They passed away three years ago in a multi-car pileup during an ice storm. I still have trouble referring to them in the past tense." Lily refilled Brick's wineglass before pouring some for herself. "Anyway, enough about me. Were your parents first-generation American?"

"My father was. But my mother was born in Dublin. She came to the States when she was a teenager. I have dual citizenship even though I was born in Brooklyn."

Lily reached for another slice of pizza. "I think I'm getting ahead of you."

"Is this a competition to see who can eat the most?"

"No, but I have to warn you, I'd probably win. Anyway, you were saying you have dual citizenship. I've heard Ireland is beautiful; have you been there?"

"It is and I've been there a few times."

"Recently? I've heard it's changed a lot during the boom times—the Celtic Tiger, I think that's what they called it."

Brick nodded. "No, the last time I was there"—he hesitated for a moment as he did the math in his head—"twenty-four years ago." Brick finished what was on his plate and considered having one more slice before deciding he'd had enough. "It was my mother's wish to be buried in County Clare and it was my responsibility to see that it happened."

"You must have been young."

"Eighteen."

Lily reached over and touched Brick's hand. "I'm sorry, I didn't mean to—"

"It's okay."

"Then, forgive me for asking, but where was your father?"

"Missing-in-action."

"Obviously."

"It was through no fault of his own." Brick hadn't planned to talk about this, but it was too late to stop now. He leaned back in his chair and looked over at Lily. "My father was an Army officer, Special Forces, and his helicopter was shot down over Pleiku." Brick saw a hint of recognition on Lily's face.

"That's in the Central Highlands."

"Right. He and his crew were declared missing-in-action, and to this day, that's their official status."

"The fucking war." Lily closed her eyes. For a moment she seemed lost in her thoughts. When she opened her eyes, she smiled sadly at Brick. "What do you remember about him?"

"Nothing. We never met. My mother was pregnant when he was deployed, and I was born two months before she was notified." Brick picked up the wine bottle. He topped off Lily's glass then refilled his own. For the second time in as many days he was talking about his childhood, a subject he rarely shared.

"That must have been horrible for your mother. When you're in limbo, how do you get on with your life?"

"Simple answer—she never did, at least on one level. That's not to say she wasn't a good mother, she was. Her world revolved around me, but she was young and should have remarried, or at least dated, but instead, she waited for my father to return."

Lily stared into her wineglass then looked up. "This may sound strange coming from someone who's been orphaned twice, but at least I know what happened. I mean, I miss them every day and will for the rest of my life, but I'm not clinging to false hope." Lily pointed toward her wineglass. "I probably could have expressed that better, but I'll blame it on the wine."

Brick nodded. "You said it well enough and you didn't use the 'c' word."

"Excuse me?" Lily sounded offended.

"*Closure.*"

"Oh, that one."

"It's an overused platitude. When I knocked on someone's door and told them their spouse or kid was dead, I never felt like I was providing closure. I was simply giving them information. Horrible news that would forever change their lives. But without it, their lives would also be changed, maybe in a worse way. Just ask a mother or father whose kid has been missing for the last fifteen years."

"Or a man whose father's been missing for much longer?"

"Yeah, that, too. Everyone deserves answers." Brick took a sip of wine. "Several years ago, I filed some Freedom of Information requests and turned up some interesting leads. But so far, just more questions."

"Maybe all these years of paying it forward will reward you."

"What do you mean?" Brick asked.

"It seems like a lot of your motivation for solving homicides was to spare the victim's family the pain of uncertainty you've lived with."

A fleeting smile crossed Brick's lips. "I thought you were a lawyer not a psychologist."

"When business is slow, I watch *Dr. Phil.*" Lily pointed to the remaining slices of pizza in the box.

"No, I've had enough."

"Me, too. I'll put the rest in the fridge."

"Cold pizza for breakfast?"

"It's been known to happen." Lily picked up the grease-stained box and headed toward the kitchen. "We can finish our wine over on the sofa."

Brick liked that suggestion. He picked up both glasses and set them down on the glass-topped coffee table. Lily joined him on the sofa, sitting close but not too close. She took a sip of wine then set her glass back down.

"I owe you an apology."

"Really . . . why?"

"I was thinking about the day when you approached me at Pho 75; I was pretty rude to you."

"No, you were just . . . well, come to think of it, yeah you were." Brick laughed. "It's okay though, no apology needed."

"I hate to admit this but I guess I just think of all cops in the same way and you definitely don't fit the stereotype."

"I take it you think that's a good thing?"

"Yeah, I do." Lily started to say something but quickly covered her mouth. Her attempt to stifle a yawn failed. "Excuse me, it's the wine, not the company."

"I understand, but it's also been a long day, especially for you. I should be heading out." Brick stood up; so did Lily. For a few seconds, their eyes locked. To Brick, it was a now-or-never moment. Gently he cupped Lily's face in his hands and kissed her on the lips. She responded by closing the distance between them and kissing him with an intensity he had hoped for but didn't expect. Who initiated the next kiss didn't matter. All that mattered to Brick was that it happened. No need to keep score.

"Brick—" Lily's voice sounded far away as she stepped back, a look of regret erasing the passion that had been there a second before. "I'm sorry, Brick." She sank back down onto the sofa.

Brick felt like an awkward teenager. "It's my fault, I shouldn't have—"

Lily shook her head. "No, please . . . please don't apologize." Her chin quivered and she appeared on the verge of tears as she cast her eyes toward the floor. "It's not you—it's me."

Brick sat down next to her. "I don't understand, Lily. What does that mean?"

Slowly she raised her head. "Look at me, Brick. What do you see?"

"A beautiful woman." As soon as the words were out of his mouth, he had a startling thought. Unlike Ron with a photographic memory of movie scenes, not many stuck with Brick, but *The Crying Game* was an exception. "Are you telling me you're not . . . a woman?"

"What? Oh, my God!" Lily started to laugh, an infectious laugh that spread to Brick and reduced the tension in the air. "I can assure you, I'm one-hundred percent woman."

"That's a relief. Then, Lily, what is it?"

Brick noticed Lily biting her lip. It was obvious something was troubling her and she seemed reluctant to talk about it. Brick took her hand. "Lily, don't do a Guadalupe Cruz—talk to me."

Lily laughed again. "That's what I'm doing, isn't it. It's just that . . . oh, what the hell."

Slowly, Lily unbuttoned her blouse. She turned her back to Brick as she slipped it off her shoulders and let it drop to the floor. Purplish-red scars covered her back and arms. Brick had a sickening feeling in the pit of his stomach. Not because of the disfigurement he saw but because of what he imagined Lily had endured. He had seen enough scarred bodies over the years to know these weren't recent. He moved closer to her and kissed the back of her neck as he recalled images of Vietnamese kids running in the streets as fire rained down from the sky.

Brick's voice was soft, barely louder than a whisper. "Lily, please turn around." As if in slow motion, she complied. The skin on her chest, above her lacy bra, bore similar scars.

"What do you see now?" Lily asked.

"The same beautiful woman."

"Please don't patronize me."

"Is that what you think I'm doing?"

"No, and it's not fair for me to make that assumption. It's just I never know what type of reaction I might get."

"I understand." Brick glanced at her breasts as she took a deep breath. He reached over and held both of her hands in his. "We all have scars of one type or another; some are just closer to the surface."

Lily nodded but didn't respond for a minute or two. "Then is there a chance we can pick up where we left off?"

Brick leaned over and kissed her mouth. Garlic never tasted so sweet. "I think we already have."

# CHAPTER THIRTY-SIX

*First, he closed the blinds. Next, he made sure the dead bolt was locked by checking it twice. Then a third time. He'd better watch out, he didn't want to end up with OCD. He laughed to himself. OCD, ADD, ADHD, disorder du jour. It was a bunch of bullshit, just a way for doctors and drug companies to make big bucks. He knew what he was doing. It made sense to check the door. He had to make sure he'd shut out the rest of the crazy fucking world. He had stuff to do and he didn't want to be disturbed.*

*For now, he set up his computer on the dining room table. He laughed again. Maybe he should think of it as the dining corner table. And over there was the sleeping corner. He didn't care; he had more important things to spend his money on than rent. A studio suited him just fine. Not that it was cheap; even a dump in the city was expensive.*

*That's why God invented credit cards. And he had a brand-new one in his wallet. Bank of America could go fuck themselves. Threatening to turn him over to a collection agency; he'd show them he wasn't intimidated. He waited a few more seconds while the computer booted up, then logged on and entered his password. He surfed for a while before deciding on a website that guaranteed what he was looking for. Quickly he entered the number from the new credit card along with the expiration date and security code. Easy as pie, he was in. Fuck you, Bank of America.*

*After about two hours he took a break. His stash of frozen dinners was dwindling, but he had his choice of mac and cheese or lasagna. He checked the heating instructions and chose the mac and cheese. The lasagna would have taken longer and he didn't feel like waiting. Sometimes it seemed that's all he ever did. He'd been waiting all his life to meet the right woman. It's not that he hadn't met women, there were plenty out there, but he wasn't about to lower his standards. And he was sick and tired of waiting and being toyed with. All the time and money he had spent and what did he have to show for it. He took a deep breath and tried to calm himself, but it was too late. He felt the rage building and he knew he had to do something or he would explode. His eyes darted around the cluttered room and landed on his computer.*

*With both hands, he picked up the laptop and smashed it against the wall.*

# CHAPTER THIRTY-SEVEN

BRICK CRAVED A cigarette. In a previous life, he always kept a pack in his nightstand for that euphoric interval before exhaustion set in. It was the only time he allowed himself or anyone else to smoke in bed. But this wasn't his bed or his nightstand and Lily was a non-smoker; he willed himself to stay in the moment and not think about nicotine.

"Have you ever been to the ballet?" Lily asked as she snuggled against his chest.

"What?"

Lily laughed. "I know that just came out of the nowhere but I looked over at my dresser and saw the ticket envelope. A girlfriend and I were going to the Kennedy Center on Saturday but she had to go out of town. Some kind of family emergency. Anyway, I know it's not a thing most guys would want to—"

"Are you stereotyping again?"

"I guess I am. Would you be willing to go with me?"

"I do have a reputation to live up to and I can think of worse things than spending a Saturday night with you."

"Really?" Lily smiled at Brick. "Let's see if you still feel that way after sitting through two hours of *Giselle*."

Brick put his arm around Lily and closed his eyes. Thoughts of a cigarette were long forgotten as he drifted off to sleep.

*　*　*

For a moment, Brick wasn't sure where he was. Abruptly, he looked to his left then smiled at the sight of Lily sleeping on her side. He heard her softly snoring as he closed his eyes and fell back to sleep. An hour later, the clock radio jarred him awake.

"Morning." Lily raised up on one elbow then flopped back down on her pillow. "Think I drank too much wine."

Brick laughed. "Headache?"

"Kind of . . . but it was worth it."

"Good." Brick ran his fingers along Lily's thigh. "How much time do we have until you have to get up?"

Lily pouted. "Not enough." She reached for her robe at the foot of the bed. "Rain check?"

Before Brick could respond, she disappeared into the bathroom. He picked up his socks and underwear, hating putting them back on, but his only other option was going commando. He stepped into his boxers and reached down to pull on his sock but suddenly stopped. What had he done? He sat down on the edge of the bed. In the afterglow of making love, he had forgotten about the Nats-Yankee game. He couldn't believe it; he had agreed to go to the ballet . . . the ballet. Brick thought for a moment. Lily was reasonable; she'd understand, especially when he explained the potential for seeing Mariano Rivera. As he finished getting dressed, he mentally rehearsed what he would say.

Lily emerged from the bathroom wearing a black bra and panties. Brick was pleased she made no effort to conceal her scars.

"You're dressed." She seemed surprised. "I thought you might have gone back to sleep."

"I don't want to be in the way. You've got a lot to do today."

"Unfortunately." Lily wrapped her arms around Brick. "Guess I should start by putting on my court suit with the short skirt."

"All right, but let me enjoy looking at you a little longer." Brick kissed the top of her head. Now was as good a time as any to bring up his dilemma. "I just hope you'll—"

"It's okay, I'm fine. It's something I've had to deal with my whole life. You made it easy for me and I'm looking forward to tomorrow night." Lily looked up at Brick and smiled. "Kristin is one of my best friends, but I'd much rather go to the Kennedy Center with you."

Brick swallowed hard and returned the smile. So much for the words he'd rehearsed. "Tomorrow it is. But I'd better get out of here now before I'm guilty of obstructing justice. Let me know how things go."

"I'll text you as soon as I know something."

*   *   *

Brick removed his wallet from his pants pocket and set it on the top of his dresser next to the baseball tickets he wouldn't be using. He was trying to put things in perspective. Mariano was a closer. If either team had a three- or four-run lead, he wouldn't leave the bullpen. But there was always that chance he would take the mound, and the guy wasn't going to play forever. This could be the year he decided to retire. And if that were the case, Brick was missing out on his only opportunity short of a trip to Yankee Stadium. A trip to Yankee Stadium—why hadn't he thought of that before? Probably because, even though he was born in Brooklyn, New York was one of his least favorite places on the planet. But spending a weekend there with Lily could make it tolerable. Even more than tolerable, all the way to amazing if last night was any indication. He stripped off his clothes, threw his dirty underwear and socks in the hamper, and stepped into the shower.

Aside from writing some checks and answering emails, there was nothing demanding Brick's attention. A twenty-minute power nap seemed like a good idea. Two hours later, a text message woke him. He reached over to the nightstand and grabbed his cellphone.

"Hearing set for 2. Wish me luck."

He typed a quick response. "Irish luck ok?"

"I'll take that over Vietnamese any day."

Brick smiled at the message on his phone until he noticed the time. He had slept a lot longer than he planned. He threw back his bedspread and got up. He wasn't tired anymore but he was hungry. Ravenously hungry. The bills and emails could wait. He got dressed and headed off in the direction of Boland's Mill.

Even before Brick walked in the door, he knew what he wanted. Traditional Irish breakfast was a staple on the menu along with pub grub favorites like corned beef and cabbage and potato soup. He took a seat at the empty bar and placed his order with Rory.

"And a tomato juice," Brick added.

"Hair of the dog?"

"Something like that."

"How about a Red Bull chaser," Rory suggested as he popped open a can.

"Why, you own stock in it?"

Rory took a swig. "I should. Man, I'm hooked on the stuff."

"I'll stick to tomato juice."

"Suit yourself." Rory filled a tall glass and set it down in front of Brick.

"Thanks. What do you hear from Eamonn?"

"Nothing the past two days. And that worries me, but there's nothing I can do about it."

"How's everything going here?"

"Better. I got the schedule straight and I'm actually going to be off tomorrow night. First time in a while."

"Big plans?"

Rory shook his head. "No plans."

"Kelly likes baseball, doesn't she?" Brick asked.

"Yeah, why?"

"I've got two tickets for the Nats game tomorrow night. They're yours if you want them."

"Jaysus—they're playing the Yankees. Your man Mariano's in town and you're giving away the tickets. What happened, somebody die?"

Brick shook his head. "No, nothing like that. But I can't use them; somebody should. Hey, if you want to impress Kelly—club-level seats just to the left of home plate, no waiting in line for concessions or the bathrooms."

"Afraid it's going to take more than baseball tickets. She's pissed at me . . . big-time."

"What happened?"

"Something stupid."

"Wouldn't be the first time, right?" It was meant as a joke, but Brick realized too late Rory wasn't amused. He seemed genuinely upset. "Sorry, didn't mean to make light of your situation."

"It was my fault." Rory chugged his can of Red Bull. "I borrowed her laptop and forgot to erase the history before I returned it."

Brick swallowed quickly to avoid spraying Rory with tomato juice. He picked up a napkin and wiped his mouth, trying hard not to laugh. "If it's any consolation, you're not the first guy to get caught."

"Tell that to Kelly." Rory glanced toward the kitchen. "I need to go check on your food." A few minutes later he returned with a large plate of fried eggs, bacon, bangers, potatoes, baked beans, and soda bread. He set it down in front of Brick. "Okay, what I did was wrong,

I admit that, but it's not like it was kiddie porn or anything illegal. I mean, there's thousands of sites out there and this was just a couple of . . . well, you know. Do you think Kelly's overreacting?"

Brick buttered a piece of soda bread. "You're asking for my opinion, right?"

"Yeah."

"Okay, start with an apology but do not—under any circumstances—imply that she's overreacting. Got that?" Rory nodded as Brick continued. "If you're lucky, she might come to that realization on her own. But you got to remember, a lot of women—I don't know, maybe most women—find porn offensive and threatening."

"Yeah, I know, it's just—"

"Hey, what's more important to you—a relationship with Kelly or spending nights curled up with your laptop?"

"Well, when you put it that way." Rory crumpled the Red Bull can and threw it in the recycle bin. "More tomato juice?"

"Just half a glass."

Brick went to work on his second egg. It was almost gone when he felt his phone vibrate. He wiped his hands on his napkin before reaching into his pocket for his phone. The text was from Lily.

It simply read:

"my office – 15 minutes"

# CHAPTER THIRTY-EIGHT

BRICK HAD A bad feeling as he stood on the corner flagging down cabs. Two passed him by before the third one stopped. He got in and gave the driver the address for Lily's office. As he adjusted his seat belt, he thought about the text. It didn't make sense. An earlier message indicated the hearing before Newton was set for two o'clock. It was now just past one. Why would Lily leave the courthouse? Scenarios started running through his head. Had Newton changed his mind about hearing the motion? Not likely. Maybe the judge had gotten sick or had a family emergency. That could mean a postponement. But if that were the case, why hadn't Lily said so?

In less than ten minutes, the cab driver turned onto P Street. Just as he pulled over to the curb, Brick spotted Lily climbing the steps to her office. With her back turned toward him, he couldn't see the expression on her face, but it didn't matter. He could tell by her lowered head and slumping shoulders something was wrong.

Brick paid the driver and got out of the cab. He rushed up the stairs two at a time and caught up to Lily.

"He's dead," Lily said. No emotion, just a matter-of-fact statement. She unlocked the door to her office and they both stepped inside.

"The judge?"

"No, Guadalupe Cruz killed himself."

Of all the scenarios Brick had run through his head, this wasn't one of them. It took a minute for him to wrap his head around what Lily had said.

"Suicide?"

Lily shrugged. "At least that's what we were told."

Brick was conflicted. He wanted to embrace Lily and comfort her in the way lovers do. But he couldn't, not here in her office. It felt as if last night was a long time ago or had never happened. It was why he'd always kept his personal and professional lives separate.

"Lily, I know this is tough, but I need to know as much as you do." He pulled out a chair at the conference table and motioned for her to sit down. "Can I get you a glass of water?"

She nodded as she opened her briefcase and retrieved a file with Cruz's name printed on it. She dropped it on the table before sitting down. Lily took off her glasses and massaged both sides of her forehead.

"Are you okay?" Brick set a glass of ice water in front of Lily.

"I feel a migraine coming on."

"Stress will do that." Brick sat down across from Lily. He waited while she washed down an Excedrin, then two more.

Lily leaned forward, resting her elbows on the table, her fingers intertwined. "As soon as I got to court, I went to the Clerk's Office to check the docket. The hearing was set for two with an Assistant U.S. Attorney by the name of Brooks. I knew Cruz wouldn't be on the early prisoner bus so I spent a couple of hours in the library. Around eleven, I went down to the cellblock to see if he had been brought in but the deputy told me Cruz's name wasn't on the list. I was a little concerned, but he said another bus was scheduled. He tried to check for Cruz's name, but the computer was down. Typical, right?" Before continuing, Lily reached for the Excedrin bottle again.

"Haven't you taken enough for a while?" Brick asked.

"What? Oh yeah, I guess I have."

It bothered Brick to see Lily in pain. "Did you take time to have some lunch?"

"No and that's probably part of the reason I have this splitting headache."

"I can go get you a sandwich."

Lily managed a half smile. "Thanks, maybe later. Anyway, I decided to go up to the lawyer's lounge rather than hang out in the cellblock. I was there about twenty minutes when a deputy marshal, a different guy than the one in the cellblock, approached and asked if I was Lily Nguyen. Then he told me Judge Newton needed to see me in his chambers immediately."

"I bet the deputy's delivered that message a few times to attractive attorneys." Brick realized too late that this wasn't the time or place for his comment, but Lily didn't seem offended.

"Attractive, unattractive—Newton doesn't discriminate. Well, the last place I wanted to be was behind closed doors with him." Lily took a drink of water. She rubbed her eyes before continuing. "As it turns out, my concerns were unfounded. It was standing room only. His law clerk and bailiff were there along with Brooks and his boss. And *the* U.S. Marshal, not one of his deputies. That's when I knew something serious had happened, but I still wasn't prepared for what the marshal had to say."

"How could you be?" Again, Brick wanted to reach out to comfort Lily.

Lily's voice was flat and emotionless. "He didn't have a lot of details but from what he was told it appeared Cruz had ripped the sleeve of his jumpsuit into strips, tied them together, and used it as a ligature around his neck. By the time the guards found him, he was dead." Lily leaned back in her chair. "I don't get it. I spoke to him yesterday; he didn't seem agitated or depressed much less suicidal."

Brick recalled his last encounter with Cruz. He hadn't picked up on any signs that he was suicidal either, but then not everyone who is announces their intentions. "What was the reaction from the others in the room?" Brick asked.

"Shock. The prosecutors offered their condolences, and Newton told the marshal he wanted to be kept informed as to the autopsy findings and any other pertinent information. But let's face it, that's just lip service. Nothing is going to happen. It's over."

"Not as far as I'm concerned."

"Oh, come on, Brick, it's time to be realistic."

"What's more realistic than the fact Cruz didn't kill Jose or Maria."

"But you can't prove that, especially now that Cruz is dead."

"So what are you suggesting—I just forget it, walk away?"

"Do whatever you want. Here, be my guest." Lily flung Cruz's file across the table. It landed in front of Brick. "I'm sorry, I don't mean to be snarky but I feel like such a hypocrite."

"Why?"

"I have to teach a class tonight at American. Bright-eyed first-year law students, and you know what I feel like telling them? Quit . . . just quit right now. Do something else with your life. Anything has to be better." Lily looked at her watch. "I've got a couple of hours before the class; I'm going home and taking a nap."

Brick was tempted to ask if she wanted company but thought better of it. "We're still on for tomorrow, aren't we?"

For a minute, Lily looked confused. "Oh, that's right, the ballet." Lily nodded.

"Good." Brick smiled. "I'll stop by your place around six."

\* \* \*

"It's go time."

Brick reread the three-word text from Ron. At least there was some good news today. He smiled as he pictured his former partner sweating bullets but trying to look calm, reassuring Jasmine everything would be okay. And Jasmine was probably hurtling some less than appreciative comments Ron's way. But they'd bounce off him. Ron was a good man and he'd be a good father, of that Brick had no doubts. He was happy for them, but from a purely selfish point of view, he wished it wasn't happening right now. So much had changed now that Cruz was dead, and he could use Ron's help. Since he'd handed over his gun and badge, Brick had fleeting second thoughts about his impulsive decision, but this was different. Would this mean Jose and Maria's killer got away with it? This case, more than any other he'd ever worked, needed to be solved. Brick hated to think he'd join the ranks of retired detectives haunted by the unsolved mystery of a case gone cold.

Brick considered walking home, but the wind had picked up and dark clouds to the west threatened rain. He checked the weather radar on his phone. Storms were approaching, and according to the weather alert, some could be severe. For the second time in less than an hour, he flagged down a cab.

*     *     *

A deafening clap of thunder greeted Brick as he unlocked his door. He stepped inside, thankful he made it home just in time. Sheets of rain beat against the windows with a force reminiscent of driving through a car wash. Even though it was still midafternoon, the room was dark. Brick flipped the light switch, but nothing happened.

"Great, the power is out." Was he talking to himself more lately? Probably. Was it just a normal by-product of spending more time alone or should he be concerned? Either way, he had more important things to worry about than his sanity.

Brick kicked off his shoes and changed into a pair of sweatpants and a Nats t-shirt. He needed to do laundry, but it would have to wait until the power was restored. And no telling when that might be. He pulled his table and a chair over by the window to take advantage of any natural light. A lot of questions regarding Cruz swirled around in his head. It was probably unrealistic to hope Cruz left a suicide note naming names, but going through whatever personal property the jail was holding might be enlightening. He'd talk to Lily about that, but in the meantime, he needed to get started. Brick picked up Cruz's file and flipped through it. Learning everything he could about the man wouldn't be easy. Without the authority he had as a cop, he felt he had both hands tied behind his back.

The rain was letting up, but Brick noticed pellets of hail collected on the windowsill. Others may doubt it, but he believed all the talk of climate change. Violent storms seemed to be happening more frequently. He could remember a time when thunderstorms were common in August but rare in April. This was the second bad one this month. Thinking about the previous storm conjured up memories of nearly decking Travis Allen. Brick was still embarrassed by his behavior, but were it not for that, he wouldn't have met Eric Monroe. And if anyone might have some insight into Cruz's world, it was Eric. Brick reached for his phone. He scrolled through his contacts until Eric's name appeared. The phone rang three times before Brick heard Eric's voice directing him to leave a message.

Brick set his phone aside. Hopefully, Eric would call him back soon but there was no guarantee. Again, he picked up Cruz's file. This time he did more than flip through it. He read every word looking for anything that might be relevant. He booted up his computer only to be advised that the battery was low. There wasn't much he could accomplish in ten minutes. Instead, he jotted down notes about Cruz's previous arrests that he would later enter into a spreadsheet.

Two hours of reading in less-than-ideal lighting was taking its toll. Brick pushed back from the table. He stood up and stretched. It was still raining, but the wind had subsided. He grabbed a beer out of the fridge along with a wedge of cheddar cheese and a jar of olives. Searching the kitchen cabinets for crackers, he saw an unopened box of Triscuits. According to the use-by date, he'd found it with three days to spare. He headed back to the table just as his cellphone rang. With his free hand, he held the phone up to his ear.

"Hey, Brick, it's Eric. What's up?"

As far as Brick was concerned, there was no reason to waste time with small talk. "Have you heard about Guadalupe Cruz?"

"Yeah, about an hour ago when I got off a surveillance. General consensus around here—that's the second time he did something right."

"Taking a plea was the first?" Brick asked.

"Yeah."

"Well—what you and the other guys might not know—he was about to withdraw his guilty plea." Brick waited for Eric to respond. For a moment he thought his call had been dropped.

"Are you shitting me?" Eric asked.

"Check the court docket. The hearing was set in front of Judge Newton."

"But that doesn't make sense. Why would he kill himself before the hearing?"

"That's one of the things I'm trying to figure out. The other, why did he plead guilty in the first place?"

"Hey, did you forget—you're retired. If I were you, I'd take up golf or fishing."

Brick laughed. "Maybe I will after—"

"Yeah, yeah . . . I know."

"I figured you'd understand," Brick said. Listen, would you be willing to do a little brainstorming with me?"

"Sure. I'd suggest getting together tonight, but I'm beat. How about tomorrow, around noon?"

"That works. Is Boland's okay?"

"Absolutely. You can buy me a beer."

"Deal."

# CHAPTER THIRTY-NINE

BRICK PICKED UP his pint of Guinness and took a sip. "Before I forget, Rory, here you go." He slid the Nationals tickets across the bar.

Rory took one. "That's all I need."

"You and Kelly are still on the outs?"

Rory nodded. "You might say that—which is more than she's saying to me."

"The old silent treatment?"

"Yeah."

"Give it time." Brick picked up the other ticket wishing he'd be using it himself. "Eric's meeting me here. I'll see if he wants it." Brick glanced at his watch. "Guess he's running late."

"If he doesn't, I can try to sell it outside the park." Rory wiped down the section of bar in front of Brick. "Do you want to go ahead and get some food?"

"Might as well. I'll take an order of sliders with cheese."

It was now half-past noon. Brick was about to check his phone for text messages when he saw Eric rush by the window. He stepped inside and looked around before glancing in Brick's direction.

Eric pulled off his sunglasses and dropped them on the bar. "Sorry I'm late. I was taking my time, thinking I'd be early until I realized the clock was wrong. Guess the power was out last night, but not during the storm, sometime after it."

"No problem. Rory said the lights flickered here a couple of times, but at my place, the power was out for several hours. Same street, two blocks south, you'd think we'd be on the same grid, but it's D.C."

"Yeah, there's no rhyme or reason to the infrastructure. Remember when the manhole covers were exploding like popcorn? No one seemed to notice until one blew in Georgetown. Then it was national news. Tells you who rates."

Brick agreed. "Several years ago, a cabdriver from somewhere in Africa told me he felt right at home here because D.C. is run like a third-world country. At the time, I thought he was crazy, but the more I thought about it, I realized it was dead on."

Eric shrugged. "The whole country's becoming the haves and have-nots."

"I'm afraid you're right, but at least we've got baseball." Brick picked up the ticket. "It's for tonight's game, but I can't use it. It's yours if you want it."

"It's the Yankees—are you serious?"

"Yeah." Brick sighed. "Only one drawback . . ."

"Obstructed view?"

"No." Brick laughed. "You'll be sitting next to Rory. I gave him the other one."

"I think I can handle that. It's none of my business, but I can't believe you're not going."

"I can't believe it, either." Rory joined in the conversation. He leaned on the bar, positioning himself between the two men. "I don't know but I think our man here is holding out on us. Got an invite to the White House for feck's sake?"

"Something like that."

"Really?"

"No, the ballet."

Rory laughed. "Like I really believe that."

"It's the truth."

Rory shook his head. "C'mon, you're passing up a chance to see Mariano Rivera . . . the Sandman . . . maybe the greatest closer of all time . . . for the feckin' ballet?"

"Promised a friend—just happens to be the same night." Brick picked up his Guinness and took a drink.

"Friend? It better be a friend with benefits, some really good benefits." Rory turned in Eric's direction. "What can I get you?"

"How about his date to the ballet? Think I'd like to meet this woman."

"You and me both, but afraid I can't arrange that."

"Then I'll have a Harp and a corned beef sandwich."

Rory stepped over to the taps and filled a glass for Eric. He set it in front of him before turning back to Brick. "I bet it's the blond. I've seen you leave with her a few times."

"Tracy? No, in fact, she's getting married soon . . . to another woman."

"Holy jaysus!" Rory jumped back from the bar as if it had suddenly been electrified. "And all this time, I figured you two were—"

"Don't know why you're so interested in my social life."

"Well, it's not like I've got much going on in my own. I was living vicariously there for a minute, then you throw me a curveball. Kind of like Mariano—who you're not going to see tonight."

"Thanks for the reminder," Brick said. "All right, I'll say this once so we can end this conversation. I am going to the Kennedy Center with a woman named Lily Nguyen. You don't know her, but if you did, you would understand."

"Lily Nguyen, the defense attorney?" Eric asked.

"Yes."

Eric nodded. "Ah, now it all makes sense to me."

"Not me," Rory said. "On a scale of one to ten—?"

"Twelve." Brick couldn't help smiling as he said that. "And now, Rory," Brick continued, "if you're satisfied, could you check on the sliders I ordered?"

"Will do." Rory turned and headed toward the kitchen.

Brick shook his head. "I don't know what's up with him."

"Personally, I don't care why you can't use the tickets, I'm glad to have one. The game's sold out, and the scalpers will be cashing in big-time." Eric took a sip of beer. "How's Nguyen reacting to Cruz's death?"

"I haven't talked to her today, but yesterday she was devastated. She was expecting a ruling on a motion to withdraw his guilty plea then finds out her client is dead. That's tough."

"I'm sure. But does she really think he's innocent?"

"We all know Cruz isn't a choirboy, but given what we've found, there's reason to believe he's innocent, at least as far as the Delgado murders." Brick took a sip of Guinness and wiped the foam from his upper lip with the back of his hand. "We think he pled, not because he did it, but because he was being coerced."

"Not sure I follow you," Eric said.

"Looking back, I think the investigation went off the rails pretty much from the start."

"Sliders with cheese." Rory set a plate of three mini-burgers in front of Brick. "Need some ketchup?"

"Yes."

Rory grabbed a bottle of ketchup from the shelf under the bar and handed it to Brick.

"Thanks." Brick glanced at Rory's hand and noticed a couple of nasty scratches. "What happened to your hand?"

Rory quickly dropped his hand down by his side. "I don't know . . . I guess it's courtesy of Elvis."

Brick picked up one of the sliders. "You need to clip her claws."

"I'll make sure I do that in all my spare time."

"Better than getting scratched like that. Watch that it doesn't get infected." Brick could tell he'd pushed one of Rory's buttons. That wasn't his intent. "If you have a pair of nail clippers around here, I'll take care of it."

"Check the drawers in Eamonn's desk. There's probably one from a beer company—some of the trinkets and trash promotion shite they give us." Rory yawned. "Think it's time for my second Red Bull. Maybe, my third—who's counting."

Brick took a bite out of the slider. "Where's Elvis?"

Rory shrugged. "Last time I saw her, she was sleeping on Eamonn's desk." He glanced back toward the kitchen. "Eric, I'll go check on your sandwich."

"No rush, I'm going out back for a smoke."

"Thought you were going to quit," Brick said.

Eric smiled sheepishly. "I am . . . just not today."

Brick polished off the third slider and washed it down with the last swig of his Guinness before heading to Eamonn's office.

"Adding pet groomer to your resume?" Eric asked when Brick passed him at the end of the bar.

"Maybe I should—might make me more marketable."

Brick opened the door to Eamonn's office slowly. Elvis wasn't asleep on the desk. Instead, she was at the door ready to dart out if given the chance. He scooped her up and closed the door behind him.

"Good girl, Elvis." Brick set her down on top of Eamonn's desk and stroked the cat's back. The cat responded with a couple of head butts and one very loud meow. "Glad you're in a good mood." He pressed on her right front paw to expose her claws. To Brick's surprise, the cat's front claws on both paws had been removed. He checked her back paws. Those were intact and in need of trimming, but it was unlikely they were responsible for the scratches on Rory's hand. Then again, maybe it was possible, considering Elvis's contortions.

With one hand, he held her securely as he opened the middle drawer. Next to a small box of Band-Aids were some paper clips, a couple of ballpoint pens, loose change, and Post-it notes but no nail clippers. Brick felt uncomfortable going through Eamonn's desk, but he was determined to make good on his offer. He pulled open another drawer. A stack of invoices filled most of the space, but something wedged in the corner caught his eye. He bent down to get a closer look and recoiled at what he saw.

A taser. Why would Eamonn have a taser? In all the years Brick had known him, he never heard Eamonn express any concerns about his safety. So, if it didn't belong to him, in all probability, it belonged to Rory. Brick needed to think clearly, but disjointed images and thoughts collided in his brain. Was it possible this was the taser that caused the bruise on Maria's hip? If so, it could only mean one thing—Jose and Maria's killer had been hiding in plain sight all along.

"How's it going in there?"

Brick was startled to see Rory standing in the doorway. He banged his knee as he slid the drawer closed. Brick struggled to keep his voice steady. "Not so good, I . . . I couldn't find the clippers, but Elvis has agreed to pick on someone else."

Rory turned and walked away.

Brick reopened the drawer. He regretted not having a pair of the latex gloves he always carried when he was on the job. He wanted to get the serial number of the taser but couldn't risk messing up any existing fingerprints. Instead, he had to settle for a quick photo. He checked the image on his phone before slipping it back into his pocket. It wasn't great, but he could see the make and model. That was better than nothing. Brick closed the door to Eamonn's office and went back to his place at the bar.

"Find what you were looking for?" Eric asked.

"What?" Brick realized Eric had spoken to him, but his mind was elsewhere.

"Asked if you found the clippers."

"No." Brick wanted to tell Eric about the taser, but now was neither the time nor place. There were too many things to confirm and for that he would need help from Ron, which might take some time. Instead he signaled to Rory.

"Another Guinness?" Rory asked.

"Just the check, I need to get going."

"Thanks for the ticket." Eric picked up a napkin and wiped some mustard from his hand before extending it in Brick's direction.

"Enjoy the ballet." Rory handed Brick the check while attempting a pirouette that nearly sent him crashing into a case of Jameson.

Brick wasn't amused. He left a ten and a couple of ones on the bar.

# CHAPTER FORTY

It wasn't the first time Brick barely remembered leaving Boland's, but the other times he'd had more than one Guinness. He climbed the stairs to his apartment, slid his key into the lock, and opened the door. With thoughts of Rory's possible involvement in the Delgado murders, his brain was in overdrive. Why had Rory allowed him to check Eamonn's desk, knowing he might find the taser? Carelessness? Or did he want to get caught? Brick reached for his phone to take another look at the image of the taser but saw a text message from Ron.

"One of each. All doing fine. Catching some zzzzzs."

A boy and a girl—exactly what Ron had prayed for. A fleeting smile crossed Brick's lips as he looked at the texted photo of the two babies. As much as he wanted his ex-partner's insight, he couldn't disturb him now. Instead, he grabbed a pad of paper and sat down at the table. For several minutes he stared at the blank page, thinking back to the day he discovered Jose's body. He tried to recall the details of the conversation he'd had with Rory. He remembered Rory saying he'd been away for the weekend and that was why he was just finding out Jose hadn't shown up for work for a couple of days. If it was true, Rory had an alibi that should be easy to verify.

But if he was lying, all the calls and text messages were nothing more than a ruse. One Brick bought into like a sucker for a Ponzi scheme. Was Rory so calculating he went to Jose's building, knowing what he would find like a killer joining a search party after he had dumped the victim's body?

It was possible Rory was leading a double life and the question gnawing at Brick was why hadn't he suspected him before now? He knew the answer even though he hated to admit it. He was too close to the investigation to be objective. He didn't think so at the time, but the old cliché of hindsight being 20-20 couldn't be more applicable. And had he not been so blind to the possibility of Rory's culpability, a young woman in Arlington might still be alive. To Brick's way of thinking, he might never be able to adequately atone for his mistakes, but for now, he couldn't waste time wallowing in regret. He owed it to the victims to find the truth even if it meant implicating Rory.

Brick closed his eyes and tried to visualize what may have happened inside Jose's apartment. Rory's connection to Jose was obvious and that, no doubt, connected him to Maria. But how did Cruz figure into the equation? And if Rory was armed with a taser, why did he bludgeon Jose with a towel bar he ripped off the wall? Brick was convinced the taser was used on Maria, but was that before or after attacking Jose? Which one of them was his primary target?

Hurriedly, Brick wrote down the questions as they occurred to him. Despite his best effort, it was still hard for him to picture Rory committing two, maybe three, murders. What could have triggered him to act in a way that seemed so out of character? Ask anyone who frequented Boland's and there would be agreement regarding Rory. With his Irish accent and gift of gab, he was a charmer. But then, according to people who knew him, so was Ted Bundy.

* * *

Brick stood in front of his closet staring at his collection of ties hang-ing on the rack, but his thoughts weren't about which tie to select. All the unanswered questions surrounding Rory dominated Brick's focus. Bringing Lily up-to-date wouldn't exactly be typical Saturday night dinner-date conversation, but might as well get it out of the way over dinner and hopefully they'd be doing a dance of their own after the ballet. Brick grabbed a maroon and navy striped tie and closed the closet door.

Before leaving his apartment, he did a quick personal inventory. Teeth brushed, hair combed, tie knotted, and fly zipped. He discon-nected his cellphone from its charger and slipped it into his jacket pocket.

It was just after five p.m. He had plenty of time to walk to Lily's place. From there, they could catch a cab to Foggy Bottom and grab a quick dinner before heading to the Kennedy Center. The cool April air was refreshing and Brick welcomed the exercise, both physically and mentally. From experience he knew that the best way to find an-swers was to take a break from thinking about the questions. He hoped his strategy would work this time.

"We have the walk light."

Brick turned to his left and saw an elderly woman, stooped and leaning heavily on a cane.

"Excuse me?"

"The light—it says 'walk.'"

"You're right." Brick deliberately matched her pace to ensure she crossed safely. They made it to the other side as the seconds counted down to zero.

"Have a good night," she said and smiled warmly.

"Thanks." Brick returned the smile. "You do the same."

"Oh, I intend to."

Brick watched as she continued on her way halfway down the block before disappearing inside an elegant vintage apartment building. There was something about the woman's demeanor that reminded Brick of Eamonn. Through him, Brick's perspective on aging had changed over the years. What was the Irish proverb he often quoted? Brick thought for a moment before recalling the words: "Don't regret growing older; many are denied the privilege." It was heartbreakingly true. Brick knew more than his share who had been *denied*; Jose was just the most recent. And learning Rory was responsible would break Eamonn's heart.

Try as he might, Brick couldn't turn off his thoughts. Now that he was within sight of Lily's building, he'd have someone to bounce his ideas off of. He stepped up his pace and turned onto 17th Street.

Before climbing the steps to the building, Brick paused for a moment. The sweet scent of lilacs filled the air. He breathed deeply. Lilacs were his mother's favorite flower. He headed up the steps and entered Lily's security code on the intercom keypad. He reached for the door handle, bracing himself for the deafening squawk of the buzzer.

It was the last sound he remembered hearing.

# CHAPTER FORTY-ONE

Beep . . . beep . . . beep . . .

The smoke detector was just out of Brick's reach. Still, he tried one more time stretching as far as his arm could go, but it seemed the device had climbed up the wall a couple of inches. Brick opened the closet door and rooted around until he found his baseball bat. The one signed by Hank Aaron. He ran his fingers over the wood before gripping it firmly in both hands. He faced the detector like an incoming fastball and swung hard, making contact. Pieces of shattered plastic rained down on the faded linoleum floor.

Beep . . . beep . . . beep. They were getting louder and each one was like a nail being driven into his brain. *Make it stop*, Brick pleaded even though he was sure no one was listening.

"Brian . . ."

Had someone called his name or was he imagining things? Was he awake or asleep? He wasn't sure. He wasn't sure of anything except for the excruciating pain inside his head. But at least feeling pain must mean he was alive.

"Brian . . ."

Who was calling him *Brian*? He needed to open his eyes, but despite a couple of attempts, it seemed like an impossible task. Finally, he felt his eyelids flutter. Seconds passed as he struggled, but his

Herculean effort paid off. He looked up and saw a distorted face staring back.

"Brian, can you hear me?"

He tried to respond but his mouth was so dry he could barely swallow, and when he did, he regretted it. His throat felt as if it had been scraped raw. All he wanted to do was close his eyes and go back to sleep but he managed a slight nod.

"Stay with me, okay?"

He didn't know where he was or who was speaking, but her voice sounded kind. He wanted to obey, but every blink was a challenge, and the incessant beeps continued nonstop. And now there were more sounds—footsteps and a husky male voice. A white-coated figure bent over him and flashed a light in his eyes. Brick wanted to slap the hand away from his face, but when he tried to raise his arm, he realized it was tied down. The other one, too. Where was he and why was he being restrained? His head filled with crazy thoughts of torture and alien abductions.

"Brian?"

If his captors knew his name, what else did they know? *Who are these people?* Brick felt his heart rate accelerate, each beat strong enough to send his heart knocking against his ribs. And the beeps were keeping pace.

"I'm Dr. O'Keefe. I'm the attending physician. You're in the hospital because you took a nasty blow to the head, but you're going to be okay. Do you understand what I'm saying?"

Before Brick could respond to the white-coated guy who looked awfully young to be a doctor, he took a sip of water offered to him by a woman holding a straw to his parched lips. It tasted better than Dom Perignon, but sucking on the straw sapped his energy. All he could manage was a whispered "yes."

Dr. O'Keefe patted Brick on the shoulder. "Right now, you need to rest. I'm going to give you something to help you sleep."

Brick started to panic. He didn't want to sleep; he wanted to move his hands. "Can't . . . can't move my hands."

"Don't worry, it's okay. We had to restrain you in the emergency room. You probably don't remember, but you put up a fight worthy of Mike Tyson. If you promise not to throw any more punches, we'll free your right arm. The left has an I.V. so we'll leave it taped to the board." The doctor motioned to the nurse and she removed the restraint.

With his newly freed hand, Brick reached up and scratched his nose before drifting back to sleep.

*   *   *

"Looks like Sleeping Beauty is waking up."

Despite the foggy haze dulling his senses, Brick recognized Ron's voice. But was it real or a figment of his imagination? He gazed across the room to where he thought his former partner sat. Brick tried not to blink fearing if he did, the image would disappear.

"What are you doing here?" Brick asked.

"Making rounds. Checking on you, checking on Jasmine and the babies, checking on you again." Ron got up and moved closer to the head of Brick's bed. "Need some water?"

"Yeah."

"Better get you sitting up." Ron pressed the button on the remote to raise the level of Brick's bed. He poured some water into a cup. "Here you go, small sips." He handed the cup to Brick and waited while he drank. "You're looking better, man. How do you feel?"

"Like my head's going to explode." Brick handed the empty cup to Ron. "How'd you know I'm here?"

"Ran into one of the ER nurses in the cafeteria last night; she told me. And just so you know, a couple of Third District guys are working your case. I know one of them, he's good."

"Oh." Brick thought about that for a minute. "Wait, did you say last night—what time is it?"

Ron checked his watch. "Ten minutes to ten."

"Sunday morning?"

"No, man, it's Sunday night. You pretty much lost a day."

Brick closed his eyes and tried to sort out the jumble of thoughts inside his head. "But I was going to the ballet."

"They must be pumping some strong drugs into that IV." Ron whistled through the gap separating his two front teeth.

"It was for Lily."

"Lily . . . Lily Nguyen?" Ron asked.

"Yeah. And I had Nats tickets, but I promised her, and she was all upset because Cruz killed himself."

"Whoa, Brick, you're talking crazy, man. Cruz is in jail. Last I heard, Lily was trying to get his guilty plea revoked."

Brick shifted trying to find a more comfortable position. "I know what I'm saying. Cruz is dead. I was waiting to tell you."

"Why?"

"Because of the babies. Didn't want to bother you."

"So this happened on Friday?"

Brick thought for a moment, mentally going back in time to things he remembered. "Yeah, Friday." With his right hand, Brick patted the bed around him. "Where's my phone?" He started to panic. "I need to talk to Lily."

"Take it easy, man. I'll look for it." Ron opened the drawer of the tray table that had been pushed to the foot of the bed. "It's here along with your wallet and watch." He handed the phone to Brick.

Brick pressed the home button and stared at the phone, waiting for the apps to appear. Once they did, he tried to find the message icon but he couldn't distinguish one blurry icon from another. He blinked a couple of times and again tried to focus but to no avail.

"Here." Brick handed his phone to Ron. "Check for text messages. There's got to be one from Lily."

The phone all but disappeared in Ron's big hand. With his forefinger, he tapped the screen. "Okay, found it. My office—fifteen minutes." Ron glanced up at Brick then looked back at the phone. "Wait, that was from Friday at 1:03 p.m."

"There's got to be more."

"Afraid not."

"Check voicemail."

Again, Ron's finger tapped the screen. "Nothing."

"That's weird. Why didn't she call . . . even to give me hell for being late?"

"Don't know, man, but it's not like you just stood her up. I'd say you've got a valid excuse. Even Jasmine would probably agree." Ron looked at the phone again. "There is a message here from Rory. Actually, not a message, it's a photo." Ron studied it for a moment. "Looks like batting practice at Nats Park."

Bit by bit, events from Saturday were starting to come back to Brick. Vaguely he remembered being at Boland's Mill. He closed his eyes and tried to ignore the pain in his head as he struggled to concentrate. "The taser."

"What?" Ron said.

"The taser. I found a taser in Eamonn's desk and Rory—"

"Hey, there's another text from him."

"Read it to me."

"U missed great game. So did Eric. WTF." Ron set the phone down on the tray table. "Hope he paid you what that ticket was worth."

"No, I gave . . . oh my God . . . what was the time stamp on Rory's picture?"

Ron picked up the phone. "6:14 pm . . . so?"

Brick's eyes darted around the room. "I . . . I got to get out of here."

"C'mon, man, you're not going anywhere." Ron looked up at the monitor tracking Brick's vitals. "You need to relax. Your blood pressure just jumped twenty points."

"Where are my clothes? I need my pants."

"That suit's history, man. Just relax, I'll go to your place and get you some clothes when you need them."

"That'll be too late." With his free hand, Brick grabbed the IV needle and ripped it from his left arm. He pulled off the tape securing his arm to the board. A wave of nausea washed over him as he swung his legs over the side of the bed and tried to stand. He grabbed Ron's arm. "You got to help me."

"Okay, man, I will, but you need to get back in bed."

"No! Only Rory and Eric knew where I was going. It wasn't Rory, it was Eric."

"What do you mean?"

"It was Eric—he attacked me and now he's got Lily."

Ron shook his head. "C'mon, Brick, get back in bed. You're talking crazy. There's no reason why Eric would attack you."

"Yes, there is." Brick felt his knees start to buckle. He grabbed the railing on the side of his bed. "I'm not crazy and I'm telling you, Lily's in danger."

Ron opened his mouth as if to say something but stopped. He paced back and forth in front of Brick's bed before pulling out his cellphone. "I'm probably going to regret this, but I'll call over to Third District and have them send someone to Lily's apartment to check on her."

"I need to be there."

"Really? How far do you think you're going to get with your ass hanging out of a hospital gown? If you want to make sure Lily's safe, this is what we're going to do."

Reluctantly, Brick climbed back into bed just as the evening nurse entered the room. She gave Ron a suspicious look as she approached Brick's bed.

"What happened to your IV? What's going on in here?" Her tone was a mixture of confusion and anger tinged with fear.

"I'm ready to go home," Brick said.

"Dr. O'Keefe will make that determination."

"Then you need to call him."

Without any further discussion, the nurse turned and left.

Brick lay back against his pillow but didn't shut his eyes. He tried to read Ron's expression as he talked on the phone, but his blurred vision made it impossible to focus. Instead, he concentrated on what he could hear of Ron's one-sided conversation. A few "okays" didn't tell him anything.

"Holy shit! What's the address?" Silently, Ron stared at Brick. "Okay, thanks." Ron put down the phone. "That was the Deputy Watch Commander. He confirmed there's a possible hostage situation. SWAT, I mean the Emergency Response Team, is on its way."

Brick felt like he had been punched in the gut. Another wave of nausea hit him. He swallowed hard, forcing bile back down his throat. There was absolutely no satisfaction in being right.

"Find me some clothes."

Ron didn't argue. He left and returned a few minutes later carrying a set of blue scrubs. He helped Brick step into the pants then pulled the shirt over his head.

"Here's your shoes; they were in the locker." Ron slid Brick's bare feet into the loafers. He grabbed Brick's wallet and cellphone out of the tray table drawer. "You'll need these."

Brick patted the sides of his pants. "I don't have any pockets. Hang onto them for me."

"Will do." Ron slipped the wallet and cellphone into his jacket pocket and zipped it shut. "Ready, partner?" he asked.

"Where's the nurses' station?"

"Opposite end of the hall from the elevators."

"Let's go." Brick felt dizzy but figured if he could make it to the elevator, he could make it to the street. He staggered slightly, but sheer determination propelled him to put one foot in front of the other.

What would have taken a couple of minutes under normal circumstances took longer. Brick stopped to rest, but eventually they made it to the street outside the hospital's emergency room entrance. A light rain was falling. While Ron tried to hail a cab, Brick steadied himself by holding on to a streetlight. Several occupied cabs passed by coming from the direction of the Kennedy Center, the very place Brick had intended to be just over twenty-four hours ago. It was raining harder now and the chances of getting a cab diminished. Suddenly, Ron frantically waved his arms as a police car rounded Washington Circle. The car stopped and the officer riding shotgun rolled down the window.

"What's the problem?"

Brick watched as Ron flashed his badge. He couldn't hear the answer, but it didn't matter. They had a ride.

# CHAPTER FORTY-TWO

THE WAIL OF the siren intensified the pain in Brick's head, but he wasn't about to complain. He covered his ears with his hands as the police car sped east on K Street. At the intersection with Connecticut Avenue, the officer suddenly swerved to avoid colliding with a Lincoln Town Car turning illegally from the left lane. Brick dropped his hands as he banged against the side of the car. His shoulder slammed into the window, and for a moment, he forgot about the pain in his head.

"Fucking diplomats." Ron echoed the comment from the two uniformed officers before looking in Brick's direction. "You okay, partner?"

"Yeah."

Two blocks north of Dupont Circle, eastbound traffic was being rerouted, but police and emergency vehicles were waved into a Thai restaurant parking lot. The driver pulled next to an unmarked car and stopped. Both she and the other officer got out and opened the back doors freeing Brick and Ron.

"Wait here while I get a handle on what's going on," Ron said.

Brick didn't have the strength to argue. He leaned against the side of the car while one of the officers called in their location to the dispatcher. The other turned to Brick.

"We were about to go off-duty, but I don't think that's happening anytime soon." He unwrapped a stick of chewing gum and popped it in his mouth. "I don't mind, I can use the overtime."

With Lily's life possibly hanging in the balance, Brick could have reamed the rookie for his insensitivity, but he understood where the officer was coming from. He'd been there himself when he was in uniform and on the lowest rung of the pay ladder. Overtime was overtime.

Brick had lost track of how much time had passed. He glanced at his wrist to check his watch and realized he'd left it at the hospital. He didn't care about the watch but hated not knowing how much time had elapsed, and he regretted not accompanying Ron. He considered setting out to find him but dismissed the idea; he barely had enough energy to keep standing. Distant sirens grew louder as more police vehicles arrived. Brick looked up and saw a helicopter hovering over Lily's building. Police or news chopper, he couldn't tell, and looking up made him dizzy. He lowered his eyes and saw Ron sprinting in his direction.

"Okay, partner, here's the deal." Ron sounded winded as he continued. "Lieutenant Hughes from Three D is in charge. I filled her in as much as I could, but she needs to know what you know."

"Let's go." Brick tapped into energy reserves he didn't know he had as Ron guided him to the mobile command center van.

Brick had been in mobile command centers many times, and despite his concussion-induced, muddled thinking, he recognized the familiar activity. Positioning the players was like a choreographed dance with one big difference—if you didn't get it right, people might die. Lieutenant Sonia Hughes introduced herself and directed Brick to a seat. Although he hadn't met her before, he knew her by reputation. Anyone who paid attention to the local news remembered the way she'd peacefully resolved an eighteen-hour standoff at a kids' day-care center. Her fifteen minutes of fame cast her in the national spotlight, but the attention didn't go to her head. It had, however, landed her a promotion.

"Listen carefully to this 9-1-1 call. Can you identify the caller?"

Brick slipped a pair of headphones over his ears. "Ready." He strained his ears, listening to the brief, whispered plea for help. "Play it again." He needed to be absolutely certain. This time he was. "It's Lily Nguyen."

"You're sure?"

"Yes." Brick set the headphones aside.

"Okay. We know the call was picked up by the cellphone tower across the street. What we don't know is whether she's still in there, but we've got to operate as if she is. Now, according to Detective Hayes, you think she's being held by—" Hughes glanced down at some notes.

"Eric Monroe," Brick said.

"And you believe he's the same guy who assaulted you last night. Is this some kind of domestic situation? A love triangle?"

"No, nothing like that, but it's complicated." Brick took a deep breath trying to fill his lungs with as much oxygen as possible. "It's all circumstantial, but I think Eric is responsible for the Delgado murders." Brick saw Hughes knit her brow before she glanced in Ron's direction. His shoulder shrug indicated he couldn't confirm what Brick just said.

"And Eric's an ICE agent?"

"Correct."

"So there's a possibility he's armed."

"Right." Brick's earlier adrenaline surge had waned, and he felt exhaustion setting in. "Whether I'm right about the Delgado murders doesn't matter now. All that matters is Lily." He was about to continue but was interrupted when an emergency response team officer dressed in camouflage stepped into the van.

"Lieutenant, we've evacuated the other occupants in the building. We've got a team in the adjacent unit. They're setting up surveillance equipment through a vent on a shared wall. We've got another team on the roof. So far, the blinds are drawn, but we've seen a shadow behind the corner window. Do you want us to cut the power?"

Hughes didn't respond immediately. "No, not yet."

"What about setting up a landline?"

Hughes turned toward Brick. "Lily must have a cellphone. Right?"

"Yes. I've got her number and Eric's."

"Then let's go with those rather than wasting time with a landline. We need to get him talking."

Ron reached into his pocket and retrieved Brick's phone. He handed it to Lieutenant Hughes.

"Here goes." She took a deep breath. She used her forefinger to enter a number, then stopped. "Wait a minute." She turned toward Brick. "He probably thinks you're in the hospital or dead so hearing your voice might catch him off guard. Can you handle it?"

Brick thought about Lily and didn't hesitate. "I can—with your help and Ron's. Give me a thumbs-up or down so I'll know how I'm doing."

"All right, then." Hughes passed the phone over to Brick. "Once you make contact, put your phone on speaker."

Brick's vision was still blurry. He could make out the green phone app but he needed Ron's help to find Eric's number on his contact list. Brick held the phone up to his ear and prayed Eric would answer. On the third ring, someone did.

Brick listened closely. In the background, he could hear the faint rumble of the refrigerator as it cycled on. He waited for a voice but there was no response. He couldn't wait any longer.

"Eric, it's Brick." He put his phone on speaker and set it down.

"Are you fucking kidding me?" Eric broke into a high-pitched laugh that made the hair on the back of Brick's neck stand on end. "Thought I finished the job, but I guess I was wrong."

Brick exchanged eye contact with Lieutenant Hughes. "If it's any consolation, I've got one mother of a headache." It took everything he had to keep his voice calm.

Eric laughed again, but this time it didn't sound as maniacal. "You're not the only one."

"You, too? We can get you some medication."

"Not me, Lily. Wait a minute, what do you mean *we*. Where the fuck are you?"

"I'm right across the street in the Command Center van with Lieutenant Hughes from the Third District and my old partner, Ron. Go ahead, look out the window."

"Sure, so a sniper can pick me off."

"C'mon, Eric, you've been in law enforcement long enough to know that's not how it works. Everybody here wants this to end peacefully." Brick took a sip of water from a bottle Hughes handed to him.

"I'm in kind of deep. Don't see how that can happen."

"Step by step, Eric. Step by step." Brick deliberately paused to give him a chance to think about the possibility of a solution. "First step, let Lily go."

"No can do. But she's okay."

"You said she has a headache, probably a migraine. She tends to get those."

"Guess you would know. Why'd you lie to me about her?"

Brick didn't have to fake confusion. "I don't know what you mean."

"Yeah, you do. You made it sound like she was perfect."

"We both know no one is perfect, but she's pretty close."

Another laugh from Eric, but unlike the last time, this was just a quick snorting sound. "The only way you could say that is if you don't know about the scars."

Eric's comment rocked Brick to his core. At the moment, he didn't know if Lily was alive or dead or if she had been raped, but knowing

Eric had seen her scars infuriated him. It was an unforgiveable violation. Still, he knew he needed to get his emotions under control.

"Oh, the scars." Brick felt his heart pounding in his chest. "I know about them, but that doesn't change anything. Lily's been through a lot, Eric. Not just today, but most of her life." Brick glanced over at Lieutenant Hughes. She gave him a thumbs-up sign. "Do the right thing and let her go." Brick waited for a response, and for a minute, feared the conversation might end. He didn't want that to happen. "Eric?"

"She's just like the others." Brick heard an edginess building in Eric's voice. It worried him. "Every one of them—they're all the same."

"Who, Eric? I don't know who you're talking about."

"Don't play dumb with me. You're smart, Brick. Maybe too smart for your own good."

"I don't know about that. You had me fooled. After finding the taser, I thought Rory had killed Jose and Maria."

"I don't believe you."

"It's true. I got to hand it to you, Eric, pretending to go out for a smoke, but using the time to slip into Eamonn's office—that was very clever."

"You really think so?"

"Absolutely. You just need to do the smart thing now—let Lily go."

"Why? So she can go out and deceive someone else? It's got to stop, Brick. I'm telling you, for them, it's just a game, and they'll keep playing and playing and playing."

Lieutenant Hughes gave a hand signal Brick interpreted to mean "keep him talking." He acknowledged with a nod but felt as though the walls of the Command Center were closing in on him.

"You mean the women who disappointed you?" The question got another thumbs-up from Hughes, but Brick was more interested in Eric's reaction.

"Yeah, Einstein." Eric's voice rose a couple of decibels. "The ones that look so good, so perfect in their come-fuck-me photos, and then, in person, they're tattooed or have a big ugly birthmark—"

Brick hunched over the table anticipating Eric would continue his tirade, but the next sound they all heard was a tremendous shattering of glass. Lieutenant Hughes grabbed her radio and leapt from her chair.

"GO ... GO ... GO ..." she shouted into the radio as she flung open the door of the van. Ron trailed on her heels. As much as Brick wanted to follow, he knew he'd only be in the way. He sat there dripping in sweat and shivering. No longer able to fight off the exhaustion, he laid his throbbing head down on his hands and closed his eyes.

# CHAPTER FORTY-THREE

"Brick?"

At the sound of Ron's voice, Brick managed to open his eyes and raise his head. He didn't know how much time had passed—minutes, maybe hours—he had no idea. And his confusion wasn't limited to time. He looked around at his surroundings. It took a minute for him to realize he was still in the Command Center van. Slowly, he started to recall the events that had transpired prior to him passing out.

"It's over, partner." Ron pulled up a chair and sat down next to Brick.

"Lily . . . is Lily okay?"

"She's on her way to the hospital."

"Where are they taking her?"

"Georgetown."

"But is she going to be okay?"

"I'm not sure. Uh . . ." Ron cleared his throat before continuing. "The paramedics think she may have suffered a stroke."

"A stroke? That doesn't even make sense." Brick rubbed the back of his neck. "What about Eric?"

"He's dead. Apparently, after he smashed the table, he stabbed himself in the throat with a piece of glass. From all the blood, looks like he hit his carotid artery."

"Jesus Christ." Brick tried to stand up but his legs wouldn't support him. "Nothing makes sense or maybe everything makes sense." He slumped back into his chair. "At this point, I just don't know."

Ron put his hand on Brick's shoulder. "It's okay, man; we've got time to sort it out. But for now, there's another ambulance waiting outside to take you back to the hospital."

"I don't need a hospital. I'm okay."

"No, you're not." A reassuring smile crossed Ron's lips. "And besides, you got to return those scrubs I stole."

Brick knew Ron was right. He wasn't okay, far from it. He wanted to thank his former partner, but words stuck in his throat as tears ran down his face. He reached up and squeezed the hand resting on his shoulder.

Ron would get the message. Of that, Brick was sure.

# CHAPTER FORTY-FOUR

*Two Weeks Later*

"I FIGURED I might find you here, just didn't think it would be on that side of the bar."

As far back as Brick could recall, he had never seen Travis Allen here in Boland's. It wasn't the kind of pickup bar he bragged about frequenting. "It's temporary. Rory needed to pick up Eamonn at BWI, and the regular bartender is stuck in traffic on the Beltway. He'll take over as soon as he gets here."

*No good deed goes unpunished,* Brick thought as he watched Allen climb onto a barstool. Of all the ones that were vacant, he took the barstool Brick usually occupied. He already felt as though Allen was trespassing just by walking in the door; this made it worse. Brick stepped over to the beer taps, anticipating Allen's order, but Travis shook his head.

"I'll have a club soda."

Brick figured Allen must still be working. He filled a glass with ice and soda and set it on a coaster in front of him. "Thought you were off-duty."

"I am . . . and I'm on the wagon." Allen raised the glass and took a drink. "Look, I owe you an apology. That whole thing that happened at the FOP, I was out of line and it wasn't the first time. It'd be easy to say I was celebrating and drank too much, but the truth is I've lost control when it comes to alcohol. Didn't think I'd ever do it, but I started going to AA. In fact, I'm headed to a meeting when I leave here."

Brick was taken aback and unsure what to say. "Well, thanks." That seemed like a reasonable way to start. He thought for a moment. "I'm not going to pretend I ever liked working with you because we both know differently and as far as the Delgado case—there's plenty of blame to go around, but I appreciate you apologizing. And I wish you well on staying sober. It's good you realized it and decided to do something before you hit bottom like a lot of guys."

Allen shifted his weight and leaned his elbows on the bar. "Actually, as attorneys often say, in the interest of full disclosure, I did hit bottom. Karen took the boys and left."

Brick had to give the devil his due. He knew Allen loved his sons. He might not have been a great husband, but he at least made an effort to be a good father. "I'm sorry to hear that."

Allen sighed. "Well, it's not as bad as it was. She gave me a choice—get and stay sober, stop the womanizing—yeah, she knew about that, too—or get a divorce lawyer 'cause that's what she was going to do. I know she'd get custody of the boys. And I'd be lost without my kids." Allen took another drink. "But it's more than that; it's like that old saying about not knowing what you've got till it's gone. That's kind of how I feel about Karen. I'm lucky she's giving me a second chance."

Once again, Brick was at a loss for words. He noticed Allen's glass was empty. "Want a refill?" Brick asked.

Allen shook his head. "No, I need to get going." He stood up and reached in his pocket. He pulled out a couple of ones and was about to leave them on the bar. Brick waived him off.

"I think you have a future as a designated driver so get used to free drinks, goes with the territory."

"Thanks." Allen shook hands with Brick before heading to the door. He walked out without looking back.

*Don't know what you've got till it's gone.* Those words resonated with Brick, but right now, it was too painful to think about. Instead he thought about Allen. Was it possible for an asshole like him to clean up his act? Maybe. Was it possible for Roberto Morales to stop abusing his wife? Maybe. One thing those two had in common was alcohol, and if they both managed to stay clean and sober, they might start acting like decent human beings. Brick wouldn't bet the rent on either being successful, but in both cases, for the sake of the women who loved them for whatever reason and their kids, he hoped the guys would beat the odds. And he had to admit, it took balls for Allen to do what he did just then, not knowing what kind of reaction he would receive. Maybe at one of his AA meetings they talked about making amends and that may have been his motivation. Still, it's a lot easier to talk the talk than to actually carry through. At least for today, Travis Allen had earned his respect.

Brick was refilling the ice bin when he heard a knock at the back door. He glanced up at the clock on his way down the hall. He hoped it was Patrick, ready to start his shift, but Brick was in for another surprise. He looked out the peephole before opening the door. On the other side was Eamonn. Beside him, Rory stood with his arm around Kelly. Brick quickly unlocked the door and let them in.

Eamonn looked tired and a little thinner, but he also looked relaxed. He smiled when he saw Brick. "It's good to be home. How are you, lad?"

It was such a simple question, but coming from Eamonn, it brought a lump to Brick's throat. He swallowed hard. "I've been better."

Eamonn nodded. "I know. We'll talk soon. For now, I need to lay this tired old body down."

Kelly stepped around Rory and took Eamonn by the arm. "C'mon, Elvis is upstairs waiting to see you."

"I'll take his bag upstairs and be right back," Rory said.

Brick went back to the bar and poured himself an orange juice while he waited for Rory. He didn't have to wait long.

"Definite advantage to living over the bar—you don't get stuck on the Beltway."

"Just another day in paradise." Brick reached under the bar for a bag he had left. "If my services are no longer needed . . ."

"Hey, thanks a lot for bailing me out. I didn't want Eamonn to take a cab from the airport. Gotta tell you, I'm so relieved to see he's doing okay. Tired, but that's normal. Kelly's fixing him some soup, then I expect he'll sleep for a while. Feckin' jet lag, always takes me a couple of days to recover."

Brick nodded. "Speaking of recovering—what's up with you and Kelly?"

"We're doing okay."

"Good to hear. She's a sweet girl."

"Yeah, she is." The freckles on Rory's face faded temporarily as he blushed, turning his cheeks a deep shade of red. "But she's also tough. Let's just say, I'm on a very short leash."

Brick laughed. "Leash or laptop. Remember what I said, Rory, it's all about choices."

\*    \*    \*

If Brick had ever been on this tree-lined street of single-family houses in Northeast D.C. before, he didn't remember. The homes were modest but well kept. He didn't need to check the address; he knew he was at the right place by the double-stroller parked on the screened-in porch. He rang the doorbell and waited. A minute or so later, Jasmine opened the door. Brick handed her a bouquet of spring flowers and a small gift bag.

"They're lovely, thanks so much." Jasmine stepped aside. "Come on in. Ron's out back getting the grill ready, and the twins are asleep. Enjoy the quiet, it won't last." Jasmine set the flowers down on a table in the hallway. "Can I look in the bag?"

"Of course."

Jasmine reached into the bag, and Brick heard the rustle of tissue paper. "They're so cute!" She held up two infant bodysuits—one blue, the other red. On both were the words "Washington Nationals" separated by their trademark curly W. "These kids better be sports fans or Ron will be convinced we brought home the wrong babies."

"Maybe by the time they go to their first football game, there will be a new stadium in the District."

"Oh, please don't get him started on that." Jasmine picked up the bouquet of flowers. "I need to put these in water. There's beer and soda in the fridge. Grab yourself something to drink and go check on the Iron Chef."

Brick hadn't taken any pain medication in a couple of days but still passed on a beer. He picked up a can of Coke Zero and headed outside.

"Good timing, my man. Think the coals are ready. Hope you're hungry."

"I am."

"How do you like your steak?"

"Medium rare."

"That can be arranged." Ron threw a couple of large steaks on the grill and stood back. The meat sizzled as it hit the hot grill. "Shouldn't take too long. How are you doing?"

"So, so." Brick was relieved to be talking to Ron. "Physically, pretty good but still some trouble sleeping."

"Par for the course. I tell Jasmine, it's okay, I'll get up when the babies cry, but the truth is, I'm usually awake before them anyway. It's going to take time, man, for both of us."

"You're right." Brick pulled back the tab on his can of soda and took a drink. "You'll never guess who I talked to this morning . . . Travis Allen."

Ron almost dropped the bottle of beer he was holding. "No way. What, did he call you?"

"No." Brick explained the unexpected encounter. "And it's like I told him, as far as the Delgado case, there's enough blame to go around. I'm sure he'll share that with Blancato, which is what I intended."

"Do you think Blancato feels responsible?"

"No. but it doesn't matter. Enough people know his role in the clusterfuck."

"That's for sure. I don't think there will be another joint task force with ICE anytime soon." Ron used a fork to lift a corner of one steak. "Looking good. Have you talked to Kyle Thibodeaux?"

"He called once to see how I was doing, but that was it. Why?"

"Seems that big investigation he's working on has to do with abuse of power by several ICE agents."

Brick almost choked on a mouthful of soda. "Really?"

"All those files and crap in his office—he's had to go through every case in which ICE was involved since 2003."

"Wow. That explains a lot."

"Yeah, I ran into him on his way to the grand jury, and as he put it, Eric Monroe may be just the tip of the—"

"Let me guess, ICE-berg." Brick shook his head. "That sounds exactly like something Thibodeaux would say."

"He also said, stay tuned 'cause heads are going to roll." Ron checked the steak again. This time he flipped it then turned back in Brick's direction. "I'm sorry I couldn't attend Lily's memorial service, but that was the same day Jasmine came home from the hospital."

"I understand."

"How'd it go?"

"It went well. Maybe because she had dealt with her parents' sudden death, she was very specific about her wishes. Lily wanted it to be a celebration of her life and it was. I'm not sure she envisioned it would take place in the Ceremonial Courtroom to standing room only, but she was well respected in the legal community. Lots of her students from AU were there and they hosted a reception afterward." Brick smiled as he recalled all the boxes of Luciano's pizza that were delivered. "I think she would have been pleased."

Ron nodded. "It's still kind of shocking to me what I read in the autopsy report. I mean, she was young and looked to be healthy. Do you think she had any idea she had a brain tumor?"

"No, although looking back, there were some signs. She was having migraines, but millions of people have migraines, and they don't have a brain tumor. Sometimes, her logic seemed off, but I thought she was just thinking out loud. When you do that, not everything makes perfect sense."

"Right." Ron sprinkled some salt and pepper on the steaks.

"And a couple of times, I sensed her mood swings, but let's face it, I didn't know her well enough for it to set off any alarms. Still, sometimes I think if I had only—"

"Don't go there, man. You can't beat up on yourself for something you had no way of knowing."

"Easier said than done." Brick needed a minute before he continued. He finished off his Coke Zero. "Since Lily didn't have any family to speak of, she had designated a girlfriend to be her advocate in case she got sick or was incapacitated. Anyway, I spoke to her, and from what she was told by the neurosurgeon, the tumor was inoperable and very aggressive. Within weeks there would have been serious indicators like vision loss, disorientation, seizures, things like that. At best, she probably had six to nine months."

Ron looked shaken. "That's horrible, but even so, she shouldn't have been cheated out of whatever time she had left by a lowlife douchebag. If Eric had lived, do you think he would have been charged with Lily's death?"

"Possibly. The prosecutors would argue the hostage situation caused the stroke, and the stroke killed her, but it's complicated by the preexisting condition. It's a little like the situation with Cruz. It seems to me that photoshopping those pictures and leaving them in the cell led to Cruz's suicide."

"Having seen those pictures, I totally agree." Ron shook his head as if trying to clear the images from his mind. "The one of his wife was bad enough, but the baby . . . he had to be a sick motherfucker to even fake pictures like that." He took a sip of beer. "Note to gangbangers—don't post family photos on Facebook."

"All in all, it probably wouldn't have really mattered since the case in Arlington was a capital murder. If he was convicted, he'd get the death penalty."

"For sure, and in Virginia, they fry 'em first, ask questions later."

Brick knew Ron was exaggerating but not by much. "Eric saved taxpayers in at least two jurisdictions a lot of time and money."

"True, although we're going to be working this for a while. It's going to take a couple of weeks to finish going through all his computers. He had three or four plus a couple of hard drives. I wouldn't be surprised if there are other victims. I told you about his wallpaper, didn't I?" Brick nodded. "He definitely liked petite women with long dark hair. He must have subscribed to a lot of magazines to find all the pictures he pasted on his wall." Ron picked up a bottle of Worcestershire sauce, unscrewed the cap, and shook a few drops onto the steaks. "And what's really weird, these women were all fully clothed, but then the stuff on his computer, whoa. I mean, I'll admit I've surfed some porn sites, like every other guy on the planet, but there's a limit."

"Are you talking kiddie porn?"

"No, we haven't found that, at least so far. I'm talking hard core and the quantity. And that stuff gets expensive. He had credit cards up the wazoo—most were maxed out."

"Some claim porn can be just as addictive as alcohol or drugs or gambling."

"Apparently, it was for him." Ron looked perplexed. "I just don't get it—some things aren't meant to be spectator sports."

"Like sex?"

"Exactly."

"Unless you're a voyeur."

"But that's another thing that doesn't make sense. He went beyond voyeur by abducting or holding his victims hostage, but he didn't have sex with any of them. And he left these rambling tirades about women pretending to be perfect then betraying him."

"He made a comment like that to me, remember?"

"Yeah, you're right, I forgot about that. But these were long rambling rants calling women sluts and whores. He wrote about how disgusting they were and how it turned him off. Then we found other stuff that was the complete opposite."

"What do you mean?"

"We found a couple of love letters to a fantasy girlfriend. He described how perfect she was and how he'd search until he found her. Bullshit like that." Ron took another sip of beer. "Can you hand me those tongs."

Brick picked up the tongs and handed them to Ron. He watched as Ron picked up one of the steaks, set it on a platter, and tested it with a meat thermometer, but he was thinking about the love letters Eric had written. He felt as though he had found the missing puzzle piece.

"Says medium rare."

"It's starting to make sense, Ron."

"Say what?"

Brick didn't respond immediately. So many thoughts were running through his head, he needed a minute to sort them out. He took a deep breath. "I get it now. Eric was searching for his Galatea."

"His what?"

"Galatea. In Greek mythology, the sculptor Pygmalion was so disgusted by prostitutes and immoral women that he vowed never to marry. Instead, he created an ivory statue of what he believed to be the perfect woman. He named it Galatea and fell in love with the statue."

"I don't know, man." Ron's dreads swayed as he shook his head.

"Think about it," Brick said. "It's obvious Eric liked certain physical characteristics, and he sought out women who met his requirements. But when they failed his expectation of perfection, he either rejected them, or in some cases, killed them."

"And then started his search all over again." Ron looked over at Brick and nodded. "I guess that does make sense. And it seems he abused his ICE authority to prey on at least two of his victims." Ron added the other steaks to the platter. "I think we're ready to eat."

Brick held the screen door for Ron.

"Thanks, man." He hesitated before climbing the stairs. "Greek mythology . . . damn, you need to go on *Jeopardy*."

"No, I'd probably get too many movie trivia questions." Brick smiled at his former partner. "Think I missed my chance . . . I should have gone on that other show, the one where you could phone a friend."